A dropped pin would have sounded loud in the absolute silence

Noah felt half the room staring at his unprotected back. The other half stared at his heated face. He couldn't leave the diner without paying for his breakfast, or he would have been gone.

"What are you talking about?" Abby pushed between the chairs and the tables, arriving at Officer Hayes's side. "I think you've been drinking, Wade."

The officer shook his head and gave her a righteous smile. "Nope. Haven't touched a drop all week."

Her face set in a skeptical frown, Abby crossed her arms and stared up at the big man. "So what are we talking about here? A speeding ticket in one of those traps you guys like to set up in small towns?"

"No, ma'am." Hayes looked around, making sure he had everybody's attention. "Noah Blake was paroled from a state of Georgia correctional facility in Atlanta on Monday morning after serving three years of a seven-year sentence."

"For what?" Abby's voice wobbled.

"Manslaughter," Hayes announced. "Mr. Blake, here, killed a man in Georgia. And he went to prison for it."

Dear Reader,

After "Where do you get your ideas," the most frequent question an author hears is "How long does it take to write a book?" The idea for the AT THE CAROLINA DINER series came to me in 1999 as I was writing other stories. I got the go-ahead from my editors in the summer of 2000 and submitted the first completed book in January of 2001. So in one way or another, then, I've been working on *Abby's Christmas* for more than five years.

All that time I've been visiting a diner of my own—a small "restaurant/deli" near my home, where they cook a good breakfast (including grits) and keep my iced-tea glass full. The waitresses know me by sight and can usually predict what I'll order. (I change my mind occasionally, just to keep them on their toes.) They call me "honey" and sometimes "darlin'" and they remember I want unsweetened tea. During the thirty or forty minutes I spend with them, I feel cosseted and cared for. Mothered.

Abby Brannon mothers her customers at the Carolina Diner. She longs for adventure, but accepts the chains of friendship and love binding her to her hometown...until Noah Blake returns. Noah's had enough adventure to fill several lifetimes. Now he's looking for a connection to the places and people of his past. Abby is definitely a part of that past. But is he part of her future?

I hope you enjoy the time you spend with my friends in New Skye, especially Abby and Noah. I love to hear from readers through the regular mail and by e-mail. My personal Web site is in transition, but you can reach me—and other great Superromance authors—at www.superauthors.com.

All the best,

Lynnette Kent
PMB 304
Westwood Shopping Center
Fayetteville, NC 28314

Abby's Christmas
Lynnette Kent

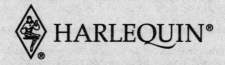

TORONTO • NEW YORK • LONDON
AMSTERDAM • PARIS • SYDNEY • HAMBURG
STOCKHOLM • ATHENS • TOKYO • MILAN • MADRID
PRAGUE • WARSAW • BUDAPEST • AUCKLAND

ISBN 0-373-71245-6

ABBY'S CHRISTMAS

www.eHarlequin.com

Printed in U.S.A.

A friend who talks me through my fears and doubts and
celebrates my successes without reservation.
A writer who pushes me—and my characters—in
the right direction with one little word: "Why?"
A woman who blesses my life and my work.

For Pam, with love

Books by Lynnette Kent

HARLEQUIN SUPERROMANCE

 765—ONE MORE RODEO
 793—WHEN SPARKS FLY
 824—WHAT A MAN'S GOT TO DO
 868—EXPECTING THE BEST
 901—LUKE'S DAUGHTERS
 938—MATT'S FAMILY
 988—NOW THAT YOU'RE HERE
1002—MARRIED IN MONTANA
1024—SHENANDOAH CHRISTMAS
1080—THE THIRD MRS. MITCHELL
1118—THE BALLAD OF DIXON BELL
1147—THE LAST HONEST MAN
1177—THE FAKE HUSBAND
1229—SINGLE WITH KIDS

Don't miss any of our special offers. Write to us at the
following address for information on our newest releases.

Harlequin Reader Service
U.S.: 3010 Walden Ave., P.O. Box 1325, Buffalo, NY 14269
Canadian: P.O. Box 609, Fort Erie, Ont. L2A 5X3

CHAPTER ONE

THE BELL ON THE DINER'S front door jingled, and Abby Brannon glanced up from the miniature Christmas tree she'd just started to drape with a string of shiny red beads.

A man stepped out of the bright December sunshine, then halted for a moment just over the threshold, blinking his eyes against indoor shadows. His black hair had been cut short, without much skill or style. He looked a little sunburned across his arrogant nose and high cheekbones. His broad shoulders filled out a scarred leather jacket, while dusty biker boots and lean hips in faded jeans completed the bad-boy-drifter picture.

The beads slipped through Abby's fingers to clatter on the counter. *Noah Blake.*

Only when the newcomer looked at her across the empty room did she realize she'd said his name aloud. He narrowed his eyes and tilted his head slightly. "Is that you, Abby?"

At the sound of his husky voice, her heart jumped like a startled frog. She swallowed. "Who else would you expect to find at the Carolina Diner in the middle of the afternoon?"

She rounded the counter and confronted him where

he stood, grabbing the lapels of his jacket to shake him a little. "You've been gone a long time, but things haven't changed that much. Welcome back!"

His hands closed over her shoulders and he grinned down at her. If she hadn't been stunned by his sudden arrival, she certainly was at that moment. Noah's one-sided grin was a sugar high she'd never been able to resist.

"Thanks." He leaned in and kissed her cheek, then let her go. "Kinda quiet in here, isn't it?"

Abby fought to keep from touching the kissed cheek with her fingertips. "The usual lull between late lunch and early dinner. Come sit down. You look a little chilly—what can I do to warm you up?" Good thing she'd turned away before she asked that stupid question, so he couldn't see her blush. "Coffee? Tea?"

"Got any hot chocolate?"

When she glanced at him in surprise, he shrugged. "I haven't had some in…a long time. I just thought it would taste good."

"Well, sure. I can make you hot chocolate. Give me a couple of minutes." She stepped through the kitchen door, then poked her head out again. "The menu hasn't changed since you left, but in case you don't remember…"

Propping one hip on a stool, Noah pulled the plastic folder out of the clip on the counter. "Right here."

"You got it." Abby smiled, then went into the empty kitchen to hyperventilate.

I can't believe he's here. She drew hot water from the pot and blended in cocoa powder and sugar until they melted. *I thought he'd have got himself killed by now. Or arrested.* Adding vanilla, then milk, she heated her brew on the burner. *Why has he come back? Should I ask him? There's no way it could have anything to do with me. Right?*

The suggestion left her too shaky to pick up the mugs of cocoa. She bought time by squirting whipped cream on the tops, then dishing up a couple of cherries for decoration. When she thought her hands could handle the strain, she grabbed a thick white mug in each hand, dragged in a deep breath and headed back to the counter.

"Here you go." Setting his drink in front of him, she backed up against the service counter and took a sip from her own. "Enjoy."

Noah toasted her with a lift of his cup. "Thanks." After one taste, he looked at her in surprise. "How'd you make this?"

"Cocoa, sugar, water, vanilla and milk. A little salt. Is something wrong?"

"I just…expected the usual powder." He shrugged. "Not many people make hot chocolate from scratch."

"I'm an old-fashioned girl, I guess." She felt her cheeks heat up. Again. "So, how long have you been in town?"

Noah squinted at the clock over the counter. "Almost thirty minutes now."

"You came here first? You haven't seen your mom?"

"Not yet."

Surprised in her turn, she raised an eyebrow. "She doesn't know you're coming, does she?" When he shook his head, she nodded. "I talked to her just yesterday, when I took her to the grocery store. No wonder she didn't say anything." Noah's mother was not the kind of person to enjoy surprises. "Would you like to call her from here? Give her a little warning?"

Now he was the one with flushed cheeks, and a storm in his dark gaze. "You think she needs warning?"

"This will be a pretty big shock—you showing up after fifteen years away. And she's been sick. Did you know that?"

"Uh, no."

"She's supposed to use her oxygen all the time."

"I—"

"It's not good for her to get upset."

In a sudden hurry, Noah downed the last of his chocolate and stood up. "This was a bad idea, after all. I think I'll just keep going. Don't mention I was here." His long strides quickly took him outside.

Abby rushed after him and found him standing beside a big Harley. "Noah, I didn't mean… Noah!" She grabbed his arm as he jerked on a glove. "First of all, you owe me one-sixty for the hot chocolate."

He shoved his bare hand into the pocket of his jeans.

"More important, you can't run away like this."

"Who says?" He crammed a couple of dollars into her fingers, still wrapped around his sleeve. The leather was cold, the bills warm from his body.

"You'll hate yourself if you do."

"So what's new?" His mouth hardened into a straight line.

She squandered the only leverage she had left. "You can't let your mother die without ever seeing her son again."

He stared at her a long time. The resistance in his expression made her want to weep. "She's…dying?"

"She's got diabetes, heart and kidney problems. Her health has been precarious for several years now."

They stood still, gazes locked, while the sharp wind whipped up dust in the gravel parking lot. A small, dirty dog trotted to the bike, sat by the rear wheel and lifted a paw to touch Noah's leg.

"You've got a friend." Abby let herself be diverted. "He wants a lift."

"Yeah, I helped him out of some trouble back in South Carolina. Now he thinks he owns me." Noah pulled out of her grasp. He bent to pick up the animal and stowed the dirty little guy in the backpack hanging from the bike's seat.

"You brought him here with you?"

"Didn't have much choice." Swinging the backpack onto his shoulders, he threw his leg over the bike and pulled on the other glove. "If I'd left him, the kids would've shot him to death with BB guns."

Abby shuddered. "Where are you going?"

He gave her a resigned look as he buckled his helmet. "Where do you think? One-fifty Boundary Street. I'll ride slow, in case you want to call and announce me."

She smiled, but before she could say anything, he revved the engine and left the parking lot with a spray of gravel. Abby watched as he waited for the traffic light at the corner to change, then saw him head up the hill across the highway, toward his mother's house.

Her heart sang. *Noah is home!*

Back inside the diner, she punched in the familiar telephone number, then hung up before the first ring. Noah's mother might need more than just a call to warn her. She'd been in the hospital last week with her insulin wildly out of control. Maybe somebody should be there when Noah got home in case something happened.

By the time she'd finished thinking things through, Abby had the diner doors locked, the Closed sign on the door and her keys in her hand. She would stay just long enough to be sure Mrs. Blake was all right, then rush back to her usual routine.

Come to think of it, though, with Noah Blake in town, her life might never be *usual* or *routine* again.

NOAH GLANCED ACROSS the street at New Skye High School as he waited through the traffic light over the intersection beside the Carolina Diner. Not much had changed since his time, except for a row of portable classrooms added along the side. Hard to believe he'd ever been confined inside those orange brick walls. With a shake of his head, he left the school behind, rolling through the intersection, accelerating up the hill toward Boundary Street.

The rough, run-down neighborhoods he passed through hadn't changed all that much, either. Some of the beer joints bore different names, some were gone, and others had opened since his time. More of the advertisements in the store windows were in Spanish and most of the men loafing in the parking lots and on the street corners looked Latino.

Passing through a business district of bars, pawn-

shops and gas stations, he caught a yellow light and
rolled to a stop with time to spare before red. The driver
in the truck behind him sat on the horn, but traffic stops
threatened trouble. Noah preferred to avoid any unscheduled encounters with the police.

A glance to the right showed him a parking lot
stretching down the side street, deserted but for a white
Toyota parked next to an overflowing Dumpster. As
Noah watched, a little kid stood up in the front passenger window, fingers curled through a space between the
top of the glass panel and the door frame. The child put
its face up to that crack of air.

In a second of relative quiet, Noah heard the kid's
cry. "Da-a-ade-e-e!"

He turned the bike down the side street and parked
in the empty lot, a short distance from the car. With the
Harley locked and the keys in his pocket, he approached
the vehicle slowly, giving the child a chance to see him,
hoping not to cause a panic.

But the little boy stopped crying as Noah got closer,
and stared through the window with the tears still wet
on his thin, dirty face. His hair was cut too short, his
head practically shaved. He wore a cheap quilted vest,
an orange T-shirt, jeans, mismatched socks, but no
shoes. The afternoon was chilly, with a temperature
somewhere in the fifties, but the windows of the car had
steamed up, so the little guy probably wasn't cold.
Noah remembered how warm a car could get if you
cried enough, jumped up and down on the seats, beat
on the windows.

He tried the back door handle and swore when he
found it unlocked. At least *his* dad had locked him in.

Noah poked his head inside. "Hi," he said quietly. "My name's Noah."

The child hiccuped and sniffed but didn't speak.

"What's your name?" No answer. "Where's your mommy?"

"Mama," the little boy said, and shuffled sideways to lean against the back of the seat he stood on. "Mama." His movement stirred up the air in the car, along with an aroma of sweat, onions and wet diaper. "Mama." He smiled, showing new teeth.

"Are you here by yourself?" Noah didn't expect an answer.

But the boy said, "Daddy. Da-a-ade-e-e."

So maybe the dad was somewhere nearby. And maybe he should be punched for leaving his kid alone like this. Or maybe he could just suffer when he came back to the car and the kid wasn't there. Then again, a kidnapping charge would spell disaster for Noah.

And when had he ever let something like that stop him?

On the thought, Noah straightened up and opened the front passenger door. "Want to go for a walk?" he asked the kid. "We can find your dad."

Again that smile. "Daddy." Without hesitation, the little boy held out his arms to be picked up.

Rolling his eyes, Noah did just that, settling the child easily on one arm. The dog in his backpack hadn't so much as stirred.

"Right." Noah shut the car door and turned toward the street. "Let's see—"

"Hey! Hey, put him down!" The shout came from

behind. "Leave my kid alone!" Noah pivoted to see a man running toward him from the alley behind the building across the street.

"Daddy," the boy in his arms cried, laughing now. "Daddy!"

"Hurt him and I'll kill you," his dad yelled. Nothing about him seemed dangerous—he was just a guy in sneakers, jeans and a dark blue windbreaker.

"I'm worried," Noah yelled back. "Real worried."

The man slowed as he reached the back of the car. "Just put him down. Tyler, come to Daddy. Come on, Tyler."

Noah didn't doubt that Tyler recognized his father. He just wasn't sure he wanted to leave a child with such an irresponsible jerk.

He walked back toward the car. "Are you crazy, leaving a little kid alone like that? You're lucky he didn't just get out and wander away. Or that some pervert didn't steal him."

"He was okay. I was only gone a minute." The guy looked beyond Noah to the street, then over his shoulder in the direction he'd come from. "Put him down."

"He was crying his eyes out. And the doors were unlocked, for God's sake."

"I thought I locked the door. Just give me my kid and butt out, damn it."

Noah put Tyler on the ground, steadying the little body until he got his balance. Tyler took off across the broken, rocky pavement, straight for his dad. "Daddy!"

The guy scooped up his kid. "Let's go home, Ty." Without another word to Noah, he buckled the kid into

the car seat in the back of the car, slammed himself into
the driver's seat and started the engine. Gray smoke
belched from the tailpipe and the motor ran rough. But
within five seconds, the car shot across the lot, turned
into the street and disappeared.

Noah went back to his bike, put on his helmet and
headed toward Boundary Street. Abby had wanted to
warn his mother. He'd sure given her plenty of time.

Thinking about that meeting in the diner, he shook
his head in wonder. Whatever kind of greeting he'd expected when he came home, Abby's generous welcome
had totally surprised him. Her gold-green eyes had
sparkled like polished topaz, and her smile had been
genuine, without a trace of malice. He recalled the
smoothness of her skin against his lips. She wasn't
slender, but who wanted slender when he could have a
woman with such wonderful curves? His hands
clenched as he thought about playing with the thick,
reddish brown hair curling softly on her shoulders.

Slow down, son. Noah shifted on his seat. His body
reacted to just the hint of sex with more enthusiasm than
the circumstances warranted. Then again, until this
week he hadn't even seen a woman for a long, long
time, let alone been with one, so maybe he could be pardoned for an overactive imagination.

He laughed at himself. Pardoned. Now, there was a
word. No pardon had come down for Noah Blake. Just
early parole and time off for good behavior.

And, maybe, a chance to start over.

Just below the top of the biggest hill in town, Boundary Street performed the function for which it was

named, cleanly separating the already-haves in New Skye from the wish-I-could-gets. The north side of the street was heavily wooded, sheltering the upper class from the harsh realities of life on the south—and poor— side.

Noah pulled the bike to the curb in front of a little house midway along the south side of Boundary. The white siding cried out for paint, the blue shutter on the right side of the living room window hung by one nail, and the roof needed replacing. But the chain-link fence, rusty and sagging though it was, still enclosed the well-tended flower beds that had always been Marian Blake's pride and joy. Neatly raked and weed free, the garden displayed flowers even in December. Camellias bloomed pink, red and white. Pansy faces danced in pots on the steps, while ivy and periwinkle twined underneath the azaleas.

With his helmet braced under his arm, Noah stared at the garden he'd spent hundreds of hours on. He struggled for a deep breath, but a pair of giant hands seemed to have closed down on his windpipe.

Across the street behind him, a car door slammed. With quick steps, Abby joined him. "She loves her garden. There's always something blooming, which is a miracle as far as I'm concerned."

Noah cleared his throat. "I…I'm surprised she keeps it up." He pulled himself together. "What are you doing here?"

"I wondered if even a call might be upsetting. So I thought I'd—"

"Introduce me? Like a butler or something?"

Abby put her hands on her hips. "I'm just trying to help."

"I don't need any help with my own mother, thanks."

She returned his glare without flinching. "I didn't for a minute think you did. But maybe she needs some help with you."

Without waiting for his answer, she pushed open the lopsided gate and marched up the sidewalk to his mother's front door. The bell hadn't worked fifteen years ago. Judging by the fact that Abby used the knocker, it still didn't.

After what seemed like a long time, the door creaked open. Noah heard his mother's voice—high, a little hoarse—and Abby's warm tone. Like it or not, he was being introduced.

In the pack on his back, the dog wiggled, fighting to get out. Noah shrugged out of the bag, stepped into the front yard and secured the gate, then let the dog run free.

The few steps he took along the front walk required more guts than Noah had expected. Finally, he came to a stop just behind Abby and looked up into his mother's face. He might not have recognized her if he'd met her anywhere else. Her skin was pale, and not just from shock at his arrival. She'd gained forty or fifty pounds since the last time he'd seen her. Once a warm brown, her unkempt hair was now streaked with white and faded to almost beige.

She stared at him, eyes wide, mouth a circle of surprise. "Noah?"

He managed a smile. "Hi, Ma. How are you?"

"I can't believe…" she said faintly. Then she looked beyond him. "Get that dog out of my flowers! What the hell is he doing in my yard? Get him out, get him out!" There was nothing at all faint about the order.

Noah turned at the same time as Abby, and they both went after the dog. The mutt, of course, decided the chase was all a game. He dashed from corner to corner, wagging his tail and panting, refusing all pleas to come, to be a good dog, to get the hell out of the flower bed.

Marian Blake stood on the porch step, yelling instructions. "There he is! He's heading toward the back—don't let him run over the irises! Don't you step on my daylilies, Noah Blake!"

Vaulting over the fading lily leaves, Noah bent to crawl under the camellias next to the wall of the house. "Stupid dog. I'm gonna strangle you when I get my hands on you."

"That's not incentive." Abby crawled in beside him. "I wouldn't come if you talked to me in that voice."

"Yeah, you've been real successful in getting hold of him so far."

"I came closer than you did." She eased farther down the house wall, peering under the bushes, crooning, "Come on, sweetie. It's okay. Nobody will hurt you."

The dog sat halfway between them, among the fallen camellia blossoms, feinting one way, then the other, every time one of them reached for him.

"I've had enough," Noah growled.

"What are you going to do?"

She gasped as he lunged toward the house. He

slammed his shoulder into the concrete block foundation, but he came up with an armful of dog. "Don't hurt him," she cautioned.

"I'm not going to hurt him," he told her irritably. As proof, the dog proceeded to lick as much of his cheeks and chin as he could reach. "Stop it." Noah pushed the scruffy head away. "Yuck."

Abby started to laugh, then stopped suddenly. "You're hurt." Holding the dog's head away, she pressed with her fingertips to turn Noah's cheek toward her. "You must've scraped your face against the wall. Does it hurt?"

"No." He pulled his head away from her scrutiny, from her touch. "This is nothing. I've been punched by some of the best." He walked ahead of her, wondering how much worse the day could possibly get.

His mother had come down to the sidewalk and was surveying the garden anxiously. "I hope he didn't dig something up. I bought some new daffodils this fall, just got them into the ground."

"I don't think he had time, Ma." Noah moved up beside her. "He's a pretty small dog."

She turned toward him and glared at the dog. "What are you doing with a dog, anyway? You know I don't like dogs."

"Sorry. I forgot."

"Like you forgot to call and tell me you were coming? Like you forgot to come home since you were eighteen? Like you forgot to let me know you were still alive for the last four years?" She snorted and turned toward the house. "You have a serious memory problem."

Noah took one step in the same direction.

"And don't think you're bringing that dog into my house," she said, without looking back. "I won't have any filthy animal in my home." The screen slapped shut, then the front door.

The dog squirmed in his arms, but Noah stood still. His first impulse was to run as far and as fast as the full tank on the bike would take him. His second impulse was to slam inside the house and tell the bitch exactly what he thought of her, *then* take off for the farthest corner of the country.

"Noah?" He'd forgotten Abby entirely. "Noah, I'll take the dog."

He looked over at her, not understanding. "What?"

"I'll take the dog home with me. We've got a fenced yard and an enclosed porch where he can sleep."

"I can just—" He didn't really have another option. "I guess that'll work for tonight."

"What's his name?" she asked, reaching around the dog so that she was practically in Noah's arms. He got a whiff of the sweet flower scent in her hair. When she drew away, with the animal cuddled against her own chest, he missed her warmth.

"I don't know."

Her eyes widened. "You didn't name him?"

"No. I didn't—" This might not be the best time to confess that he hadn't planned to keep the mutt. "I didn't have time to think up a name."

"I guess not." Her smile was a flash of brightness in the darkening afternoon. "We'll work on that tomorrow. See you then."

"Sure." She made tomorrow sound like something to look forward to. Noah watched her leave the yard and cross the street to her car, an old red Volvo, where she settled the dog on the passenger seat before getting in herself. The sound of the engine, when it finally started, called for a major tune-up, but Abby gave him a cheerful wave and another smile before she pulled away from the curb.

As she left, Noah realized his first impulses had weakened, letting a certain degree of reason take hold of his brain. He wasn't going to run out on his mother again. Not before they'd had a chance to…settle things. Not before he made sure she would be taken care of for as long as she needed. He owed her that much.

So he opened the screen and pushed back the door into the house. A wave of heat hit him—the thermostat must be set at eighty degrees—along with the scent of onions and hot grease. His stomach churned, but he forced himself to walk to the kitchen.

His mother glanced at him. "I was beginning to think you'd just run off again." With a tilt of her head, she directed him to the table by the window. "I was cooking when you showed up. Sit down. Go on, sit. This'll be done in a minute."

Noah eased out of his jacket and hung it on the back of the chair. Even his sweatshirt was too hot. Since he wasn't sure he was staying, though, he wouldn't take it off.

"There." A plate thumped onto the table. She still used the same dishes he remembered from fifteen years ago, made of unbreakable white glass, with blue flowers around the edges. Two hamburgers anchored the meal, framed by a pile of potato chips and a couple of pickles.

"Here's some rolls." A bowl of hamburger buns plopped onto the table. "I've got mustard and mayo. No ketchup."

"This is good, Ma. Thanks." He only hoped he could eat without choking.

She set a soda can by his plate, and then brought her own dinner plus a cola to the table and joined him. Her eyes closed. "Thank you, Lord, for this day and the blessings it has brought. Amen."

Noah barely got his own eyes shut before she finished, and was a little slow in opening them. The first thing he saw was his mother's fork, carrying a piece of dull gray hamburger, pointing into his face.

"So why don't you tell me," she suggested, "just where you've been for the last fifteen years?"

He took a deep breath.

"And why the hell," Marian Blake continued, "you bothered to come home now?"

CHAPTER TWO

The Diary of Miss Abigail Ann Brannon

September 2, 1981
Dear Diary,
The first day of fifth grade was just like the last day of fourth grade. We got our books and they all look boring. Why do we have to study North Carolina history? We live here, so what's to learn? I want to know about England and Africa and Japan. No such luck.

They mixed up the kids in different classes, like they do every year. Dixon and Rob and Jacquie are with me in Mrs. Davis's room, but Adam and Pete have Miss Lovett for a teacher. We get to see one another at recess and lunch, though.

Mrs. Davis made us sit in alphabetical order. How stupid is that? The boy in the desk next to mine is Noah Blake. He's shorter than me and really skinny. I heard he went to Porter Elementary but got transferred to New Skye Elementary because he caused so much trouble. I didn't see him do anything wrong today. His T-shirt was too big and his jeans were too short and his arms were covered with purple bruises. He didn't say

anything all day, and sat by himself at lunch and recess.
I think he's scary.

And I think Dixon has a crush on Kate Bowdrey.
I'm glad it's not me—boys are too much trouble.

April 1, 1982
Dear Diary,
Mrs. Davis assigned partners for our end-of-the-year
project today. April Fool's for me—I have to work with
Noah Blake. He hasn't said a word to me all year long,
now we're supposed to work together on the biggest project all year. We have to pick a historic building, make a
model and write about it. A North Carolina building,
of course, not something neat like the Taj Mahal or the
Eiffel Tower. We got fifteen minutes at the end of the
day to talk about what building we want. Noah just
shrugged when I asked him what he wanted to do. But
when I named some buildings—the state capitol, the
courthouse here in New Skye, the lighthouse at Cape
Hatteras—he rolled his eyes or sneered. He doesn't like
my ideas, but he doesn't have any of his own. Stupid boy.
I don't think he has lunch money—I hardly ever see him
eat.

June 4, 1982
Dear Diary,
This was the last day of fifth grade and the worst day
of my life. I stayed up until almost midnight writing the
paper for my history project with Noah. He built the
model of Fort Fisher at his house and was bringing it in

this morning for our presentation. When I got to school, the model was on my desk—smashed to pieces, like somebody punched their fist into the fort about ten times. Noah didn't show up for school. I read the paper to the class, and Mrs. Davis said she wouldn't take marks off on the model—you could tell it had been beautiful, made out of little sticks like the boards at the real fort, with bunkers covered by green felt for grass and a flag and cannons. I don't know what happened to it. I'm wondering if Noah's okay.

August 13, 1982
Dear Diary,
I saw Noah at the county fair tonight. I was behind this guy in line, and something about his shoulders, about the way he stood, made me sure it was him. But he was with a girl—she looked like she was about sixteen. I didn't say anything to make him turn around. I decided I didn't want a funnel cake after all and went for a pretzel instead.

He looked really cute.

September 4, 1982
Dear Diary,
The first day of middle school was weird. Changing classes freaks me out—I'm sure I'm going to be late every time. I have at least one class with just about everybody I know, but I only have lunch with Pete and Adam and Rob. Dixon still stares at Kate like he could eat her up, and she doesn't even realize it.

Even weirder than the classes was when Noah came up behind me at the water fountain after lunch. I turned around and—boom!—he was there. I had water dripping off my chin, of course. He grew about six inches over the summer, because he's taller than me now. His jeans weren't too short. He had a black eye, and his hair was longer.

He said he was sorry about the history project last June—he'd tripped when he was carrying it in and smashed it all up. I said it was okay, because I got an A on the paper. He said Mrs. Davis made him write a paper on his own and he'd managed to pass. I asked him about the black eye, and he said he got hit by a baseball he meant to catch. Why do I feel like that's not how it happened?

I thought about him a lot this summer, and I can't stop thinking about him now that I've seen him again. But we don't have classes together and Dad wants me to start working afternoons at the diner to give Mom a break, so unless Noah comes over after school, I probably won't see him at all this year.

He won't miss me. And I shouldn't miss him. But sometimes when Mrs. Davis would say something really silly, I'd see Noah trying not to laugh. I'm going to miss sharing the laughs.

I'm going to miss Noah, period.

STOPPED AT THE RED LIGHT two blocks from home, Abby glanced down at the dog on the passenger seat. "What am I going to do with you? You're too dirty to let into the house, and I'm pretty sure you have fleas, because my arm itches. Where can I get you a bath?" He hunched his skinny shoulders but wagged his tail at the same time. "That's not an answer."

In the end, she left Noah's dog with Carly Danvers, a friend from high school who'd built a nice little business grooming and boarding dogs. Carly promised to bathe and dip the little guy and then leave him on the porch at the Brannon house when he was dry, with food and water and a soft dog pillow to lie on. All he needed now was a name.

That would be Noah's contribution, Abby hoped.

She returned to the diner well before the dinner rush started, to find her dad stressing out over her absence.

"You just lock the place up and disappear?" Charlie Brannon stood in the kitchen with his hands on his hips, a squarely built man with the posture and haircut of a marine drill sergeant. "You don't call or leave a note? I was looking in the broom closet, expecting to see your body headfirst in the mop bucket."

Abby winced and went to fold her arms around his bulky shoulders. "I'm sorry. I didn't think I'd be gone long enough for you to notice." To be strictly honest, though, she hadn't given him a thought since Noah had walked through the diner door.

"Yeah, well." His voice softened with the hug. "Where'd you go?"

To gain some time, she shrugged out of her coat and went to hang it up in that same broom closet. "Um...I went to see Mrs. Blake."

"Weren't you there just yesterday? She call you and complain, as usual?"

"No, no." Abby took a deep breath. "Actually, Noah stopped by this afternoon."

"Noah?" Her dad's heavy dark brows drew together. "You mean Noah Blake?"

"That's right. He's come back."

"What's that troublemaker want here? I thought he was gone for good."

"He's not a troublemaker, Dad." The accusation made her furious.

"I don't know what he's like now. But when you kids were in school, he raised more hell than this town could handle. Including burning down the school two weeks before graduation."

"He did not burn down the school." She stomped into the cold room, brought back the pot of stew she'd made for tonight and slammed it onto the burner. "Nobody burned down the school—there was a fire in the principal's office, that's all. And Noah didn't set it."

"Of course he did. I saw his motorcycle over there not ten minutes before the fire truck showed up. So why is he back now?"

"He didn't say."

"And why did you go to his mother's house? Did he forget the address?"

Abby bit her tongue. "He thought he would...surprise her. But I thought Mrs. Blake might need a little support, since she's been sick so much. So I went along to...smooth the way."

"Did you?"

Trust Charlie to ask the really hard question. "I...don't know." Bitter and sick, Mrs. Blake was never easy to get along with. But her reaction to Noah's arrival hadn't been anything like Abby expected. "Noah brought a dog with him, a stray he rescued on his way here."

Charlie snorted in disbelief.

"And the dog got loose in the flower beds—"

"And Marian Blake started squealing."

Abby sighed. "Something like that." With belated guilt, she realized she should probably warn Charlie about the dog.

"Doesn't surprise me," her dad said, starting on the salads for dinner. "Bad enough the boy didn't let her know he was coming. Showing up with some mutt has to be the stupidest thing he's done in a while. I was there the day in third grade when Marian got chased across the playground by a dog. German shepherd, it was."

He shook his head. "Dog just wanted to play and when Marian ran away screaming, it thought she'd invented a new game. By the time the rest of us kids got there, the shepherd had her flat on her back under the pine trees and was licking her face off. She didn't come back to school for a week, she was so hysterical."

"That's horrible." Abby stirred the stew and then went to the pantry for cans of green beans. Noah couldn't know his mother's story, or he wouldn't have brought the dog home with him. But there was obviously no hope of convincing his mother to take the poor animal into her house. Which meant...

"So you chased the dog off, and then what?"

"We didn't exactly chase him away."

"Well, Marian didn't change her mind after all this time."

"N-no."

Charlie glared at her. "Don't tell me that."

"What?"

"Don't tell me you kept the stupid dog."

"You don't know it's a stupid dog. You've never even seen it."

"I don't have to see a stray to know I don't want it."

"He's sweet, and scared to death."

"If he's in my house, he's got a good reason to be scared."

Hands on her hips, Abby glared at her dad. "I live there, too. And I'll put *my* dog on the sunporch with a blanket and a bowl of water and some food."

"It's not your dog, it's Noah Blake's dog."

"I'm keeping it." She'd had no intention of doing any such thing when she took the dog home, of course.

Charlie pinned her with his drill-sergeant glare. "Abigail Ann Brannon, I will not—"

Out front, the bell on the door jingled once, and again, and yet again. The dinner rush was starting.

"We'll discuss this later," he promised, and left the kitchen. Abby heard his brusque voice out in the dining room, greeting familiar customers. She stood still for a few seconds longer, recovering from the argument with her dad. When was the last time she and Charlie had seriously disagreed?

Never, was the first answer that came to mind. Sure, they argued a lot. And he could be hard to get along with sometimes. But she hadn't seriously defied her dad since she was fifteen and wanted to attend a summer camp in Wyoming. Her parents had said no—they needed her to work in the diner. She'd given them the silent treatment and sulked through the entire summer until she went back to school and saw Noah again. They hadn't talked much, except when she passed him a few sheets of paper if he needed them, or a pen when he didn't have one. Just seeing him had always made a major improvement in her day.

And she hadn't seen him in fifteen years.

"Fried chicken, stew and meat loaf," Charlie announced as he came into the kitchen. "Hamburger, cheeseburger, tuna sub, grilled cheese and soup. Two more stews."

Abby shook herself from head to toe. Time to get to work. "Right. I've got the grill. Two burgers and a grilled cheese, coming up."

NOAH FOUND IT AMAZING that his mother still watched the same roulette-wheel spelling show and supply-the-question quiz program after dinner as she had when he'd been in high school. The sitcoms that came afterward had changed actors, if not story lines, but after half an hour of watching, he felt sick to his stomach. Or maybe that was the hamburger.

"I'm gonna go see a couple of people," he told his mother during a commercial break. "I still have my key, unless you changed the locks."

She stared up at him for a long minute. "No, I didn't change the locks." As he crossed to the front door, she said, "Do you want breakfast?"

He looked back over his shoulder. "Sure." He hadn't been given the choice for years. "That'd be good."

"You better show up in the kitchen at eight, then."

"I'll be there. 'Night." If she responded, he didn't hear her.

Standing outside the chain-link fence, he stopped to take a deep breath of cold, dry air. He hadn't remembered the house being so small, so…so tight. On the other hand, he must have had some reason for running away, right? Besides knowing that if he stayed, his life would be over before it began.

With the Harley rumbling underneath him, Noah admitted to himself that he didn't really have anywhere else to go. Most of the guys he'd hung with in high school were probably in jail. Even if they weren't in the joint right now, they surely had been, and seeing them could constitute a violation of his parole. Not a smart move for his first week of freedom.

The nightly rituals in the neighborhoods south of Boundary Street hadn't changed in fifteen years, either. And they differed not at all from the usual agenda on the "bad" side of most towns he'd ever been in. The bars did a booming business. Working girls lingered on street corners and beside alleys. He fielded a couple of waves as he waited at a stoplight, remembered how long it had been since the last time, and gave the possibility a second's consideration—until Abby's sweet face appeared in his mind's eye.

Suddenly, a hooker in black leather and chains didn't seem to be what he needed. With a shake of his head and a lift of his hand, Noah rolled on down the hill, to another light and through an intersection, then into the gravel parking lot of the Carolina Diner.

The lights were still on and half a dozen cars sat in the parking lot. He'd be safe enough going in for a cup of coffee, maybe a piece of pie. He remembered liking Charlie Brannon's chocolate pie.

As the door shut behind him, he realized he'd made a mistake. Every table in the room was empty except for a few square ones pushed together in the center, where people sat with papers spread out in front of them, working.

Working, that is, until they all stopped and turned to stare at him. Noah felt his cheeks heat up at the same time as he started to recognize the faces. The names popped into his head a second or two later.

Abby got out of her chair and came toward him, one hand extended. "Noah! It's good to see you again." Before he could back out, she caught his wrist in her cool fingertips. "I'm sure you'll remember almost everybody here."

"I didn't mean to interrupt...."

"You're not." The tall, brown-haired guy at the end of the table got to his feet, offering a handshake and a grin. "Welcome back, Noah."

"Dixon." Noah gripped Dixon Bell's hand. "Thanks."

Dixon turned to the woman in the chair next to him, who was standing as well. "You remember Kate Bowdrey? She's now Kate Bell."

"I remember she was the smartest person in the class." He smiled at the slender and beautiful Mrs. Bell. "How are you?"

"Glad to see you again." To his surprise, she gave him a hug and a kiss on the cheek. "You've been gone too long."

All of a sudden, he was surrounded by people he'd gone to high school with, returning handshakes and hugs, trying to catch up with a lot of changes very fast. Kate's sister Mary Rose, as blond as her sister was dark, had married Pete Mitchell. Adam DeVries, who didn't seem to stutter anymore, was the mayor of New Skye and married to a woman named Phoebe. Jacquie Lennon was now Jacquie Lewellyn and shoeing horses for a living, which meant she must still be horse crazy.

And Abby was still Abby. "What can I get you to drink?" With her hands on his shoulders, she leaned forward as he sat in the chair she'd just left. "More hot chocolate? Iced tea? Coffee?"

"I came for coffee. And—" He glanced around the table to see that most of the others had enjoyed some kind of dessert. "And some chocolate pie?"

"You got it." Her hands tightened for a second before she let go. Noah noted a sudden hollow in his chest where his breath used to be. He turned to Adam, on his right. "Looks like there's some serious planning going on tonight."

"We're the committee for the big Christmas Dance. Or maybe it's called the Reunion Dance."

"Holiday Reunion Dance," Jacquie put in from across the table. "Our fifteen-year high school class reunion is gonna be a holiday bash."

"Fifteen years?" Noah said. "Hard to believe it's been so long."

"Or that we're so old." Abby set a mug down by his left hand. "I still feel eighteen."

"I usually feel like I'm eighteen when I get up in the morning," Pete said with a grin. "But by the time I get home, it's a lot closer to thirty-three."

After more than two years in prison, Noah felt as if he was closer to fifty. "Uh…sounds like a good time. Do you expect a big crowd?"

The question did what he'd hoped, which was to get all of them talking, explaining the plans for the dance, the guest list, the decorations and music. All he had to do was nod and listen and try to make sense of this unfamiliar world he'd stumbled into.

Abby brought him his pie and then sat in an empty chair across the table. Between bites—the pie was every bit as good as he remembered—Noah took the opportunity to watch her with her friends. She'd pulled her hair back in a ponytail, so he could see the long column of her throat and her delicate pink ears, dusted with the same freckles that sprinkled her face. Her hazel eyes glowed as she talked, and a smile always hovered around her sweet, full lips. She was the most alive woman he'd ever seen. And the most desirable.

Not in this life. He gave himself a mental punch and refocused his attention on the discussion.

"What we need to decide is how to decorate the gym," Jacquie said. "People will feel like they're supposed to play basketball if we don't do something."

"We can hang mistletoe from the hoops." Dixon winked at his wife, who blushed.

"It's drafty in there, too." Mary Rose pretended to shiver. "My dress has short sleeves and a low back."

Pete put an arm around his wife and gave her a squeeze. "That's why we're going to do lots of dancing. Slow dancing." Noah noticed for the first time that Pete's left arm was in a sling, under which he wore a cast from shoulder to fingertips.

Abby rolled her eyes. "After two years, you two still act like newlyweds. Consider the rest of us who aren't so besotted, why don't you? Noah, what do you think?"

He put his hands up in defense. "I don't have a clue about stuff like this."

She frowned at him. "You're not helping."

That was supposed to bother him? He started to shrug, then realized he didn't like disappointing Abby. "Well, you could make a smaller space within the gym, if you used dividers of some kind."

"Dividers? Like screens?"

Noah nodded. "Yeah, or curtains. I think there are curtains on stands you can rent for that kind of thing."

"Or we could build something easily enough," Adam said. "Plywood sheets and two-by-fours would do the job. Paint them whatever color you want and make a room within a room. Good idea, Noah."

"Red and green for the season?" Pete suggested.

"We could do holiday designs." Mary Rose sat forward to look at her sister down the table. "Or use wallpaper."

"Or wrapping paper. Or…" Kate thought for a second. "Or we could paint a whole scene on the boards. A party scene, with Christmas decorations and trees and people—"

"A snowy landscape," Jacquie said, "with horses and sleighs and lighted houses."

"We could do a street scene—downtown New Skye all decorated for a white Christmas." Abby's face shone with pleasure. "We haven't had snow at Christmas here since I was six. But we could paint one, and maybe even scatter snowflakes on the floor and hang them from the ceiling. Coach Layman is making us put mats over the floor as it is, so piles of fake snow shouldn't be a problem. And we could dance in the snow without getting cold!"

By the time the meeting broke up at almost eleven o'clock, a contest had been decided on. Individuals or groups could register to paint a Christmas-scene panel. The entry fees would add to the budget for the dance, Abby pointed out, and prizes would be awarded to each participant.

"Some can be gag gifts, like 'Most Glitter.'" Abby grinned at Noah. "I love glitter."

"'Colored Inside the Lines,'" Noah suggested. "That's the best some of us can hope for." Abby and her friends burst out laughing, and he stared at them in surprise. His reputation did not include being funny.

Folks said good-night as Abby gathered up the dishes from the table and walked them into the kitchen. Before leaving, Dixon put a hand on Noah's shoulder. "Speaking of basketball, we have a friendly game going on Saturday mornings about seven, over at the school. Pete usually plays with us, but he got hurt on the job a couple of weeks ago, so we're short a man. Want to join us?"

More surprises. "I'm not sure—"

Dixon nodded. "Give me a call, let me know. Or just show up. Good to see you."

"You, too." He stared after the Bells for a minute, then followed Abby into the kitchen with the glasses and mugs from the table. "You don't have to stay and wash up, do you? It's late."

"There's a dishwasher." She nodded toward the contraption in the back of the kitchen. "Load and run."

Once she'd flipped the washer switch and locked the back door, Abby turned off the lights. With the only illumination coming from the dining room, the shadowed kitchen felt small. Intimate.

One-track mind. Noah leaned his hips back against the stainless-steel counter, shoving his hands into the pockets of his jacket. "I haven't seen your dad. He still work here?"

"He does, but I make him go home for a couple of hours in the afternoon and for good about eight o'clock. He's just not as young as he was." She pulled the dark red coat he'd seen her in earlier out of the nearby closet, then turned to smile at him. "None of us are, I guess."

"You work by yourself all the rest of the time?" He made a conscious decision not to help her with the coat, though she was struggling with the inside-out sleeves.

"I have help until about three in the afternoon. Billie Underwood comes in to cook up vegetables, pot roasts and stuff while I make the desserts. She goes home to take care of her grandkids after school, but still does a lot of baking and cooking for us then, too." Still fighting with the coat, she blew a frustrated breath off her lower lip. "Would you please come over here and untangle this stupid cloth from my arm?"

Warily, Noah straightened up and stepped close enough to catch the collar of the coat and the end of the sleeve. "Why don't you just stopping wiggling for a minute?"

Abby dropped her hands and was still. She'd gotten him where she wanted him, finally—alone in a dark room. This was the moment she'd been dreaming about for most of her life, at least since the first time she thought kissing a boy didn't sound like the grossest idea on the planet.

But now she wasn't sure what to do next. She'd never seduced a man before. As he dragged the coat off her shoulders and arm, she turned to face him, without stepping back.

He did, though, holding out the coat to the side and pulling the arms straight. "There." He pushed the coat toward her. "Now you can put it on."

Abby turned her back to him, extending her arms in a demand for help. After a pause, Noah sighed very loudly, slipped the sleeves over her hands and pulled the coat up. She didn't take any responsibility for getting the collar up to her neck, and he huffed again as he settled the wool over her shoulders.

For a moment, nothing happened. Abby feared she'd lost.

Then she felt the lightest of touches in her hair. A slight tug told her he'd wrapped a strand around his finger. She could hear his breathing, rough in the dark.

When she didn't move away, he stroked his knuckles over her head, just above her ear, then his fingertips. His shaking fingertips.

Now she could turn, and did, setting her palms on his chest. She'd always wondered how far she would have to look up to see his face when they were this close. He was taller than she remembered. Taller than he looked. The perfect height for kissing, her head just level with his shoulder.

One of his hands had tangled in her hair. The other traveled down her arm to cup her elbow. His dark eyes were narrowed, suspicious. "What are you doing?"

"Welcoming you home," she whispered back. Then she went up on tiptoe and pressed her mouth against Noah's.

For a few miraculous seconds, he took everything. She offered comfort and he seized it all. Desire and his need flamed over them both. His mouth was firm, agile, demanding. Abby sank into the kiss, sank into Noah until his hands, his body were all that kept her upright. She would have given him whatever he wanted.

Abruptly, he shoved her away, with enough force that she stumbled backward and probably would have fallen if she hadn't backed into the wall.

"I don't know what kind of game this is. But I'm not playing." His voice grated like sandpaper on her skin.

"No game." She caught her breath, fought back tears. "I'm not a tease. I wanted to kiss you."

"Why?"

She straightened up. "Because I care about you, of course."

"Yeah, right." He paced to the door of the kitchen, then came back. "What's the problem, Abby? Are you tired of the good ol' boys in town? Looking for something different? A little excitement?"

"That's an obnoxious thing to say."

"Or do you come on to every single guy who walks in the door?"

"I don't know that you're single." She wiped her hand across her mouth. "I just offered a kiss."

"You offered a hell of a lot more than that, and you know it. But I'm not taking."

"Obviously." Trying for dignity, she stalked past him without a glance, picked up her purse and keys off the counter and left the kitchen.

At the front of the diner, she turned off the lights for the dining room and took a great deal of pleasure in listening to Noah stumble against tables and chairs in the dark. Still swearing, he brushed through the door as she held it open, but the touch only chilled her. Or maybe it was the cold night wind.

He watched from his bike as she bolted the door. "You lock up by yourself like this every night?" His growl took her by surprise. "In the dark? With nobody around?"

"Yes, as a matter of fact." She started toward her car and heard the bike rolling along behind her.

"Your dad lets you do that?"

"I've never had a problem."

"Dumb luck. You should never be here alone. Especially at night."

"Don't lecture me on safety, Noah." She didn't look at him as she spoke. "You don't know the first thing about this town or my life. You haven't been here for fifteen years. So just…just put a sock in it."

He was silent as she unlocked the Volvo and got in. But before she could close the door, he was looming over her.

"You probably think New Skye is a sweet little place where nothing bad ever happens. But I'm telling you, there are nasty people here, like everywhere else. And if you aren't careful, one day you're gonna find that out the hard way. Your friends and your family should take care of you."

Abby stared up at him. "Yes, I guess they should, *friend*." She pulled on the door with both hands and, when he stepped out of the way, slammed it shut. The engine started with a purr, thank goodness. Engine trouble would have been too mortifying. Needing to get away, Abby shifted gears and set her foot on the accelerator.

But then a thought struck and she rolled down the window. "Come get your dog," she yelled.

Noah turned and stared at her. "I don't want the damn dog."

"Well, if you don't come get him, I'll send him to the shelter. My dad doesn't want to keep him."

"What's your dad got to do with it?"

"I live in his house. He makes the rules." She couldn't believe they were shouting at each other across the parking lot in the middle of the night.

Noah wasn't shouting now. He'd gone quiet, and stood still as he gazed at her. "You live with your dad?"

CHAPTER THREE

NOAH MISSED BREAKFAST. After finally falling asleep as
the sun came up, he stumbled into the kitchen at ten to
find a pot of cold coffee and his mother's note.

"Drs appt. Back sometime."

"Love you, too," he told her. He had no business feeling resentful, since he was the one who'd been gone for
fifteen years. A warm welcome was the last thing he deserved.

Especially a welcome like the kind Abby had offered
last night.

He groaned and rubbed the heels of his hands into
his burning eyes. He'd put up with a lot of punishment
in the last few years, but last night just hadn't been fair.
He shouldn't have been required to turn down a generous, willing woman like Abby. He would have made
sure she enjoyed the night as much as he did. They both
could be feeling pretty good this morning.

Instead, he felt like hell. Nothing new there. He
flicked the switch for the coffeemaker to warm up, then
bent over to rest his folded arms on the counter and hide
his face from the bright light coming through the window. A hangover would be bearable. This ache inside
him was too much.

The phone's ring interrupted his pity party and Noah straightened up, reaching automatically for the place on the wall where the phone hung. His hand met air, then wall. No phone.

"Damn." He tracked the noise into the living room and pounced on a cordless model set up by his mother's chair. "Hello? Hello?"

"Good morning, Noah. It's Kate Bell. How are you today?"

Best to settle for a polite answer. "I'm good, Kate. How are you?"

"Just fine. But I have a little problem you could help me with, if you would."

He dropped into the chair. "I'll do what I can."

"Thanks so much. After your brilliant idea last night, Dixon volunteered to take some measurements in the gym to determine how large the painted panels should be. But when he volunteered, he forgot that he's flying to Nashville this afternoon on business. Since he can't be here, he wondered if you would take those measurements for him. We want to give people plenty of time to sign up and complete their paintings."

"Nashville?"

"He writes songs—rock, country. You've probably heard them on the radio. Every so often, the folks in Nashville want to see him up there, and this is the week."

"I'm impressed. You'll have to give me a list of his songs. But—"

"He also wanted me to remind you that you're expected at the basketball game Saturday morning. Seven o'clock."

"I appreciate the offer. But—"

"I know Rob Warren will want to see you—y'all spent time together in high school, didn't you? Rob's just married a really lovely woman with two children. He was married to Leah Rodes—do you remember her?—but she died having their baby, Ginny. So it's great that he's found somebody to share his life again."

"Sounds really nice, but—"

"Then I'll tell Dixon to expect you on Saturday. And if you don't mind, get those measurements to me as soon as possible. I've got a flyer ready to print and send out, as soon as I figure out the size of the panel."

"I'll get that done today, Kate. But—"

"Thanks so much. I really appreciate your help. I'll give you a call soon and have you over for dinner. I'd love you to meet my children, Trace and Kelsey. Till later, then. Bye."

She clicked off before he could say another word, but Noah continued to stare at the phone.

What had just happened? People like Kate Bowdrey and her sister had barely given him the time of day in high school—now all at once they wanted him to help out with their dance? Maybe Abby was behind this sudden friendliness, trying to make him fit in somehow.

He clenched his back teeth at the idea of being anybody's charity project, especially Abby Brannon's.

Then he remembered the welcome he'd received last night at the meeting, from Dixon and Adam and Pete. So, okay, Abby wasn't trying to treat him like the stray dog she'd taken home and now wanted him to retrieve.

With a groan, Noah slammed the phone back in its

cradle and headed for the shower. Kate had given him an assignment—measure the damn gym floor. There were other chores ahead of him, too, like checking in with his parole officer and his new boss.

Life hadn't been this complex in a long time. Until three years ago, he'd done what he wanted, when he wanted, without consulting anybody else. In prison, he'd had no choices, so no complications. Now he was trying to do the right thing, not sure what the right thing really was.

If he'd expected coming back to be so tricky, he might have chosen to serve out his sentence. In jail, at least, he knew what he was in for.

Since he'd come "home," he didn't have a clue.

KATE SHUT OFF HER CELL PHONE and looked across the table. "I have never sounded like such an airhead in my life."

Mary Rose grinned. "And I loved every second."

"Oh, hush." Kate pretended to frown at her sister. "I hate to strong-arm anybody, but I do think we owe Noah the opportunity to be part of the community. He didn't get a fair break in high school—from the kids or the teachers, certainly not from Principal Floyd and the police. Dixon and I want to let him know we trust him."

Beside Kate, Jacquie Lewellyn pushed her breakfast plate away. "I could tell last night—he expected pretty much the same treatment he got back then. Why are kids so cruel?" She sighed, then shook her head. "I hope I can count on Erin to behave better. In the meantime, we'll just work on making Noah part of the gang.

He won't know what hit him until it's too late, and by then he won't be able to leave."

"And won't want to," Mary Rose added. "That's more important."

Abby caught part of their comments as she brought fresh coffee and hot water for tea. "What schemes are y'all hatching this morning? Who's leaving where?"

"Oh…I—I'm planning a surprise for Rhys," Jacquie said. "A Christmas present."

"What kind of present?" Abby rubbed her eyes with the back of her wrist as she poured more coffee into Kate's mug. "And what's it got to do with hitting?"

"Oh, no. No," Jacquie said, blushing. "I was talking about boxing. Boxing lessons for when he gets tense and hard to live with."

"I'm sure you're not referring to me." Rhys Lewellyn walked up to the table. Wearing riding breeches, tall boots and a blue sweater that matched his eyes, he was definitely the best-looking man in the diner at that moment. "Because there's no one easier to get along with than I am."

"Oh, of course." Jacquie reached up to hold her husband's hand. "There's never been a cross word at our house—not even when Andrew decided to try out pierced ears."

"I only said what I thought," Rhys said, smiling.

"Along the lines of grounding him until the age of twenty-one."

"A reasonable reaction, in my opinion, to earrings on my son."

Abby smiled. "Spoken like a father. Charlie would

have skinned me alive for doing something like that without permission. As a matter of fact, I never did get my ears pierced." Her dad had been furious to find the dog on his sunporch last night, and he'd been prepared to rant about the problem for a good long time after Abby came home.

But she'd been so worn out, so sad, that she hadn't added fuel to the fire. She'd drifted to her room and Charlie's rage had leaked away.

"I remember last year when Erin dyed her hair red." Jacquie shook her head as she slid out of the booth. "I have never been so pleased to see a haircut as when the last of that red hit the floor."

Mary Rose and Kate got up, too, and soon said their goodbyes. Abby loved her friends, but she was very glad to see them leave this morning. They tended to understand without needing an explanation. Today, Abby had too much to hide.

Although nothing had actually happened between her and Noah. Really, it had just been a kiss. She had been kissed before, many times. After all, she was thirty-three years old.

But Noah's kiss had been more than she'd ever known with any other man. More than she'd dreamed. And over so fast, she felt as if he'd slapped her.

She moved through the rest of the breakfast shift in a kind of daze, half smiling at the customers she knew, half conscious of their orders and the flow of business in the diner. The crowd gradually thinned, until she was actually alone in the place. Pouring herself a glass of iced tea, Abby slid into a booth where the sun warmed the green vinyl seat and propped her head on one hand to stare out the side window. A little caffeine and a few minutes off her feet seemed like heaven.

But it wasn't to be. The doorbell jingled, announcing someone who wanted a late breakfast. Dredging up a smile, she looked across the dining room into Noah's distant gaze.

He cleared his throat. "Hi."

She didn't have the first idea of what to say, so she just stared.

He looked away, and then back at her face. "Could I get a cup of coffee?"

Abby felt too weary to stand up, but she pressed her palms into the tabletop to push herself to her feet. "Of course."

At that moment, Charlie came out of the kitchen. He leaned back against the service counter with his arms crossed over his big chest, the marine tattoo on his hand clearly visible.

"What can I do for you?"

Noah held the gaze of the man across the room, but it took more will than he wanted to admit. Despite a bum leg earned while tangling with a land mine in Vietnam, Charlie Brannon was not a guy to mess with. Back in high school, Noah had known better than to come within sighting distance of Charlie if he had something to hide.

Just like he should have known better today. "Good morning, Mr. Brannon. I thought I'd get a cup of coffee."

Charlie looked him up and down but didn't budge. "What are you doing back in town?"

"I came to see my mother, that's all."

"You waited long enough."

Not having an answer for that one, Noah shrugged.

"And when you do show up, you palm off a mongrel that kept me up all night whining. God only knows where that dog's been. But now he's in my house."

"I…" He glanced at Abby for some help. She was staring at him with her chin up, her eyes defensive, her fists clenched.

In the second that their eyes stayed connected, hers melted. She closed her eyes and shook her head, then got to her feet.

"I told you, Dad, that I wanted the dog. Noah didn't impose anything on you. Or me."

Which was an outright lie. Noah remembered those minutes in the kitchen last night. He'd imposed a hell of a lot on Abby and would have been glad to extend the damage.

Charlie snorted, as if he knew the truth. Maybe Abby had told him?

Noah waited, prepared to die.

But Abby's dad just turned to the coffeepot. "I'm not happy having you in here. But, hell, your dollar's as good as the next guy's." He set a filled mug down on the counter. "Drink up." With a shrug, Charlie returned to the kitchen.

Thanks didn't seem necessary. Charlie wouldn't care if he was polite. As Noah went toward the counter, Abby moved in the same direction. They ended up facing each other across the long, stainless-steel surface.

"How is your mom this morning?"

"She went to the doctor. I haven't seen her yet." He sipped at the strong, hot coffee, digging up words. "Did the dog really whine all night?"

Abby nodded. She sure looked like she hadn't slept much—her face was pale, her eyes tired. Under the white button-down shirt, her shoulders weren't as straight as they'd been yesterday.

The dog might be part of her problem. But after a sleepless night himself, he suspected she'd had other reasons to lie awake.

"I'm sorry about last night." Meeting Abby's gaze took even more courage than confronting Charlie.

"The dog, you mean?"

"And…other things." He wasn't about to go into details with Charlie in the building.

She looked in every direction but his. "No apologies necessary. It wasn't your fault. Just come get the dog, and everything will be okay."

"I can't take the dog." He seized the chance to argue about something practical. "You saw my mother yesterday. She won't have a dog anywhere near the house." Noah couldn't help grinning. "And when it comes to a knockdown, drag-out fight, I'm betting on my mother over your dad."

Abby's full lips twitched in an almost-smile. "No way."

"Oh, yeah."

He took another draw of coffee while she wiped the counter down and then adjusted the drape of red beads on the fake Christmas tree at the far end. For a few minutes, there was actually peace in the air.

Until she glanced at him from the other end of the counter. "So when will you come get the dog?"

"What am I gonna do with the dog if I get it?"

"What did you think you were going to do with it when you brought it with you?"

An uncomfortable question. "I didn't think," Noah admitted. "I only knew I wouldn't let a gang of kids kill him just because they could." He waited a beat. "Why can't you take care of him?"

"What makes you think I want the dog?"

"Don't you?"

She blew out a breath. "Whether I do or not doesn't matter. It's Charlie's house. He makes the rules and he wants the dog gone."

"Well, what the hell are you doing still living with your dad, anyway?" That question had been one of many bothering him last night. "You're an adult—you should be out on your own."

Abby froze in the act of refilling a napkin canister and stared at the man across the counter. He looked fierce, formidable. She was suddenly very aware of the strength in his hands and arms, the tension in his every move that spoke of experiences she didn't know, couldn't imagine.

"You don't have the right to ask me that question." She fought to keep her voice steady. "You don't know anything about me. You never did, never wanted to." Slamming the napkin holder onto the counter, she crumpled the empty napkin wrapper in her hands. "Leave a dollar by the register when you go."

"Abby—" Noah stretched out a hand.

But she'd had all she could take for the morning. Ignoring the gesture and the tenderness in his voice, she stomped into the kitchen and back to the office behind it, slamming the door for good measure. Then she plopped down in the desk chair and clutched her hands in her hair, pulling until tears burned her eyes.

He might have been gone a long, long time, but as far as she could tell, Noah Blake was just as hard to handle as he had been fifteen years ago. Why in the world had she spent even one moment hoping for anything else?

WALKING INTO NEW SKYE HIGH was a lot like walking into a Georgia correctional institution for the first time. Noah took a deep breath, but there didn't seem to be enough air to fill his lungs. He glanced behind him, just to be sure there were no chains on the door, no bars on the windows.

In the front office, he introduced himself to the young woman at the desk, someone he didn't know.

"That's right," she said with a flirtatious smile. "Dixon Bell called just a few minutes ago to say you'd be coming in his place. Since he'd already spoken to Mr. Floyd about visiting the gym, I don't think there's any problem with you going on down there." She nodded toward the closed door on her right, with its Principal Floyd sign. "He's in conference with parents and a student. If you'd like to wait—"

"No, that's okay." Noah hid his appalled reaction to the idea of meeting the principal. "I'll just walk down, do my job, then clear out." He gave her the smile she wanted. "Thanks for your help."

"Oh, you're welcome." As he reached the door, she said, "Are you sure you know the way? I could take you to the gym."

Another smile, not quite so friendly. "I remember the way." He stepped out before she could try again.

The bell for changing classes rang above his head—had it always been so loud? The halls filled with bodies and noise as kids exploded from every doorway. Noah passed through the crowd like a ghost, without really being seen. At the gym door, he met a swell of students pouring out of their daily class, their relief demonstrated by the rush. Standing to the side, waiting for the hall to clear, Noah reflected that he'd always liked gym class, welcomed the chance to blow off steam. He'd been good at sports, but never had the grades to make a team.

Which pretty much summed up his whole life.

Inside, the gym was blessedly quiet. He stood at the edge of the basketball court, fingering his industrial-size tape measure and taking in the banners hanging from the rafters that proclaimed New Skye High championships. Pictures of individual students who had exhibited special success hung on the wall. He recognized Rob Warren's picture among them, with Rob as a tall, lanky basketball player. Though he'd been one of the "good" kids, Rob had also been Noah's friend. Probably his only friend who invariably stayed on the right side of the law.

On that thought, Noah decided to start the job he'd come to do. He didn't expect or intend to attend the dance, which made explaining to himself what he was doing here tough. But he'd agreed to help Kate Bell.

The only virtue he claimed in life was sticking by his word.

He was down on one knee, recording the measurements he'd taken, when quick footsteps echoed at the far end of the gym.

"What are you doing in here?" Noah didn't have to look up to identify the speaker. "Who gave you permission to enter the school building unescorted?" Principal Floyd stood over him, a heavy man breathing hard, red-faced and sweating.

Noah couldn't get to his feet without shoving Floyd out of the way or crawling back. He wasn't ready to do either. "The secretary at the front desk gave me permission. You know that, because she's the one who told you I was in here."

Floyd clenched his fists. "Dixon Bell had my permission to enter the school building. You, of all people, did not."

"Dixon couldn't come. If you get out of my way, I'll be done in a couple of minutes and then I can get out of yours."

"What are you doing back in town, anyway? I thought we'd gotten rid of you for good."

Tired of looking up, Noah heaved to his feet, forcing Floyd to take a couple of steps back. "This is my hometown. Why shouldn't I come back?"

"Because we don't want you." The principal stood with his fat hands on his dumpy hips. He'd gone bald in the last fifteen years. "Because you're a troublemaker, and if you stick around, there's going to trouble for everybody. Nobody in New Skye needs you."

Noah had to admit the truth of that statement. "Don't have a stroke, Mr. Floyd. I'm not interested in making trouble." He ignored the flash of memory that gave him back the sweet, rich taste of Abby's mouth.

"I'm going to stand right here until you've finished whatever it is you think you're doing. And I'm going to keep my eye on you until you get off this campus. Don't plan to come back. We do have security guards, and I will be leaving orders that you should not be admitted to the grounds or the building."

"Knock yourself out." Noah finished his measurements as slowly as he could, for the pleasure of watching Floyd fume. He only regretted the job didn't take longer.

The walk back to the front of the school, however, seemed to take a century. Floyd didn't actually handcuff Noah, but in every other way he acted like a prison guard, to the extent of waving off the kids who came at them with curious faces. They didn't stop at the office, for which Noah was thankful, but continued through the front door onto the steps outside.

"Don't come back," Floyd warned again. "You've got no business at my school."

"You're right about that." Noah took his time getting down the steps. At the bottom, he turned back. "I don't suppose too many of the teachers remember me. But I did expect Ms. Lacey to be here for the rest of eternity. Did you fire her or did she finally get fed up with your pompous attitude and quit? She was a pretty good secretary, over all. Not to mention easy on the eyes."

Floyd's face turned an even darker red. "Your mouth

was always one of your biggest problems, Blake. Ms. Lacey left us years ago, to be married. Now, get off school property before I call the police."

That was a threat Noah took seriously. He didn't rush to the bike, but he didn't hesitate or falter, either. His unavoidable appearance at the police department would come all too soon.

"And stay off," Floyd yelled over the rumble of the bike's engine. Noah buckled his helmet, gave the principal a wave and wheeled out of the parking lot.

ANDY FLOYD HELD TRUE to his promise, watching until Noah Blake's motorcycle had disappeared in a swirl of dust on the highway. Inside the warm school building, he scanned the halls for tardy students, but wasn't lucky enough to see any he could nab. They had probably seen him first, and were hiding until he went back to his office.

When he reached his desk, he dropped into the chair and rubbed his hands over his face. The last person he'd expected or wanted to see this morning was Noah Blake. Nothing but trouble, he'd been, since the day he first set foot on school grounds.

Worse was the trouble he brought with him. Floyd grabbed the phone and pressed an auto-dial number. "Hey," he told the man who answered. "We've got a problem."

"What now?"

"Noah Blake is back."

"Who?"

"Noah Blake. The kid who ran away before the 1989 graduation, remember? After the fire?"

"Shit."

"Exactly."

"What's he want?"

"Who knows? But he looks like he usually gets whatever he sets his mind on. A real tough character."

After a second, the man on the phone laughed. "A tough character, is he? Good for him.

"Because I'm a pretty tough character myself."

FRIDAY MORNING, NOAH WENT to see the one person in town who knew the truth about him, the one person who had expected him to show his face in New Skye again.

Rob Warren lived in a peaceful neighborhood on the north side of downtown, in a comfortable-looking house surrounded by plenty of grass and trees. A green pine garland draped the porch rails, tied to the posts with big red bows. Lightbulbs twinkled in the garland and on the holly trees beside the front steps—nighttime would bring on a terrific light display, sure to please the kids. He'd always enjoyed Christmas lights himself.

Noah rang the doorbell, then stared at the huge wreath on the front door until the panel swung back with a draft of sharp, sweet pine scent and the jingle of small silver bells.

"Hey, Noah, good to see you. Come on in."

Warm and simple, cinnamon-scented, Rob's house immediately felt like home. Not any home Noah had ever experienced, but somehow he knew this was the way life was supposed to be. The Christmas tree by the front window stretched from floor to ceiling and, even in the daylight, shone with hundreds of lights, as well as ornaments of every kind. A nativity scene took up the entire mantel over the fireplace, complete with camels, cows, sheep, donkeys, chickens, dogs and angels. Noah smiled when he saw an obviously handmade dog near the manger.

"Yeah, the kids wanted Buttercup, my sister's golden retriever, at the stable," Rob explained. "I whittled and Valerie painted her." He shook his head. "Good thing we never thought about being artists. I don't think we can claim a thimbleful of talent between us. Have a seat."

Noah sat on the reclining armchair in the corner. "Looks like y'all will have a very merry Christmas morning." Presents wrapped in colorful paper and decorated with ribbons and bows were piled high at the base of the tree.

"We've gone overboard, I guess. It's so much fun to be a family—not two single parents with kids—that we're a little crazy." Rob shrugged, and his grin displayed not one morsel of regret. "That's what credit cards are for. Want some coffee?"

"No, thanks. I'm great." Between anxiety over this interview and the need to choke down his mother's scrambled eggs, he'd downed four cups this morning.

"Okay, then." Rob folded his long body onto the couch. "Thanks for coming here. My daughter Ginny had some surgery last week, and she's still recuperating in bed."

"I hope she's okay." Noah couldn't imagine coping with a child who needed surgery. Maybe Rob didn't have such an ideal life, after all?

"She'll be better in a few months. Ginny has cerebral palsy, and as she grows the doctors want to make adjustments in her tendons and muscles. We don't always agree with what they suggest, but she's been through a growth spurt recently and it seemed like the right thing to do. Even this close to Christmas."

Noah started to get up again. "Maybe this isn't a good time—"

Rob waved him down. "No, no, we're fine. This just happens to be my day to stay home—Valerie and I are alternating. Next week, my sister Jen will be off duty as an EMT, and she'll stay with Ginny." He smiled. "We're blessed with family who help out. And each other—I don't know what I'd do anymore without Valerie. Plus Grace and Connor, who will play with Ginny for hours while she's in bed. When they're not squabbling, of course."

Rob picked up a file folder lying on the coffee table and paged through it. "So let's get business out of the way and then maybe Ginny will be awake and I can introduce you. I haven't told anybody you were coming back—haven't mentioned, even to Valerie, that we've talked about this job. I figure your past is your business, and you'll decide what you want people to know and when."

"Thanks. I appreciate it."

"I've got a lot of paperwork here, forms to be signed and then delivered to your parole officer, forms I'm supposed to keep, information you're required to read. I guess we'll go over it one page at a time, make sure we've got everything covered. But first…"

Setting the folder back on the table, Rob braced his elbows on his knees, linked his fingers and then looked straight into Noah's face.

"First, I want to hear what you've been doing the last fifteen years or so. Tell me where you worked, where you lived, what you did in your spare time. Explain to me how in the world you ended up in prison.

"And then, give me one good reason I should trust you with a job."

CHAPTER FOUR

ABBY CLOSED THE DINER at nine Friday night and went home. As soon as she turned the last corner, she saw the big Harley parked by the curb across from her dad's house. Noah sat in the saddle, arms folded over his chest. He'd come for the dog, or to argue about the dog. She hadn't yet forgiven him for the argument yesterday morning.

"What are you doing here?" She bumped the car door shut with her hip.

"I came to get the dog."

"To do what with him? Your mother won't let him in the house, remember?"

"I'll hide him in my room." His smile gleamed white for a second. "She'll never know."

Now she crossed her arms. "Are you crazy? Of course she'll notice."

"She never knew about the mice I kept, or the lizards. I had a rabbit for a couple of years without her finding out."

"How in the world did you do that?"

"Kept my room clean, clothes washed, bed changed. She didn't have a reason to come in and snoop, so the rabbit stayed in the closet except when I was there and locked the door."

Abby couldn't help but laugh. "All these years, the teenagers of the world never realized the secret to true privacy was simple neatness."

"Give people what they want and they pretty much leave you alone."

"Words of wisdom." She stared at him through the darkness for a moment, watching the streetlight beam shimmer across his hair. "Well, come on in. Dad's usually in bed by now, so the coast should be clear."

She could have taken him around the back of the house to the sunporch. But she didn't want to sneak Noah in, as if she were ashamed of him. Noah Blake was as good as anyone else in town.

Still, she was thankful to see no sign of her dad as she led Noah through the front rooms. When they reached the kitchen, she could hear the dog snuffling on the other side of the door to the porch. As soon as she opened that door, the little guy was all over Noah.

"Hey, buddy." He knelt by the door so the dog could lick his face. "You're looking pretty good after a couple of days of inside digs. You even got a bath." Noah looked up at Abby. "That must have been fun. He can't have had too many in his life."

"I took him to a friend of mine who runs a dog-grooming business. She said he did okay. Maybe he belonged to people at one point and got lost."

"Maybe. Thanks, anyway." Cradling the dog against his chest, Noah got to his feet. "You've been a big help."

He intended to go, and take the dog with him. They

would both disappear from her life. After the way Noah had acted, she should be glad. But...

"Would you like something to drink? Coffee? Tea?"

He'd reached the door between the kitchen and the hallway. "No, thanks. I'm fine."

"Hot chocolate?"

Noah stopped and turned back. "That's a low blow."

"Does it work?"

"As long as your dad won't come in and yell at me."

Abby closed the doors to the hall and to the dining room. "He'll never know you're here. Have a seat at the table. This'll just take a second."

Noah set the dog on the floor and took a chair. He observed the kitchen while she worked. After a few minutes of companionable silence, he said, "Let me guess—your favorite color is red."

She grinned as she poured milk and cream into the chocolate mixture. "Can't put anything over on you."

"Red pots and pans, red-checked curtains, red apples on the table and a red rug on the floor. I'd have to be pretty dense."

"Red dishes, too," she pointed out, taking two big mugs out of a cabinet. "Add green napkins and I'm all decorated for Christmas."

When the chocolate started to simmer, she moved the saucepan off the burner and poured the beverage into the cups. She handed him a mug, then sat across the table with her own. The dog settled between them on the red rug, his chin resting on one outstretched paw.

Noah took a sip of chocolate. "You sure do work

miracles—this is even better than the stuff you made the other day."

"At home, I can use expensive chocolate and cream. At the diner, I have to remember cost control."

"It's worth the price. Maybe you could put Abby's Special Hot Chocolate on the menu and charge more."

She shook her head. "Charlie's pretty rigid about keeping prices down. He's the boss."

"So open your own place. Charge anything you want."

"And compete with the Carolina Diner? I don't think so."

"You'll just stick with the status quo?"

"I haven't been offered any other options." Beside them, the windowpane rattled in the wind. Abby glanced down at the dog. "It's a cold night to take him out on the motorcycle. He doesn't have too much hair."

"I brought the backpack. He'll be warm enough."

"And he still doesn't have a name."

"No." Noah stared down at the mutt. "Spot?"

She huffed in frustration. "He doesn't have spots."

"So?"

"A dog's name is supposed to mean something. Everybody's name should mean something."

"Who says?"

"I do." Holding her mug with both hands, she closed her eyes. "Loner? Ranger?"

"The Lone Ranger?" He grinned at her disgusted stare. "Why make such a big deal? Call him Harry."

"But he's not. How about Scruffy?"

"I'm not hanging around with a Scruffy."

"I don't see you hanging around with him at all."

Noah glared at her over the top of his mug, then took a long swig, effectively hiding his face. They dropped the argument long enough to enjoy the hot chocolate, and Abby gathered the courage to ask a question.

"So tell me…where have you been for the last decade or so, anyway?"

"Around." He set the drink on the table, pushing the handle of his mug with the pointer finger of one hand to the other, and back again.

When she didn't say anything, he seemed to realize he hadn't given enough of an answer. "Atlanta, mostly, for the last few years."

"What do you do?"

"Do?"

She slapped her palm on the table. At their feet, the dog jumped and sat up. "You're infuriating! You have to eat, right? What do you do to earn money?"

He chuckled at her temper tantrum. "Calm down, Abigail. I've worked a lot of different jobs over the years. Landscaping, moving furniture, construction, restaurant work—"

"Really? What kind?"

Noah gave a one-shouldered shrug. "Short-order cook, maître d', dishwasher, waiter. I did some sous-chef work at one place in Florida, but didn't stay long enough to get anywhere."

"You've been to Florida? And Georgia. Where else?"

When he shook his head, she insisted. "Come on, Noah, tell me where all you've traveled. I've been stuck in this little town since the day I was born, and as far as I can tell, I'll be here till I die. But I love hearing about other people's adventures."

Still, Noah hesitated. Abby didn't really want to know about the majority of the adventures he'd had—too many low-rent apartments and bar fights, too much experience with the police and the prison system, too few good meals to eat and good people to talk to. Wherever he'd been, he hadn't spent time on the right side of the tracks.

But he tried to give her what she wanted. "I hitched my way to California when I left here. Learned to surf and do some in-line skating." The entire two years had passed in an alcoholic haze. "Then I went to Wyoming and learned to ski at Jackson Hole. I was a lift operator for a season." He pretended to shiver. "Talk about cold."

"I can't imagine that much snow. And the Rocky Mountains—are they just spectacular?"

Somehow, she got him to describe what he'd seen of the Rockies…and Hawaii, where he'd only been able to afford a couple of months. He had stuff to tell about New York, Chicago, Dallas and San Antonio, too.

"And yeah, I have been overseas," he said finally, getting to his feet. "But it's after midnight and I need my beauty sleep. I'll just take the mutt and go on back to my mom's."

"Wait." Abby put her hand out as he bent to pick up the dog. "I—I feel bad about deceiving your mother."

Noah straightened up, leaving the dog on the floor. "You wouldn't be. Don't worry about it."

"But—" She grabbed his arm and held on tight. "Noah, why did you come home?"

"I…" He glanced away, rubbing a palm over his chin. "What difference does it make?"

"Because if you came to make peace with your mom, sneaking a dog into the house is not the way to go about it."

He put his palm over her fingers where she clutched him. "Abigail, this isn't your problem."

Her hand turned, linking their fingers. "I'd…like to see you stay around. For…a while."

Dangerous words. Her gold-green gaze searched his face, and Noah didn't know what to say.

The next moment became even more dangerous, as Abby stood, stepped closer and brought the fingertips of her free hand to his cheek. She tilted her face up, looking at him through half-lowered lashes. "Would that be so bad?"

"I—" Resisting temptation had never been one of his strong points. The sane half of his brain fired every possible weapon of logic in an attempt to keep things from going any further. But Noah touched his mouth to Abby's, and sanity popped like a soap bubble on the point of a pin.

She filled his arms sweetly, her generous breasts soft against his chest, her back supple and warm under his hands. Her kisses invited anything he chose to give, and Noah explored the entire spectrum, from tender to harsh, innocent to erotic, testing, playing…hell, resurrecting feelings he thought he'd killed years ago.

He came back to consciousness with one hand tangled in Abby's hair and one hand under her shirt, cupping her breast, while he could feel both of her hands gripping his butt.

"Abigail." He closed his mouth, settled for a few more innocent kisses, managed to drag his lips across her cheek, into her hair and finally away. "Not smart. Not smart at all."

"Who cares about smart?" She pressed a deep kiss against the base of his throat, and he felt his knees start to shake.

"You. Me…maybe." He groaned as her teeth nipped at his collarbone. She could devour him right here, right now, on her dad's kitchen floor….

Shit. With a growl, Noah jerked his head back, gripped Abby's shoulders and pushed her away to arm's length. "Stop it. Just stop."

She closed her hands around his wrists. Her lips were swollen, probably bruised, her eyelids heavy with desire. "Why?"

"Because your dad could decide to get a glass of water, for God's sake. Because it would be criminal—" What a word to choose. "It would be ridiculous for this to go any further."

Abby lifted her chin in defiance. "I'm not pretty enough?"

"What? Where'd that come from?"

"Not sexy enough? Talented enough? What does it take to catch Noah Blake's interest?" She shook her head. "I wondered all through school what was wrong with me, that you wouldn't actually ask for a date. I finally decided you just didn't want to be seen with me in public."

Noah swore again, dropped his hands from her shoulders and walked to the other side of the room. "Believe me, Abigail, you would have been a lot more miserable—then and now—if I had asked."

He shut the hall door silently behind him, the front door not quite so gently. Only when he reached his bike did he realize he'd completely forgotten to take the dog with him.

ABBY USUALLY LIKED getting to the diner early on Saturday mornings to enjoy the peace and quiet before the big crowd started arriving around eight. Even in December, folks in New Skye got up early on Saturday to get breakfast before they went shopping, before the golf match or the horse show, before they spent the day decorating the house and yard for Christmas. And Abby usually enjoyed hearing about their plans for the day. This morning, after yet another sleepless night courtesy of Noah Blake, she didn't want to wait tables, didn't want to cook or clean up, didn't want to hear about other people's lives. She wanted to crawl back into bed, pull the blanket up to her eyebrows and sleep the day away.

Not an option, of course, especially when the rush started almost an hour early.

"If you're cookin', you'd better get hoppin'," her dad ordered as he came into the kitchen. "I got two over medium, bacon, two scrambled, sausage, pancakes and ham, biscuits."

Almost by reflex, Abby started the food. She pulled trays of biscuits her dad had made out of the oven, slid them into the warmer, then turned to flip the fried eggs, pour out the scrambled onto the grill. Charlie went out with a coffeepot and two glasses of orange juice, returning in a few minutes with three more orders.

She noticed he was breathing a little fast. "Want to take over the grill, Dad, and let me do the running for a while?"

He started to refuse, then nodded and held his hand out for the spatula. "Sounds good." Billie would be in at seven-thirty to cook and so Charlie could go to the register and the counter. The three of them together could handle the breakfast rush just fine.

Abby took the first order out, brought in four, served the next three. The tables were filling up fast. As she waited for a customer at the corner table to decide between grits and hash browns, she glanced across the street to see that the weekly basketball game was under way. Dixon, Adam, Rob, Pete and Tommy had been playing Saturday mornings since high school—maybe even junior high. The sixth person varied, though for the last couple of years Dixon's stepson, Trace LaRue, had been a regular. Afterward, the guys came in for a huge breakfast, as predictable as clockwork.

This morning, though, the game looked different. Abby stared for a minute and finally realized that she missed seeing Pete. His arm had been broken by a bullet when he was on duty, taking him out of the game for a good long time. She recognized Adam, dark-haired like Pete but not as tanned. Dixon wore his dark brown hair longer. Tommy was the shortest player, compact and strong. Rob stood tallest, with silvery blond hair under the edge of his baseball cap. Trace was a darker, spiked blond.

The sixth man had a chopped-up cut to his black hair and a sharp look to his face. He wore black sweats hanging loose on a frame that needed filling out. Noah.

"I'll have potatoes," the man at the table said.

Abby looked down at him. "I'm sorry. What did you say?"

"Potatoes," he said with impatient emphasis, as if she was the reason he'd been dithering.

"Right." Abby scribbled down the order and turned away from the window.

She glanced back in time to see Noah go for a layup. When he and Dixon slapped hands, she gathered he'd made it, and couldn't help smiling.

She brought the guy by the window his breakfast then had to go back for potatoes because she'd written down grits. She poured regular coffee for her decaf trio, and brought milk to a little girl she knew was lactose intolerant.

When she'd added up the fourth—or fifth—ticket incorrectly, Charlie scowled at her. "Where's your brain this morning? You're acting like you're sick or something." His eyes widened. "You're not sick, are you?"

"No, Dad. I'm fine." She patted his shoulder, set four mugs and a coffeepot on her tray and headed back to the tables. Almost nine o'clock...the game would be ending anytime now. And then he'd be coming in to eat.

She happened to be by the window again when the six guys crossed the parking lot toward the front door.

Noah hung back, shaking his head. He didn't want to come inside.

But Dixon and Adam walked on either side of him. Rob, Tommy and Trace blocked escape to the rear. Noah would have breakfast whether he liked it or not. Pete Mitchell pulled his car to a stop in the parking lot just in time to join them at the door. Heart thumping, Abby hurried to set up their regular table.

NOAH KNEW HE COULD HAVE—should have—insisted on leaving without sitting down to breakfast. He didn't have the money to be spending on meals in restaurants, even the relatively cheap food at the Carolina Diner. And he didn't have any business seeing Abby again.

But there appeared to be a conspiracy aimed at getting him inside the diner and seated. Most of the tables in the place were full, and conversation hummed in the air. In the center of the dining room, though, three tables had been pulled together and set with places for all of them. Glasses of iced tea and cups of coffee already sat in front of most of the chairs.

"Somebody's drinking hot chocolate." Dixon claimed an iced tea chair and leaned over to sniff the steam coming from the mug on his left. "Smells good."

Noah glanced around and decided no one else was moving in that direction, so he sat down and took a sip of chocolate. The richness of the taste echoed Thursday night's expensive brew. Recklessly, he searched out Abby's face in the crowd. She stood at Pete's shoulder, across the table. Catching his gaze, she gave him a wink and a quick smile, then looked at Dixon. "Who won the game?"

"There was no beating Bell, Blake and Crawford this morning." Adam shook his head in feigned disgust. "The rest of us might as well have stayed in bed."

Rob Warren nodded. "Nothing like rolling out early on a cold morning just to get your butt kicked."

"Noah's long shots are impressive," Tommy Crawford explained. "All Dixon and I had to do was keep the defense back and let him throw. Whoosh, every time."

Noah felt his cheeks heat up. "Not every time. Maybe…three out of five."

"Maybe two out of three," Dixon countered. "You must have played some pretty regular ball to be that consistent." The expectant faces around him, if not the words, asked a question.

"Uh, yeah. In Atlanta, I lived in a neighborhood where we played ball most nights for a couple of hours." A prison was a neighborhood, of sorts. Right?

"I guess I'll find something else to do with my Saturdays," Pete said, to no one in particular. "I've been replaced by a professional."

"Nah, you'll come back." Tommy slapped him on the back, just as he took a sip of coffee. "We'll just find somebody else to play with us—make it four on a team. Hey, Abby—you want to play b-ball on Saturdays?"

While Pete sputtered, Abby shook her head. "I think not. Basketball's not my sport."

"What is your sport?" Trace LaRue, Dixon's stepson, spoke up for the first time.

"Aerobic burger-flipping," Adam suggested.

Pete joined in. "Long-distance table-waiting."

"Marathon pie-making," Rob added.

Abby laughed at the jokes, but Noah thought her gaze was harder than usual, her jaw set. She took orders from the rest of the table, coming to him last. "What can I get you for breakfast?"

"I'm not too hungry. The chocolate's enough, thanks."

No sooner were the words out of his mouth than his empty stomach betrayed him with a loud rumble.

Abby lifted an eyebrow. "Eggs scrambled or fried?"

"I'm okay."

"Scrambled," she said, writing on her order pad. "Bacon, sausage, ham?"

"I—"

"Sausage. Hash browns or grits?"

He could starve tomorrow. "Grits."

Her sweet mouth curved into a smile. "Biscuits or toast?"

"Biscuits."

"Coming right up."

A couple with two kids walked behind him just as Abby completed the order. She stepped to the side, giving the family room to pass, and steadied herself with a hand on Noah's shoulder. The press of her hip against his back, the weight of her palm on his collarbone, melted something deep inside of him—something that should have been harder, colder. He could not let her get to him like this.

He didn't look back as she left for the kitchen. A small victory, but he'd take it.

The other guys at the table replayed the basketball game for Pete's benefit, employing traditional exaggeration techniques that produced a lot of squabbling and laughing. Though most of them had been playing together since high school, Noah had never been part of this crowd and he listened to the jokes with a half smile. He knew nothing of what had happened in their lives for the last fifteen years. And if they'd known about his life, they wouldn't have invited him to play basketball to begin with.

Dixon took a long draw on his glass of tea and then glanced at Noah. "You've been in Atlanta all the time since high school?" The other guys heard the question and looked in their direction.

Noah slid down a little ways in his chair. "Mostly."

"What kind of work do you do?"

Careful. "My last job was in furniture construction."

"You're a carpenter?" Adam leaned forward. "What kind of furniture?"

"Better watch out," Tommy said. "DeVries'll have you on his construction crew before you know what hit you. He's always on the lookout for a good carpenter."

Noah grinned. "I'll remember. I've made desks, bookcases, cabinets—office furniture."

"For a big company?"

"No, not one of the major brands." The state of Georgia didn't qualify as a significant furniture manufacturing concern.

"How long did you build furniture?"

"Three years. Before that," he volunteered, since he had no doubt he would be asked, "I worked in landscaping." For a son of a bitch who was better off dead than alive.

To his relief, Charlie Brannon stepped up with a tray of food. "Wish I could eat like you young guys. She keeps me practically starved and loads your plates like you haven't eaten for a week." He glared at Pete, who had started to speak. "And don't give me any bull, because I know all of you have wives who put a damn fine meal on the table."

Noah's plate thunked onto the table in front of him. "Except you, I guess," Charlie muttered. "Your mother never did learn to serve up a decent meal."

Though true, the comment soured Noah's mood. "She struggled just to survive," he pointed out. "She didn't have the time or energy to cook fancy."

Charlie had moved down the table and didn't answer. Noah stared down at his huge mound of eggs and sausage, and the big bowl of grits. He'd lost his appetite completely.

"Don't let him rile you," Dixon advised in a low voice. "He's tough on people he cares about. You should hear him go after Abby."

"He yells at her?" To keep his face hidden, Noah stirred a pat of butter into his grits.

"Gives her a hard time, occasionally. And she takes it, because she loves him." Dixon turned to his own plate.

"Why's she still working here?" The question was out before Noah realized he'd intended to ask.

Adam, on his other side, stopped eating. "I ask myself that question sometimes. She's talked about seeing other parts of the country, even other countries."

"Why's she still living in her dad's house? Shouldn't she be married by now?"

Dixon shook his head. "Don't let her hear you say that. I don't know why Abby didn't marry somebody here in town."

Rob leaned around Dixon's shoulder from the center of the table. "I always got the feeling she was waiting for something…or somebody."

Noah's heart slammed against his ribs. "Waiting for somebody? Who?"

Rob shrugged. "He never came, I guess. She's never said."

Abby arrived at that moment with a pitcher of iced tea in one hand and a pot of coffee in the other. "Refills? Noah, you want more cocoa?"

He shook his head and took a gulp of the ice water she'd provided. Echoing in his brain was Abby's question about high school and why he hadn't dated her.

Had she been waiting for him?

The very idea almost sent him tearing out of the diner. He managed to stay in his seat, even managed to listen to the other guys talk about their kids and wives. Pete brought out the latest pictures of his little boy, almost two years old. Dixon announced that Kate was waiting to hear about admission to law school. After more than a year together, Adam said his wife's name with the tone of a bridegroom, while Rob talked about the challenge of blending two families with three kids between them. All of them seemed to enjoy the rewards in life that a good man deserved—rewards Noah would likely never see.

The bell on the door jangled as customers came and went, but all the tables stayed full. With a frown at the fact that he hadn't eaten his breakfast, Abby cleared Noah's dishes, along with the rest of the table, then bustled off to clear and serve yet again. Watching, Noah couldn't imagine how she and Charlie kept the diner traffic flowing with practically no help.

Just as he took the last gulp from a second mug of hot chocolate—set in front of him without his request—he felt a tap on his shoulder. Noah turned around, expecting Abby, and found himself confronting a tall, barrel-chested police officer. The badge over his left shirt pocket identified him as W. Hayes.

"I thought I'd have a visit from you this week." Hayes made no effort to keep his voice low.

The crowd noise faded as Noah got to his feet. "I only got into town on Wednesday."

"Yeah, and the first thing you're supposed to do is check in with me. I could have you sent back." Hayes snapped his fingers in front of Noah's nose. "Like that."

"Hey, Wade, what's the problem?" Pete pushed back his chair but didn't stand up.

Adam did. "Harassment isn't usually the way we welcome people to New Skye."

Hayes looked at the mayor. "Sorry to interrupt, Your Honor, but this man's an ex-con from Georgia. If he doesn't report to the police within twenty-four hours of arrival, he's in violation of his parole. I'm just trying to help him stay out of trouble, not to mention out of prison."

A dropped pin would have sounded loud in the absolute silence. Noah felt half the room staring at his unprotected back. The other half stared at his heated face.

He couldn't leave the place without paying for his breakfast, or he would have been gone.

Only one thing could make the situation worse. So, of course, that's what happened.

"What are you talking about?" Abby pushed between the chairs and the tables, arriving at Hayes's side. "I think you've been drinking on Saturday morning, Wade. Or else you never stopped from Friday night."

Hayes shook his head and gave her a righteous smile. "Nope. Haven't touched a drop all week."

Her face set in a skeptical frown, she crossed her arms and stared up at the big man. "So what are we talking about here? A speeding ticket in one of those traps you guys like to set up in small towns?"

"No, ma'am." Hayes looked around, making sure he had everybody's attention. "He was paroled from a State of Georgia correctional facility in Atlanta on Monday morning after serving three years of a seven-year sentence."

In his mind, Noah heard the massive clang of the steel gate at the end of that long gray hallway.

"For what?" Abby's voice wobbled on the question.

"Manslaughter," Hayes announced. "Mr. Blake, here, killed a man in Georgia. And he went to prison for it."

CHAPTER FIVE

The Diary of Abigail Ann Brannon

October 16, 1984
Dear Diary,
There was another fight at school today, during algebra.
Wade Hayes, the creepiest boy in the class, stuck his leg
out in the aisle as Esther Goldberg walked up to the front
of the room. She wears those thick, heavy glasses and she
didn't see what he'd done, so she tripped and fell, of
course, onto her hands and knees. The glasses fell off and
broke, which was when Esther started to cry. Jacquie
and I got up to help her, but before Mrs. Morrow even
knew what was going on, Noah Blake jerked Wade up
out of his desk and shoved him against the wall of the
classroom. Wade, of course, hit back, and then he and
Noah were going at each other like pit bulls at a dog-
fight. Mrs. Morrow called the office, and it took both
Coach Rangel and Mr. Arthur, the shop teacher, to pull
the guys apart. Wade looked bad—I think Noah might
have broken his nose, it was bleeding so much. Noah had
marks on his face, but I'm not sure Wade put all of them
there.

They've both been suspended for a week. Esther was okay, and I'm hoping maybe she'll get some glasses that make her look less geeky. I guess Noah won't be coming to the fall dance this weekend. Not that he would have danced with me if he had shown up. Jacquie says he's hanging out with Carla Robinson, the sluttiest girl in tenth grade. And she's so much older than him. I know everybody looks down on sluts. But they do seem to get the best guys.

February 14, 1985
Dear Diary,
Valentine's Day pretty much sucks when you're in middle school. The teachers don't make you give everybody a card anymore and there isn't a class party, so if your friends don't think about it and you don't have a boyfriend, it might just as well be any other day. Especially if you have to work all afternoon at the diner, like I did.

I got a few cards, from Jacquie and Kate, and one from Esther. Dixon and Pete pretended they didn't remember the date, but Adam had a bag of lollipops he handed out.

Somebody went around slipping anonymous cards into the locker vents, which was a pretty good trick. Kate got one with a picture of roses on the front and a sweet poem inside that looked like it was handwritten. Jacquie's card showed a photograph of a horse with its nose in a big box of chocolates, though she says they aren't good for horses.

The big surprise was that I got one of the anonymous cards, too. Mine was different, not funny, not sweet. Inside it just said, "Have a Valentine's Day as nice as you are," with no signature. The picture on the front was a field of daisies, with a big tree in the background and a woman on a swing. Across the bottom it says, "You make me think of sunshine and wildflowers."

I have no clue who sent it. I didn't see Noah in class today. But I can hope.

ABBY HAD FALLEN off a horse once, when she was twelve. For about a minute after she hit the ground, she couldn't speak, couldn't breathe. Her chest felt as if someone had sucked all the air out.

She felt like that now, standing in the middle of the diner, in front of her friends and customers—and, dear God, her father—as she heard that Noah Blake was a convicted felon. He'd come back home after being paroled from prison.

"That's right," Noah said, his eyes fixed on Wade's face. "I served my sentence and I'm on parole. You want to head down to your office right now?" He gave an open-handed shrug. "I'm finished here."

Wade shook his head. "Now I've seen you, we can wait till Monday. I'll expect you in front of my desk at eleven o'clock sharp." The policeman grinned, turned on his heel and went to sit at the table his friends occupied.

All eyes in the room were still on Noah. He lifted his shoulders and blew out a deep breath, then turned back to the table. Pulling his wallet out of his sweat-pants pocket, he put a fifty-dollar bill on the table.

"That should cover breakfast," he told Dixon. "Thanks for the game. I had a good time."

Abby waited for him to say something to her, but Noah gave her a brief half smile and left the diner with quick strides. As soon as the door shut behind him, talk flooded the room.

Pete, Dixon, Tommy and Trace joined Adam in getting to their feet. Dixon picked up the fifty-dollar bill. "I guess we'll let Noah pay for breakfast. You need more?"

Abby lifted her hand with the check for the table crushed between her fingers. "It's too much."

"Maybe he'll come back for his change." Adam put a hand on her shoulder. "Delicious, as always. Thanks, Abby."

She nodded, dazed, as the other guys took their leave. When she took the check and payment to the cash register, her dad was there, primed to point out how right he'd been.

"I told you I didn't want him here. A murderer, that's what he is. I always said Noah Blake was no good."

"Yes, you did." Abby handed him the fifty. "Though I notice his money's not too filthy for you to take."

"You don't talk to me like that, young lady." He put out a hand as if to keep her from walking away, but she was on the other side of the counter and out of reach.

The next hour passed in a blur as she took orders, cleared tables and evaded questions about Noah. Every time she went near Wade Hayes's table, the policeman gave her a grin. As she poured coffee for him and his friends, he looked up into her face.

"Whatd'ya say, Miss Abby? How about dinner tonight, and maybe a movie?"

He'd asked before, and she'd given him the same answer. "Thanks, but I have to work."

"Aw. Come on. Your old man can't chain you here twenty-four/seven. You gotta have a life."

"No, I don't." She stacked their plates on one arm and picked up the coffeepot with her free hand. "Y'all have a good day."

On Saturday, the breakfast crowd morphed into the lunch crowd practically without a break, so it wasn't until three o'clock that she had a chance to sit down and drink a glass of iced tea. Charlie was still in the kitchen, cooking for dinner, which might or might not be crowded.

The doorbell jangled and Abby automatically started to get up. A firm hand pushed her onto the seat again.

"Stay put," Valerie Warren said, sitting down across the table. "I didn't come for food."

"Want something to drink? Coffee? Iced tea?"

Valerie shook her head. "I haven't gotten used to drinking iced tea in the wintertime yet."

"You northerners." Abby shook her head in pretended disgust. "Maybe when you've been married awhile longer, Rob will get you into the habit."

"Maybe." The smile on Valerie's face was the kind usually described as "starry-eyed." She and Rob had married last June, and Abby had been delighted to be the maid of honor. "Rob told me what happened after the ball game this morning. Were you aware…?" She let the words trail off, as if she didn't know what to say to them.

"Of course not." Why would Noah tell her anything really important about his life?

"Do you think his mother knows?"

"I'm almost positive she doesn't."

Valerie wrapped her arms around herself, shivering a little. "It's kind of scary, knowing we've got a man in town who went to jail for…killing somebody."

There was no denying the truth, hard though it was to accept. "I can't believe we have to be afraid of him. But…I would never have thought he could do something like that." She had to admit Noah did have a reputation as a fighter. And fifteen years was a long time—who knew how he might have changed?

"But you don't have the details on what happened, right? I mean, there might be an explanation that makes sense. A reason for what he did. Not just cold-blooded murder—surely he wouldn't be out in only three years."

"Well, he certainly didn't hang around this morning to provide one. He was gone almost before everybody got the gist of what Wade said." And he hadn't called later to say…what? What could he possibly say?

"There must have been news reports when it happened," Valerie said. "Whatever 'it' was. Maybe you could check the Internet, see if you can dig up some old stories."

"Then I'll have information, but what good does it do me?" Abby slid out of the booth and headed toward the coffeemaker. "If Noah doesn't want to explain, what excuse do I have to go snooping into his private business?"

"You might feel better, knowing he had a reason."

"I think I'd feel better if he just left town altogether."

"But you've waited—"

She didn't have to finish. Valerie had only moved to New Skye last summer, but the two of them had struck up a deep friendship almost immediately. This Yankee stranger was the only person to whom Abby had confessed her childish crush on Noah Blake.

Abby brought a mug of coffee back to the booth and slid it across the table for Valerie. "Could be it's time for me to grow up and get over it, you know? Some things we just aren't meant to have, and I'm beginning to believe that Noah falls into that category, as far as I'm concerned." She sank back onto the seat. "Maybe the next time Wade Hayes asks me out, I'll have to say yes."

NOAH KNEW THE NEWS would reach his mother sooner or later, and probably sooner. He'd meant to tell her the truth when he first arrived, but somehow the opportunity hadn't presented itself. Or maybe he had refused to recognize an opportunity when presented with one.

Either way, the choice had been taken out of his hands. Today was the day.

His mother was seated in her chair in the living room when he got home. "I'm going to get cleaned up," he told her, and received a nod in reply. With the old shower nozzle dribbling water over his head, he tried to think of a way to begin what he had to say. But all he could really hold in his mind was the memory of Abby's shocked face, the horror in her eyes as Hayes unloaded his big secret.

How to lose a girl in ten seconds.

Not that Abby had been his to lose, of course. She was much better off knowing the truth and staying out of his way.

Wearing clean jeans and his only dress shirt, face shaved, hair combed, Noah went back to the living room and sat down on the couch. He waited until a commercial to say anything, in case his mother didn't want to interrupt her program.

"Ma, can I talk to you a minute?"

"What?" she said, without looking at him.

"I need to explain a couple of things. About why I'm here."

She lifted the remote and turned off the set. "I figured you were out of a job and out of cash."

Noah smiled ruefully. "I've been in that place plenty of times. No, this is different." He leaned his elbows on his knees. "I just got out of jail."

His mother nodded. "No surprise, there, either. I imagine that's something else you've done a lot of, the last fifteen years."

"No, just the once—for three years. I got paroled on a seven-year sentence."

"What'd you do, steal that bike you ride around on?"

He took a deep breath. "I killed a man."

Eyes round, mouth open, she stared at him for a long minute. "You killed a human being?"

"Yes."

"They only gave you seven years for murder?"

"Manslaughter. Involuntary manslaughter."

"Do you think that makes a difference?" She rolled

her eyes. "Even your bastard of a father didn't kill any-body. Not before he left this town, anyway."

Noah didn't react with an automatic defense, the way he would have before three years in prison. "My parole was transferred to the New Skye police depart-ment, and I'll be allowed to stay as long as I have a set-tled address and keep a job."

His mother slapped her knees with her palms, then clapped her hands on either side of her head. "That's just great. How am I supposed to look people in the face, knowing my son is a murderer?" She struggled to her feet, breathing hard, and walked to the window overlooking the garden. "If you'd told me this when you first showed up, I wouldn't ever have let you in the house. Maybe I'm just poor white trash, but I don't want a murderer living with me."

Before he could quite believe what he'd heard, she turned around to glare at him. "Does Abby know about this? Did she send you over here the other day, know-ing what you'd done?"

"No. Abby didn't find out until this morning."

"Well, that's something." Some of Marian's anger died. "She's been good to me, that girl. Better than my own son was. And now…this."

Noah got to his feet. "I can leave."

His mother crossed her arms and gave him a curt nod. "You'd better."

Funny, how easily she could hurt him. His gut felt hollow, but he nodded. "No problem."

He packed up in five minutes and stopped at the door on his way out. "I'll let you know where I'm staying."

She'd turned the television on again and didn't look at him.

"Right," Noah said, and walked out without the least idea of where he would spend the night.

THE DOOR SHUT, AND MARIAN heard the roar of the damn bike. She clicked off the TV, dropped the remote control and doubled over with her head in her hands.

My son's a killer. There'd never been much hope that Noah would escape the taint. His father's family held a well-deserved reputation for violence, and her people weren't much better. Her shotgun wedding to Jonah Blake, which had upset all his plans for a bright future, had guaranteed the cycle would continue.

She hadn't been surprised when Jonah left her and their son—he blamed them both for costing him a football scholarship and big-league career. Noah's disappearance hadn't been much of a shock, either, given the trouble he'd been in. She'd never known whether he started the fire at the school or not, and he hadn't given her the chance to ask. Chet Hayes, county sheriff for the last twenty years now, had assured her he held proof of Noah's guilt. Then he'd told her he didn't want her anymore and walked out the door.

Her luck with men had always been lousy.

So her son had run away, left her by herself with a lousy job and no friends. A few phone calls—Christmas, her July birthday, sometimes Valentine's Day—and a couple of letters a year had been the extent of his communication. Did he think she'd spent all these years, day by day, just waiting for him to come back?

That was exactly what she had done, of course. Only now he was here—a man she might not have recognized if she'd seen him on the street, with lines on his face and a hard look in his eyes—and she didn't know him at all. She couldn't find the boy she'd raised in his guarded expression. The words died in her throat when she tried to talk to him. Her son, the killer.

Where would he go? Was he leaving town, or just finding somewhere else to sleep? Who would give him a job? Would somebody tell her where he ended up, or would she go on wondering, as she had for fifteen years?

With no energy to get up and turn on a light, Marian sat in her chair as the shadows crawled across the wall. She was hungry, but couldn't face cooking. Her disability check didn't come till next week, so she couldn't even afford to get herself a bite to eat at the diner. Abby always took care of her….

As if somebody had flipped a switch, the answer came to her. She reached to the side for the phone and dialed a number that hadn't changed in twenty years. "Abby, this is Marian Blake."

NOAH FOUND A PAY PHONE at a gas station and dialed Rob Warren's number.

"Hey, Noah. What's up?"

"Sorry to bother you, but I think I'm going to have to back out on that job we talked about."

"I'm sorry to hear that. I hope that's because you got a better offer."

"N-no. I'm not going to be staying in town after all."

"Noah, if it's about this morning—"

"Only partly. My mother asked me to leave, though, and without an official residence…" He let his thought trail away. "I guess I'll go back to Georgia."

"But—" Rob hesitated. "I kinda hate to see you do that. This is your home."

Noah didn't have a polite answer for that comment.

"What if I hunted up another place for you to live?"

If he'd ever had any pride, today had broken it down. "I can't afford—"

"Give me a few minutes. I've got an idea." When Noah called back ten minutes later, Rob said, "Dixon's got just what you need. He's waiting for you to show up at his house."

Dixon Bell still lived where he'd grown up, Magnolia Cottage—a plantation house his family had owned since before the Civil War. After Noah cut his engine, he sat for a few seconds admiring the stately home and the sheen of new paint on its white siding and green shutters. The grass was clipped close, the flower beds edged and covered with a deep layer of mulch. Somebody put in a lot of time and effort to keep this place looking so good.

As he swung off the bike, the front door opened and Dixon stepped out onto the porch. "Come in and warm up with some coffee. It's got to be cold riding that bike around."

Noah put his helmet on the seat just as Trace came around the corner of the house. The boy's eyes shone with a hunger Noah remembered in himself. "Can I look at your bike?"

"Sure." He put the keys in his pocket, just to be safe. If somebody had left him alone with a bike like this when he was sixteen, he would have roared away as soon as he had the chance.

Inside the house, Dixon ushered him into a room on the right of the hall, where an elderly lady sat on one of the small sofas facing each other across the fireplace.

"Yes, do come in." She smoothed a hand over the light blue brocade beside her. "You can sit right here."

"How are you, Miss Daisy?" Everybody in town knew Mrs. Crawford, Dixon's grandmother—she was as close to an aristocrat as New Skye would ever get. Noah stepped forward, but hesitated to make contact between his jeans and the expensive fabric.

"I'm fine." She beckoned him closer, then reached out to catch his wrist and pull him down onto the couch. "That's better. It sounds like you're having a rough day."

"Well, things started out pretty good." Was this elegant little woman aware she was entertaining a killer? Noah glanced at Dixon, on the opposite sofa.

"I told Miss Daisy what happened at the diner this morning," he explained.

Noah looked at his hostess again. "You'll probably get some comments from your friends about renting a room to an ex-con."

Miss Daisy patted the smooth white hair on the back of her head. "My friends know better than to question my judgment at this point in my life. Ah, Kate," she said, looking over his shoulder. "That smells heavenly. Give Noah a cup so he'll relax."

Kate smiled and set a big tray down on the table at Noah's knee. Then she handed him a mug. "Here you are. Help yourself to cream and sugar." Miss Daisy's coffee was delivered in a fancy flowered cup, but Dixon and Kate both had mugs like his.

Noah took a sip and nearly groaned. He hadn't eaten at all today, even though Abby had set a king's breakfast on the table in front of him. The rich coffee eased the ache. "Terrific," he said. "Thanks."

The four of them drank in silence for a minute. The window behind Dixon and Kate looked out onto the driveway, and Noah grinned a little as he watched Trace crouch down to check out the Harley's back wheel.

With a clink of china, Miss Daisy set her cup on the tray again. "I wondered when we'd see you smile." She put her fingers lightly on his arm. "I understand you've been in prison, for a serious crime. And the details are your own business. But I know Dixon wouldn't suggest having you stay if you were any kind of danger to us."

He could feel his cheeks heating up. "I appreciate his confidence. And yours. I—" Damn, but he hated having to explain. "Just so you'll know, I didn't set out to kill anybody. I got into a fight with a guy, he hit his head and died. That's what happened."

Her pale blue gaze captured his own. "Very well. And just so you know, I expect you to behave yourself as long as you're in this town, Noah Blake. Do you understand me?"

"Yes, ma'am. I'm not here to hurt anybody, Miss Daisy." He pulled in a deep breath. "I promise."

"HI, MRS. BLAKE." Upon hearing the scratchy voice, Abby rubbed her eyes with the fingers of one hand. This was probably going to be another conversation she would have preferred to avoid today. "How are you feeling?"

"No better than usual. Listen, I need you to do something for me."

"If I can."

"Noah moved out this afternoon."

The news left Abby speechless. "I—"

"I want you to find out where he's staying. I want you to let me know what he's doing, where he's working. That kind of thing."

Abby found the breath to speak. "Mrs. Blake—"

"He told me he just got out of prison for murder."

"I believe it was manslaughter, not murder."

"He killed a man, didn't he? Just because he's not living here doesn't mean I don't intend to keep an eye on him. I can't count on him to come see me. But I can count on you to find him and let me know."

"I don't—"

"Call me when you know where he's staying." The line went dead.

Abby hung up the diner phone with a shaking hand just as the bell on the door jingled and the Torres family, all twelve of them, came in for dinner. Kate Bell's daughter, Kelsey, had joined them—Sal Torres, the oldest of the kids, had been her steady boyfriend for several years. To Abby's relief, the minutes after Mrs. Blake's call were occupied with pulling tables together to make room for so many people, taking drink orders, handing out menus and providing silverware.

After delivering the drinks, she started on orders for food. The youngest kids wanted hamburgers and fries, and the Torres parents asked for meat loaf and mashed potatoes. Abby worked her way around the table until she reached Sal and Kelsey.

"How's it going, Kelsey?"

"Good." The pretty blonde nodded her head. "How about you, Miss Abby?"

"Can't complain." Only because it wouldn't do any good. "Have you got all those college applications sent off?"

"I mailed the last one yesterday. Now all I have to do is wait."

"What's your first pick?"

"I'm hoping to hear really soon about early acceptance at Vanderbilt, in Nashville. It's a great school."

"So far away!" Abby looked at Sal. "You're going to let her escape?"

He gave her one of his beautiful smiles. "They need good car mechanics in Nashville, just like everywhere else. I figure I can get a recommendation from my boss and relocate."

"Um…does Kate know about this, Kelsey?"

Now the girl blushed. "Well, kinda."

"'Kinda.' Okay." Abby patted Kelsey's shoulder. "You might want to talk things over with her and Dixon. Soon. Parents aren't crazy about surprises like that."

While she put salads together, Abby's mind went back to the surprise of her day. Surely somebody in town, besides the police department, had to have known that Noah was coming home. Weren't paroled inmates—she winced at the "i" word—required to have a job and an address to go to when they left prison? Somebody in New Skye must've promised Noah a job.

How would she discover who? Would she have to worm the information out of Wade during a date? Carrying the tray of salads back to the Torres table, Abby shuddered at the thought.

"Here you go." She put a bowl in front of little Marguerite, who wrinkled her nose.

"Are there onions in it?"

"Would I put onions in your salad?" Abby smoothed her palm over the girl's sleek black hair. "Of course not."

Kelsey came next. "He drives this great bike," she said to Sal, as Abby set their salads down. "Trace is still out there staring at it, I bet."

Sal nodded as he speared a tomato. "I saw it when I picked you up. Hot machine."

"Dixon said he'd be staying in the garage studio for a while, so maybe he'll give us a ride sometime." Kelsey slanted a glance at Sal. "He's really cool, you know?"

The young man's dark gaze sparked with anger. "No, I don't know." He turned a shoulder to Kelsey and said something to his brother across the table.

Kelsey's jaw dropped at being so abruptly dismissed. "Sal?"

Abby put a hand on the girl's shoulder to get her attention. "Who's really cool?"

"The guy Dixon has staying at our house." With obvious reluctance, Kelsey turned away from her boyfriend. "Noah Blake. Dixon said he went to high school here."

"He did." She blew out a deep breath. "So Trace likes the bike?"

"He's been bugging our dad for a motorcycle for a year now. But Kate's really not happy with the idea, and Dixon backs her up." Kelsey sighed. "Me, I'd just settle for a little VW Bug, instead of having to drive Kate's stupid Volvo. Or Dixon's beatup truck."

"You do have it hard," Abby said, hiding her smile.

Kelsey stuck her tongue out in pretended disrespect. Sal continued his jealous pout.

The Torres family usually came in for late lunch or early dinner, so their crowd didn't take too much room away from other customers. At the moment, all the other tables were empty, so once the Torres table had received their food and drink, Abby felt free to take a break.

She went into the office behind the kitchen, sat down at the desk and picked up the phone. With a sigh of relief, she heard Kate Bell's "Hello."

"Kate, it's Abby."

"Hi, there. Hold on just a minute."

Kate asked Dixon to hang up the phone when she picked up in another room. Abby waited without saying anything—she didn't want Dixon to know about her call. Half a minute later, Kate came back on the line. "I've got it, Dixon. Thanks." After the click, Kate said, "Sorry to keep you waiting. How are you?"

"Not too bad. Um…can I ask you a question?"

"Yes, and the answer is yes."

"Noah's there?"

"Sitting on a love seat in the parlor as we speak." What else did she need to know? "I…thanks."

"Dixon told me about this morning. Are you okay?"

"Sure. Why not?"

"Abby," Kate said, in a reproving voice.

"Do I have another choice? I hadn't seen the man for fifteen years until Wednesday. He doesn't owe me anything."

"There's more to the story than you've heard so far."

"There always is. I'm just not sure that I want to know." Or, to be more truthful, that Noah cared what she knew or thought. "We've got a reunion dance meeting tomorrow afternoon, right?"

"That's right. I'll see you there."

"Sure."

After hanging up, Abby folded her arms on the desk and rested her forehead on her crossed hands.

Now what? Call Mrs. Blake and report on Noah's whereabouts, then forget about him? Let his life take its course without further interference from Abby Brannon?

She argued with herself through the dinner rush, which wasn't much of a rush since a cold rain had started about five o'clock. While cleaning, setting up for tomorrow morning, locking the doors and driving home, Abby debated her options.

Charlie was waiting in the living room when she went into the house. "Took you long enough."

"I made some breakfast casserole for tomorrow."

"Did you get some dinner?"

Abby had to think back. "Um…no. But I'm not hungry."

"You didn't have lunch, either. Or much breakfast. I'll make you some toast, at least."

She wanted to protest but was too tired. Dropping into her usual chair by the window, she waited for her dad to bring her a plate of cinnamon toast and a big glass of orange juice.

"Six pieces?" She savored the taste of buttery cinnamon sugar. "I'm going to get fat."

"Not if you don't eat anything else all day. Everything go okay with closing tonight?"

"Sure."

"No last-minute orders?"

Abby looked at him closely. "What do you really want to know?"

He shrugged, fingering the remote for the television. "Just wondered if anybody came in right before closing."

"Noah Blake, for instance?"

"I don't want him hanging around."

"He won't be. He doesn't… He's not… I don't expect to see him any more than I see anybody else in town."

"But with him working for Rob Warren, he's likely to show up fairly often."

She gazed at him with her jaw hanging loose. "He's working for Rob?" Something Valerie hadn't mentioned. Maybe Rob hadn't told her yet?

"Yeah, in that new security-system business he's setting up. Though how anybody's supposed to feel secure with an ex-con involved is more than I can see."

"How did you find out?"

He had the grace to look embarrassed. "I...called Wade Hayes when I got home tonight. He didn't mind telling me."

She still had four pieces of toast left and absolutely no appetite. "Well...it's good Noah has...a job. I expect Rob can reassure his clients about their security."

"How, for heaven's sake? The boy left town after setting fire to the school office. Doesn't that tell you something?"

"It tells me he knew he'd be blamed, whether he'd done it or not."

"You think somebody went to the trouble of making it look like Noah Blake set the fire? That they parked a motorcycle like his out in the school parking lot for me to see just about an hour before the alarm sounded?"

"I think Noah's too smart to leave his bike where it would be identified if he wanted to pull a stunt like that."

"He was still a kid. Kids aren't too smart."

Abby gazed at her dad for a minute without saying anything. "That's right. He was a kid. A kid whose dad beat up on him pretty regularly until he deserted the family completely. A kid trying to hold his life together without much help. Nobody ever gave Noah the benefit of the doubt. Nobody tried to reach him with kindness, or the gentleness he didn't get at home. He made a lot of mistakes. But did anybody offer help?"

Her dad swiped a hand over his face. "I did."

"What?"

"I tried to give him a job."

"I didn't know that. You never told me."

He shook his head. "Not a big deal. He happened to be the only one in the place that afternoon, drinking coffee for lunch because that was all he could afford."

She made a sound, and her dad nodded. "He did that pretty often. So I told him I'd hire him to bus tables and do dishes. If he wanted to learn to cook, I could promote him someday, with a pay raise."

"But he never worked for you."

"No. I went to the kitchen, let him think for a few minutes. When I came back, he was gone…along with a hundred bucks."

"He left the register open?"

Charlie shook his head. "I was short when I closed that night. I talked to the sheriff, but I didn't have any proof that Noah Blake had taken the money."

Abby blinked back tears.

"The next week the fire at the school happened and the kid disappeared. Your mom was sick and I had more to worry about than missing cash." He got to his feet. "Now we know he's a killer, as well as a thief. And you think he's a good choice to work in a security business?" Shaking his head, her dad headed down the hallway to his bedroom. From his doorway, he called, "'Night."

"Good night, Dad," she responded automatically. Minutes went by—ten, twenty?—while she tried to make sense of the puzzle that was Noah Blake. Had she been wrong all these years? Was the sweet, struggling soul she'd seen in him just a mirage?

She realized she'd never taken off her coat, which made going out again easy. Grabbing her purse and keys, she went to the near end of the hallway. "I forgot something at the diner, Dad. Be back in a little while." He argued with her, but she finally managed to get out of the house.

The rain had stopped on her way home. As she walked to the car, her breath formed white clouds in the cold night air. The car's old heater took a long time to warm up, so she traveled in pretty much the outdoor temperature—thirty degrees by the bank clock—as she crossed town. She made a hard left at Dixon's lane, then a right onto the circular drive. But instead of following the circle to the front walk, she drove toward the back of the house, where the old stable had been converted to a ground-level garage with an apartment upstairs.

Lights shone behind the shades of the second-story windows. Abby closed the car door quietly and went to the outside staircase leading to the second-floor veranda. Breathing a little too hard, she walked straight up to the door and, without giving herself time to think, knocked hard.

The door opened almost immediately. Noah glared out at her, his dark eyes narrowed, his mouth set hard. Then, as he recognized her, his expression changed to pure surprise.

"Abby? What the… What are you doing here?"

CHAPTER SIX

NOAH SHUT THE DOOR and backed up against it as Abby stalked to the counter separating the living room from the kitchen. She looked as if she was prepared to do battle—eyes flashing, cheeks flushed, fists clenched.

"What are you doing here?" he asked again. "Does your dad know where you are?"

"I'm not sixteen. I don't have to tell my dad where I go every time I step out the front door."

"Oh, sure. He doesn't mind when you walk out at ten o'clock at night to visit a man who just got out of prison. I believe that."

"You didn't complete the thought." He lifted a brow in question and she went on. "You should say 'a man who just got out of prison where he served a sentence for manslaughter.'"

"You're right." Amazing, how ugly the word sounded coming from her. "That still doesn't explain why you showed up at my door."

She glanced into the kitchen. "Do you have anything to drink?"

"Tap water. The glasses are in the cabinet to the right of the sink."

Abby threw him an annoyed glance and disappeared into the kitchen. A good host would have offered her a drink and filled the glass himself. But Noah was keeping a firm hold on the doorknob behind him. That way, they might both get out of this unscathed.

The water ran and then shut off. The seal on the refrigerator released, caught again. He counted the clack of six cabinet doors being opened and closed, plus the slide of three drawers going out and in. "Find what you're looking for?"

She came back around the counter. "Dixon and Kate have done a great job with this place, haven't they? I love the soft orange on the walls with the dark green carpet." Abby toasted him with her mug. "Cheers."

Noah had spent the last couple of hours in awe of the comfort and convenience he'd dropped into this afternoon. "Yeah, this is definitely a step up from a two-man cell on block C."

The mug clanked onto the countertop. "Good point. Now I'd like an explanation. I'm assuming you were wrongly convicted?"

"Oh, I did it." He nodded when Abby's eyes widened. "That's right. I killed a man."

"Accidentally?" Her voice wavered on the word.

"No. I'm glad he's dead. And if he wasn't…" He shrugged. "I'd be happy to try again."

She was quiet for a long time. "Why?"

Stupid. He'd been prepared for her to walk out, but not for another question. The smart answer he wanted to give wouldn't materialize.

"Come on, Noah." Abby pulled out one of the bar

stools and sat down, her heels propped on a rung and her elbows on her knees. "I want to know why you killed the guy. Money? Drugs? Self-defense?"

"He was…dangerous. A threat to anybody who went near him."

"He attacked you?"

"No…I pulled him off somebody else, and he turned on me."

"Who were you protecting?"

"A friend." When she nodded in satisfaction, he knew he had to change her attitude, and fast. "Don't shine some kind of heroic spotlight on this situation. It was a brawl, pure and simple. I got a lucky break and the other guy ended up dead. Things could just as easily have gone the other way."

She held up a hand. "Okay, okay, I get it. You're a bad man. Why didn't you tell your mother the truth right away?"

"I did. Just not all of it."

"What did you say?"

"I said I'd been in Atlanta for the past few years, working different jobs. And I decided to come back because I wanted to be sure she was taken care of."

"Would you be here if you hadn't gone to prison and then been paroled?"

Noah slapped his hands against the panel of the door. "What difference does it make? I'm here and I'll be staying for a while. What else does anybody need to know?"

"I haven't even asked you yet why you stole a hundred dollars from the register at the diner."

"Today?"

"In high school."

He hadn't thought about that episode for fifteen years. There were other sins to remember, so many of them so much worse. "I guess I wanted something for my bike. I think I had my eye on mirrors that spring."

"And thought my dad should pay for it?"

"Why not?" This kind of indifference was a lot harder to project than when he'd been a kid and hadn't really cared what people thought of him.

Except for Abby Brannon. Unfortunately, he'd cared about what she thought pretty much since the first day they met.

"My dad offered you a job. And instead of taking it, you took the money."

He hated the look of betrayal on her face, but he intended to use it. "You shouldn't be so surprised. It's who I am, Abigail—a liar, a thief, an arsonist…a killer."

"I don't believe any of that."

"Then you're a fool."

She nodded. "Maybe. Why are you so determined to make me hate you?"

"Because you're so damned determined to redeem me."

"Somebody has to."

"Well, I don't want redemption."

"What do you want?"

That stopped him for a second, because he had never put the idea into words. "I want to stop making mistakes." He passed a hand across his face. "I appreciate you trying to help out. But I am not somebody you have to worry about. Just go home and—"

"Be a good girl?" She slipped off the stool and walked toward him. "Mind my own business? Don't bother you anymore?"

"That's right." Without his brain's cooperation, his hands wrapped themselves over her shoulders. She didn't feel as sturdy as she looked.

"I don't want to. How's that for an answer?"

He echoed her question. "What do you want?"

Abby shrugged. "A walk on the wild side."

Noah started to pull back. "What the hell are you talking about?"

She gripped his wrists, kept his hands on her. "I've been everybody's good girl all my life. I want a chance to make my own mistakes. To be dangerous."

If she only knew. "The wild side isn't a safe part of town."

"So everybody says. I want to find out for myself."

"Using me as your playground?"

"Sure." She took a step, closing the small distance between their bodies. "Sounds like fun to me."

With a curse, Noah pushed her away from him for the second time. "I am not going to help you ruin your life. I don't want the responsibility."

Abby recovered her balance and straightened up under Noah's hot glare. "I wasn't asking you to take responsibility. This planet doesn't depend on you to keep it moving around the sun, and neither do I. Kiss off, Noah Blake. I'm not wasting any more time waiting for you."

She stomped past him, stepped outside and slammed the door as hard as she could. Never, *never* had she been this angry. Rage boiled up inside of her, a pressure on her bones, against her skin, that she didn't know how to release. Throwing rocks at Noah's windows appealed to her, but they were actually Dixon's windows, and she didn't want to hurt Dixon. Driving downtown, she visualized the owners of the shops and businesses and knew she couldn't damage their property out of spleen. Even Kate's ex-husband didn't deserve vandalism, though she was terribly tempted after what he'd put her friend through.

In the end she went home and was relieved to find her dad sound asleep. She changed into her favorite nightgown, a bright red flannel granny gown softened by years of washing, and went to the kitchen for a cup of cocoa. When she turned on the light, she heard Noah's dog scratching at the door to the sunporch.

"You're still awake? Come inside," she told him. As he did every time he came in, he checked out the kitchen, sniffing at the baseboards, the oven and the refrigerator, before settling with a sigh on the braided rug in front of the sink. When her drink was ready, Abby sat at the table and stretched out a foot to rub the dog's shoulder.

"You really do need a name," she told him. "I appear to be the only one who cares, so I suppose it's up to me." She considered the scruffy animal for a minute. "How does Elvis strike you? You're nothin' but a hound dog, after all. Are you lonesome tonight? We can listen to 'Heartbreak Hotel' together."

He wagged his tail a couple of times and then rested his head on his front paws and dozed off.

Abby sat there for a long, long time, wishing she could do the same.

NOAH FELL ASLEEP as the Sunday sun rose. He woke up much later with the sound of voices underneath the window. A quick peek outside revealed Dixon and family returning from church, to judge by their clothes. Sunday dinner after services…a custom he hadn't grown up with or believed in, until now.

He had just turned away from the window when someone knocked on the door. The wrinkled clothes he'd slept in didn't seem to matter, until he peered out to see Kate standing on the porch.

"Good morning." She looked like a princess, wrapped up in a thick, soft, dark brown coat. "I hope I didn't wake you."

"No, not at all. Something wrong?"

"Dixon and I hoped you would join us for lunch. We should have asked earlier, but the kids didn't want to get up for church, and by the time we could leave, we were running late. I'm sorry there's not a phone up here yet. We'll have to get one installed this week."

She made it seem like everything was her fault. Noah shook his head, wondering where to start. "Don't worry about that. I don't really need a phone. But I shouldn't barge in on your family dinner."

"You won't be barging. Miss Daisy usually cooks enough for at least another family of five. We'll all be glad to have you, if you'll come."

He might be a killer, but he couldn't be rude to Kate Bowdrey Bell. "Sure. Have I got time to get cleaned up?"

"Of course. Why don't we plan to eat about one o'clock?"

They shared a smile, and Noah watched as she went down the steps again and across to the house. He'd been at the bottom of their high school class when Kate had been valedictorian—the distance between them had been like that between the Queen of England and the next peasant scheduled to be tarred and feathered. Not much had changed.

Dixon belonged to the same New Skye aristocracy but hadn't been quite so unapproachable.

"I remember you used to sit around at school with a guitar," Noah said, when he arrived for lunch, noticing Dixon's instrument leaning in a corner of the parlor. "You always had some tune going, with your eyes closed and your fingers flying."

"Yeah, I was a real space cadet. Sometimes I wonder how I managed to graduate at all." Dixon froze for a second, then muttered a curse. "Sorry, man. That was about as tactless as it gets."

Noah held up a hand. "No problem. I earned my diploma eventually, even took some college courses on the Internet."

Dixon toasted him with a glass of iced tea. "You probably worked a lot harder for your certificate than I did. My senior year was pretty much a write-off, and it took me a good ten years to get my head straightened out. Then another three to get up the guts to come back home."

"You left town?"

He nodded. "Yeah, I thought I belonged in Nashville.

Nashville had different ideas at the time, however, so I drifted on to Texas, Colorado, Europe and then back to Colorado. By then I'd actually done some living to write songs about."

"So what brought you home?"

"The lady, here." Dixon held out a hand to Kate as she came in from the dining room. "Seemed like we were finally at a place where we could be together, so I came home to work things out. Not to mention Miss Daisy."

"I should think so," his grandmother said, joining them. "Lunch is ready. Call the children, please."

Noah sat down at the lace-covered dining room table and swallowed down a big gulp of nerves. He'd rarely seen this much silver and china and crystal all in one place, outside department stores. Two forks rested beside his plate, and an extra spoon lay at twelve o'clock. He wouldn't go thirsty, for sure—he'd been given a water glass and another for iced tea, both with stems. Could he manage to eat without breaking something?

Two teenagers sat across the table from him—Trace, the basketball player, and his sister Kelsey, a cute blonde with a pout on her pretty mouth. Noah wasn't sure whether to hope he'd get to witness the explosion she was brewing, or to be smart and escape before the fireworks display.

For a few minutes after Dixon said grace, they were all occupied with passing around platters and bowls of heavenly food—roast chicken, mashed potatoes and gravy, several bowls of vegetables and salads, plus the best biscuits he'd ever put in his mouth. It was all he could do to keep from grabbing the silver bread basket and running out with it.

"This is delicious, Miss Daisy," he said instead. "I haven't had anything so good in years."

"I'm glad you're enjoying your meal, Noah. We'll fix up some boxes for you to take back to your refrigerator. I do have to say, Kate made the biscuits. She has the lightest hand I've ever known."

Noah looked at Kate, on his left. "Is there anything you can't do?"

She blushed and laughed. "Ride a horse, for one thing. Dixon's been working with me for a long time, but I still can't feel comfortable in the saddle."

"You have horses?"

Dixon nodded. "I brought my cow ponies with me from Colorado. They stay at Phoebe DeVries's farm."

"Wait—wasn't Jacquie Lennon the one who was all about horses?"

"She still is," Kate said. "She's a farrier and trainer in the area. Her husband, Rhys Lewellyn, is an Olympic rider. I imagine their children will be, as well."

"Children." Noah shook his head. "Hard to imagine having kids." He looked across at Trace and Kelsey. "But it looks to me like it turns out okay."

Trace grinned at him, eating as steadily as a sixteen-year-old guy could. Kelsey clinked her fork onto her plate. "Well, I'm not so sure it's turned out okay. Some parents are just too…too primitive to be believed."

Noah hid a smile. So he would get to see the fireworks.

Kate looked at her daughter. "We don't have to talk about this at lunch, Kelsey."

"Why not? We're all here, right? We don't have to wait for somebody to come home."

"Noah doesn't want to get involved in this argument."

Kelsey turned her big brown eyes in his direction, giving him an innocent stare. "He doesn't mind, do you?" Before Noah could answer, she hurried on. "See, I plan to go to Vanderbilt University in Nashville for college. I even applied for early decision, 'cause I really do want to go there. And my boyfriend, Sal, wants to come with me. He's an automotive technician," she clarified. "He's really good with engines, and he races, too. Stock cars. So anyway, he can get a job in Nashville, and I can go to school and it will all be cool. I'll live in the dorm," she emphasized, with a glance at her mother. "And Sal will have his own place, like he does here. Doesn't that sound great?"

"Well—" Noah started.

"Don't feel obligated," Dixon said. "Kelsey, this isn't the right time."

"So why do you get to decide when's the right time? I want to talk now. I want to know why you don't trust me enough to believe I'll do what's right, whether I'm here or in Nashville. Sal and I are together all the time—"

"And I'm not always happy about that," Kate said.

Kelsey rolled her eyes. "We're good kids. We don't get into trouble."

"College is very different." Dixon sat back in his chair. "You've got more responsibilities to manage on your own. A boyfriend will be a real distraction."

"Or maybe a real help. He could fix my car."

"What car?"

"The one I'm getting for graduation, duh, because I can't go to college without a car."

"I'm the one who needs a car," Trace broke in. "I have ball practice every day and it's a pain always getting a ride with Kate or somebody else."

Kelsey whipped her head around to look at her brother. "If I didn't have a car in high school, you certainly won't."

Dixon held up a hand. "That's beside the point. Your mother and I don't think it's a good idea for you and Sal to move away together. Not your first year, Kelsey. Maybe when you've settled into college life—"

She jumped to her feet. "You want me to leave him for a whole year? You think he won't find some other girlfriend?"

"If you don't trust him…"

"Of course I trust him. But…you're not even my real parents. I don't have to listen to anything either of you have to say." With a sob, she left the table. Her footsteps pounded up the stairs and along the hallway floor above, then a door slammed hard enough to rattle the pictures on the walls.

After a minute, Dixon took a swallow of tea. "Sorry about that," he said, with a wry look at Noah. "We're under a little stress these days."

"No problem."

"Of course it's a problem." Kate's face was white. "She ought to know better than to behave like that with a guest at the table."

"It's hard to think about manners when your life is falling apart," Noah remarked.

Dixon chuckled. "If you understand that, you've definitely got the material to be a dad. Sal's a nice kid, but you just hate to see them tie themselves up so early."

Noah nodded. "People change a lot after high school." The understatement of the decade.

Kate sighed. "They do. And Nashville is far enough away that we couldn't get there quickly if she was in trouble." She blinked her eyes. "I'm not coping too well with the idea of my daughter—even if only my 'adopted' daughter—going off to college."

"Plus, Kate might be going back to school herself. She's applied to law school," Dixon explained. "So we're waiting to get two acceptance letters."

"I hope the news is good," Noah said. "You were planning on law school back before high school graduation, right?"

"Right. I took a detour when I married Trace and Kelsey's dad. I've loved every minute of being their mom." She took a deep breath. "But now that they're getting older, I need to find something new to do."

Starting over was something Noah understood. "You'll get it all straightened out."

"I hope so," she said, with a worried look at her husband. "I do hope so."

The rest of the meal passed comfortably enough. Noah allowed them to persuade him to have two helpings of Miss Daisy's devil's food cake and to carry a stack of plastic containers filled with leftovers when he left.

"You should keep some of this," he insisted as he stood at the door. "I feel bad taking all this great food."

"Enjoy," Dixon said. "Miss Daisy will cook again tomorrow." He patted his stomach. "I'd be the laughingstock of the roundup, if those guys could see how many pounds I've put on in the last couple of years."

"You were too thin when you came home," Kate said, putting her arm around him. "You needed every ounce. Will we see you later this afternoon?" she asked Noah, as Dixon opened the door.

"What's going on?"

"The Christmas reunion dance committee, remember? We've got a meeting at four o'clock. At the Carolina Diner."

Great. Another dose of Abby. "I wasn't planning on going. I'm not—"

"Of course you are. We've only got two weeks and there's so much to do—we need everybody's help." She backed into the house and started to close the door. "So we'll see you at four. Right?"

The panel shut before he could protest, and Noah was left staring at the bright green wreath with its gold velvet bow. Who wanted a convicted felon on their dance committee?

Kate Bell, that's who. And he couldn't be rude to Kate.

WHEN NOAH WALKED INTO the diner Sunday afternoon, Abby almost dropped the coffeepot. She hadn't reminded him about the meeting and hadn't expected him to attend if he remembered.

But if he thought she'd go back to being good old Abby, everybody's favorite waitress, he could think again. She turned to Pete Mitchell. "Hey, Pete. More coffee?"

"Sounds good." The state trooper pushed his mug closer. "Joey was up last night, teething, and I'm walking around in a fog today."

Abby clucked her tongue. "Poor little guy."

"He's with his grandmother this afternoon just so we can have some peace. She's good with fussy babies. And Joey can be a hellion."

"Kind of dampens your enthusiasm for having another one, I guess."

"Not really. Kids are great." Pete looked at his wife, who stood at the other end of the table talking to Kate. "But Mary Rose isn't thinking about more kids right now."

"She wants to go back to work?"

"We're still working through the fallout from this last 'work accident' of mine." He sighed and shifted his injured arm with his good hand. "The job is great most of the time. But every so often…"

"You get hurt. Or somebody else does." Sometimes, state troopers got killed on the job. But then, other people died, too….

She glanced at Noah, and quickly away again.

Pete shrugged and winced at the same time. "Right. We're working things out. But until we do, Joey'll have the nursery to himself."

"Hey, I was an only child. I liked it just fine. I got all the Christmas presents and all the Easter candy."

Abby set the coffeepot on the counter and perched on a stool as Kate called the meeting to order. "Cass Baker, who's doing the catering, couldn't be here this afternoon, and she asked me to report on the food. She's got the menu set up to meet our budget—dips and cheeses for appetizers, roast beef and chicken for the main course, cookies and chocolate mousse for dessert, which sounds kind of ordinary except you know it'll arrive with that special touch Sugar and Spice always delivers. Attendance looks really good—I've got acceptance cards from about sixty percent of the people we invited. How are the decorations coming?"

Phoebe DeVries sat forward in her chair. "We sent flyers about painting a Christmas panel to everybody who got an invitation, and we've received ten replies. If we put five scenes on each side, that's forty feet of space." She shrugged. "I'd hoped for more, but time is getting short. Folks have lots of stuff to do in the last three weeks before Christmas."

Adam put up a hand. "What if the committee members painted panels, too?"

"Because we aren't busy in the weeks before Christmas?" Dixon's grin took the sting out of his words.

"Well, as mayor, I'm willing to do my part. Phoebe and I will do one."

"I'll get Andrew and Erin to help Rhys and me," Jacquie said. "Between the four of us, we can produce something decent. Horses and a sleigh, maybe, though I guess there's never been enough snow down here for that."

"We can always hope," Abby told her. "I'll make a panel."

"By yourself?" Kate shook her head. "That's a lot of work. Noah, you can give Abby some help, can't you? I hate to see her do it all by herself."

He hesitated long enough that Abby's cheeks started heating up. "Don't worry about it," she said to the room in general. She couldn't look at Noah. "Dad will have some spare time."

"I'll be glad to work with you, Abby." Noah cleared his throat. "As long as Rob doesn't keep me at the job all hours of the day and night."

Rob rolled his eyes. "Hasn't shown up for the first day yet and already he's asking for time off. Valerie and I will work on a backdrop, too. In our spare time," he said, with a pretended glare at Noah.

"The section with the murals will make a great dance area," Kate said, nodding, "with the stage at one end and the food at the other. Cass has small tables she'll donate, and Mr. Floyd said we could borrow chairs from the classrooms."

There was more discussion concerning the budget, the band and the souvenirs to be passed out, but Abby let the talk flow over her head. She didn't like having Noah shoehorned into spending time with her. Kate had evidently made a project out of getting them together. But Abby preferred to do her own manipulating. She'd had years of practice.

And anyway, she'd decided last night that Noah Blake was a lost cause.

As the meeting broke up, she found the chance to get him alone by the window. "I want to talk to you."

"What have I done now?"

"I just want you to know that you're not required to spend time on this backdrop panel with me. I can get it done by myself."

He crossed his arms over his chest and leaned back against the side of a booth. "I'm sure you can."

"So just keep quiet and don't mention it to Kate, and she'll never know we didn't work on it together."

"So either I do a panel by myself or don't do one at all?"

"Right." She nodded, and pivoted on her toe to walk away.

"What if I want help?"

Abby stopped but didn't turn back. "Ask somebody else."

"Who? Wade Hayes? Couldn't you help me out, as a friend?"

Now she did look at him. "We are not friends."

"We were once. Remember that project in fifth grade?"

"It got broken."

"Yeah, but it looked good before then. And the paper you wrote was excellent. We make a good team."

When he gave her that smile, fighting him was beyond her strength. "Okay." Abby held out her hand for a shake. "I'll be able to work in the evenings, after the diner closes."

Noah's palm closed over hers, and that's when she remembered that there was nothing simple or friendly about the way she felt. The contact of skin against skin sent a flash of pure energy racing across her nerves.

A flicker in his dark eyes told her he'd experienced

the same connection. His grin faded, and he took a quick breath.

The next second, he was backing away. "I'll call you tomorrow night," he said, looking over his shoulder to avoid running into the tables and chairs, or maybe to avoid her eyes. "And we'll set up a time to get started."

"Sure," she told the back of his head. "Sounds great."

Then he left, along with the rest of the committee, and a few Sunday night diners straggled in. Her dad went home about eight o'clock. Abby was thinking she might get to go home early herself when Wade Hayes strolled in and sat down at the counter.

She hid an impatient sigh. "Good evening, Officer. What will you have?"

"I passed up my grandmama's apple pie just so I could come have coffee and a big piece of your spice cake, Miss Abby. With ice cream." He was a good-looking guy, if you liked them linebacker-size with blond hair and a tendency to sunburn.

"Coming up," she said, aiming a smile in his general direction. "I'm getting ready to close, so just yell if you need something."

"I got this invitation to the Christmas reunion dance," he said as she put his cake in front of him. "Sounds like fun. I wondered if you would be my date."

"Oh…" Thank goodness she had her back to him as she wiped down the service area. She had a moment to prepare. "Oh, Wade, that's nice of you. But I'm on the committee." With her expression under control, she turned to look at him. "I imagine I'll be busy all night long. I wasn't planning to go with a date."

He frowned. "Doesn't sound like much fun for you."

"Sure, it does. I'll get to talk to everybody, just to make sure they're having a good time."

"Well, you gotta promise me a couple of dances. Slow ones." The grin he gave her missed being a leer, but not by much.

"I promise." She crossed her heart, then wished she hadn't when his gaze lingered on her shirtfront.

Wade dawdled over his dessert, but finally she was able to lock the door behind him. Sweeping and mopping the dining room floor were so second nature to her that she didn't even think about the tasks anymore, and soon enough she was pulling on her coat, ready to leave.

At the back door, she realized she hadn't called Marian Blake to report what she knew about Noah's new residence. Since it was good news, there wasn't any reason to conceal the facts, right? Even though she felt like a…a quisling. Or just a sneak.

But the fact that Mrs. Blake wanted to know meant that she still cared about her son, and helping her might somehow heal the breach between them. Abby dialed the number from the office phone. "Hi, Miss Marian. It's Abby."

"I wondered if you had decided to ignore what I asked you to do."

"No, no, I just…needed time to find out, is all. Noah's staying in an apartment over Dixon Bell's garage."

"Those Crawfords, always showing off how much money they have."

"And he'll be working for Rob Warren, in his new security service."

"Hah! What does Noah know about security? Who'd let him work on their house, anyway, with his record?"

"I would," Abby said quietly.

"The more fool you. He's never been anything but trouble and never will be." Mrs. Blake hung up.

Abby set down her own receiver, then put her head in her hand. Okay, so Noah had stolen money from her dad, and probably other people, as well. Maybe he did set that fire in the school. He'd served time in prison for killing a man. And those were only the crimes she knew about. He could have done more of the same and worse during the last fifteen years.

But what chance had he ever had to avoid trouble, when his own mother was so dead set against him?

More important, how would he become whole if Marian Blake's bitterness never healed?

CHAPTER SEVEN

NOAH DOZED OFF ON the couch in front of the TV Sunday night—a luxury all by itself—and slept like a rock. His eyes popped open at 5:00 a.m., though, with the thought that he would be starting to work for Rob Warren this morning. There was no going back to sleep.

He went for a run, instead, through the dark lanes in the countryside around Magnolia Cottage. What had once been the Crawford family plantation had been sold off in pieces for business and highway development, leaving just the grand house and a few acres of estate as a remnant of glory. Boundary Street wasn't far from Dixon's "cottage," and Noah jogged by his mother's house, noting again the dilapidated condition of the building and the fence. Maybe she'd let him do some repairs on the place, even if she didn't want him living there. He'd worked several different construction jobs in Atlanta, and knew what to do with a hammer and saw.

By six-thirty, he was showered, shaved and dressed in the new jeans and shirt he'd bought last week. He had on new socks, too, and he'd cleaned up his boots. Rob wanted to see him at eight-thirty this morning. What would he do until then?

He fought a strong urge to head to the Carolina Diner for breakfast. He had plenty of food in the kitchen—besides Miss Daisy's leftovers, he'd stocked the refrigerator with eggs, bacon, bread, butter, orange juice and milk. He'd stored cereal in the cupboards, plus hot chocolate mix.

What he didn't have here was Abby. Talking to her would be dangerous, but he could watch her from a distance, see her smile and feel like everything would work out. She had that kind of power, though he didn't think she realized it. He wasn't sure what was wrong with the men in New Skye that she was still single, still living with her dad. A woman like Abby should have been somebody's prize.

Finally, he refused to give in to an impulse that would only cause trouble and cooked for himself, then cleaned up the kitchen, made the bed from yesterday and straightened the small mess he'd left in the bathroom. He hadn't lived somewhere this nice more than a couple of times in his life. The least he could do was take care of it.

He was wheeling the Harley out to the drive when Kate, Trace and Kelsey came out of the house.

"Something wrong with your bike?" Trace called, heading in Noah's direction with Kate following. Kelsey rolled her eyes and got into the Volvo parked nearby.

Noah shook his head in answer to the boy's question. "I didn't want to make a huge racket and wake everybody up. 'Morning, Kate."

"Don't worry about that," Kate said. "We're all early risers, except for Dixon. He's a night owl, but if we wake him up in the morning, he goes right back to sleep. The kids and I have to be up and out before seven-thirty. And Miss Daisy beats us to the coffeepot every morning."

"Can I start the bike?" Trace prowled around the Harley, studying every angle. "Please?"

Noah glanced at Kate, who winced and then took a deep breath. "I suppose that's okay. Not that we're buying one, you understand."

"I know, I know." Trace looked at Noah. "What do I do?"

"First thing, get on." He thought Trace would pass out from joy. "Here's the key, the gas, the brakes…"

After a three-minute lesson, Noah stepped back. Trace followed directions flawlessly, and the roar of the Harley's engine shattered the quiet morning.

"Awesome!" Trace mouthed. Noah grinned. He remembered the first feel of all that power underneath his butt.

The door of the Volvo slammed, catching Kate's attention. Kelsey stood there with her hands on her hips. "Come *on,* let's go."

Kate made a T with her hands, and Trace cut the engine. "Time to go," she said.

"Man." He looked as if he wanted to stomp his feet and throw a temper tantrum. "I wish I could…" He heaved a sigh. "Thanks, though. It's a cool bike."

Noah looked at Kate. "I could take him to school." Beside him, Trace gasped.

Refusal was the first expression to appear on Kate's beautiful face. "I don't think…"

"Please. Oh, please," Trace whispered. "I'll bring

home all A's for the semester, I promise, if you let me ride with Noah."

She laughed, a lovely, ringing sound. "That's quite a promise."

"And…and no detentions at school, either. I'll be a perfect student."

This time, Noah chuckled. "You're a better man than I am if you can keep that promise."

"Do you have an extra helmet?" Kate asked.

"Damn. No, I don't." What a stupid mistake. The boy looked like he'd been run over by a semi-truck. "I'm sorry, Trace."

"He can use mine." The three of them turned to see Dixon coming across the grass, holding out a helmet. "I heard the engine," he said in response to Kate's stare, "looked out the window and figured the next issue would be a helmet." He handed the headgear to Trace. "You'd better get your butt on the bike and get to school." He grinned at the boy, then put an arm around Kate's waist and pulled her close enough for a kiss on the cheek. "'Morning, gorgeous."

"I'm sorry we woke you."

"No problem. Just means I'll be awake when you come home again." He gave her a wink Noah had no trouble interpreting. "Have a good day, Noah."

"Thanks." He pulled on his own helmet and swung onto the Harley in front of Trace. His cheeks felt warm and there was a hollow space in his chest where his breath used to be. With an extra rev of the engine, he turned the bike onto the drive and away from the house, with Trace perched behind him.

He took the long way, to maximize the ride time and avoid traffic, giving Trace a decent experience and himself time to recover. What would it be like to have a woman who would always be there, in your arms each night, waking up with you each morning? A woman to count on every day? He'd known many women, hooked up with a few for a while, but always drifted away again. He'd never had a single positive thought about marriage.

Why now?

Ignoring Principal Floyd's orders to stay off school grounds, Noah pulled the bike up to the curb directly in front of the main entrance. Trace climbed off the back of the bike and held out a hand to Noah. "Thanks. That was too awesome."

A couple of guys joined them. "You got to ride on the Harley, LaRue?"

"How cool is that?" They asked Noah questions and examined the bike with eagle eyes until the bell rang inside the building. "Thanks again," Trace called, and the three hurried inside.

Still grinning, Noah headed the bike out of the parking lot…and found himself staring across the street at the Carolina Diner. He still had thirty minutes before he could show up for work. Who would blame him for starting the day with a cup of great coffee?

Inside, his choice of tables was small. But when he glanced at the counter, Charlie stood at the register, which torpedoed that option. Noah saw a table for two near the front, and sat down with his back to a booth crowded with construction workers, waiting for Abby to notice him.

"I always thought this was a family kind of place," said one of the guys behind him.

"I wouldn't bring my kids in," somebody else commented. "Not if they're letting murderers eat here."

"He killed a kid?" somebody else asked. There was some discussion of the issue, until they finally concluded they hadn't actually heard who he killed. "It's gotta be easier the second time, you know? He could go postal any second and we'd all wind up dead."

"Mass murder at Charlie's diner," the second guy suggested, in a TV anchor's voice. "Details at six." And then, in a changed tone, "Hey, Miss Abby. More coffee?"

"No more coffee." Her voice was flat. "And breakfast is on me. Now get out, and don't come back until you've got some sense in those thick heads of yours. Go on. Get out."

The guys left, with a lot of complaining and confusion and several stiff knocks against Noah's chair. Abby waited until the bell on the door had signaled their exit and then came around to face Noah. "Good morning. What will you have?"

"How about some pride?" He glared up at her. "I don't need you to chase off troublemakers. And I sure as hell don't want to cost your dad the price of their breakfasts."

"You didn't." She lifted her chin and stared down her nose at him. "The change left over from that fifty you stuck me with on Saturday paid for their meal. I have a right to tell people to leave if they're behaving badly, and you don't have anything at all to say about it."

Noah shook his head. "I just want a cup of coffee," he said wearily. "Is that too much to ask?"

Abby was still mad, but at the same time she hated seeing Noah so defeated. "Not at all. I'll be back in a minute."

Charlie tried to talk to her when she went past him into the kitchen, but she shook her head, snatched up an order and hurried out again. With the next tray, she carried Noah's coffee and set it down on his table after she'd delivered the other customers' food.

She hugged the tray against her chest. "You're headed to work, I guess?"

He nodded, keeping his eyes on the ribbon of cream blending into his coffee.

"How's life in your new place?"

"Okay." One black leather shoulder lifted in a shrug.

Abby thumped that shoulder with the heel of her hand. "Hey, Noah—this is me, being a friend. Is it too much to expect you to cooperate?"

He looked surprised. "Sorry. I guess I'm out of practice. What am I supposed to do?"

"Look at me when we talk, for starters. Answer with more than one word and a shrug. If you want to go for the big win, ask about *my* life."

One side of his mouth quirked in a smile. "How's your life, Abby?"

"Not too bad. I've got lots of old friends coming home for the holidays. And we'll be closed the week between Christmas and New Year's, so I'm looking forward to some time off."

"Sounds good."

"It will be." Across the room, a couple of customers wanted her attention. "There's more to life than waiting tables and cooking. Or so they tell me." Annoyed at the impatience she could see in their eyes, she tapped her fingers on the tray. "I'll be back to check on you in a few minutes."

But work took over, as it always did. When the crowd cleared and she could breathe again, Noah was gone. He'd left exact change for the coffee, plus tax and a dollar tip. She'd have to tell him not to bother with tips. She didn't want to be paid for caring about him.

Especially when he was so determined not to return the favor.

WARREN AND SONS LOCKSMITHS occupied a concrete-block building on a side street near the downtown business district. Rob's company, Warren Security Monitoring, operated out of the same building but was an entirely separate organization from his father's. Noah parked his bike in what he hoped was an inconspicuous corner and went in through the front door.

"What do you need?" The man behind the counter was Rob's double, except for being a couple of decades older.

"Mr. Warren, I'm Noah Blake. Rob hired me—"

"Yeah, yeah, sure he did." Rob's dad dismissed him with the wave of a hand. "How he thinks he's going to keep clients with an ex-con working for him is beyond me. But, hey, it's his money he's throwing away, not mine." Without another word, Mr. Warren disappeared through a side door. Noah could hear him calling for his son somewhere in the back of the shop.

Hands in his pockets, Noah faced the window that looked out over the parking lot. Maybe this was a bad idea. Maybe he could get his parole moved back to Atlanta, get a job with people who didn't know him. Being a permanent stranger was a hell of a lot easier than being a suspicious friend.

"Hey, Noah." Rob's low voice predicted the grin he wore when Noah turned around. "How are you this morning? Ready to get to work?"

"Sure. But…" He took a deep breath. "This might not be such a good idea after all. I'm getting the impression I could drive away more business than I bring in. You've got grounds for rethinking the offer."

Hands flat on the counter, Rob did appear to be considering. "Well, I can't say I haven't heard the negative side of the argument. But I think most men deserve a second chance. So, if you want one here, it's yours."

Until he felt the tide of relief wash over him, Noah hadn't realized just how much he wanted the job. "Well, then, I'm reporting for work."

The morning flew by as Rob introduced him to the company, the equipment and the procedures. So far, Warren Security Monitoring had acquired fifteen clients, including six houses Adam DeVries had built and wired for alarm systems. Pete Mitchell had asked Rob to set up a security system for his home, and Jacquie and Rhys Lewellyn had hired him to wire their barn, though the installation work hadn't been done yet.

"They wanted to wait until after the holidays," Rob said. "In the meantime, I've got four houses under contract and three I've installed and we're now monitoring." He led Noah into the control room. "This is where we take the calls. You remember my mom? Mom, this is Noah Blake—he's going to be our installer. She takes the day shift on the board," he explained, "and my brother and I alternate on the swing shift. That way I only have to hire out the graveyard shift—11:00 p.m. until seven in the morning."

With his online computer training, Noah was sure he could have run the control board efficiently. But monitoring personnel were required to be bonded, Rob had said. Fortunately, mere installers didn't need that endorsement.

By midmorning, Noah had thirty pounds of manuals to read and a handle on the basics of installation. "I've got nothing scheduled for the afternoon," Rob told him. "If you want to take these home and start reading, that'll be fine. You can call if you have questions, or use the Web sites for the suppliers. Or both."

"Sounds good." Noah shifted the thick books to his left arm and held out his right hand to Rob. "I really appreciate the chance. I know you're taking some serious flak for giving me a break."

"I'm glad to help. And you'll find out after a while that I'm not such an easy guy to work for."

"He can be downright harsh," Mrs. Warren said, leaning around the door frame opening into the hallway. "Why, I've known him to…" She shook her head, smiling. "No, it just doesn't work. Rob's the most easygoing, patient and considerate employer in town. I've always been afraid he'd get taken advantage of, but somehow he never does."

Rob rolled his eyes. "Leave it to his mother to blow a guy's cover."

Noah grinned, though he didn't know much about the kind of relationship Rob appeared to have with his mom. "I'll see you tomorrow morning. Eight o'clock this time?"

"Right." Rob clapped him on the shoulder and went back into the work area. Noah stowed the manuals in the saddlebags on the bike and pulled on his helmet. Then he kicked the motor to life and headed for police headquarters and the worst hour of this day.

Wade Hayes emerged from his office about forty-five minutes after Noah registered his name with the officer at the reception desk. The waiting room had been empty the whole time. Noah decided not to take the hint that even dead air was more significant in Wade's day than their appointment.

The cop gave him a quick glance from across the room. "Come on back." By the time Noah reached the hallway, Wade had disappeared, requiring Noah to peek in every door to determine which room to enter. Just another mind game.

Once inside the correct office, Noah waited in front of Wade's desk for an invitation to sit down. He didn't owe the guy a single slice of courtesy, but neither would he provide the smallest excuse for complaint. Wade let him stand for a good ten minutes as he thumbed through a file Noah assumed was his own.

Finally, Hayes looked up. "Go ahead. Sit. Says here you have a job with Warren Security Monitoring."

"That's right."

"And you're living with your mother at 150 Boundary Street?"

"My address has changed. I'm at 78 Magnolia Lane now."

Wade grinned at him. "The old lady threw you out, huh? Havin' a murderer for a son was too much for even her to swallow?"

Noah clenched his fists but kept his voice low. "What else do you need to know?"

Leaning back in his chair, Wade clasped his hands behind his head and put his crossed feet up on the desk. "I'd like to know how you got the balls to show up here, after all this time and after what you've done. Anybody with sense would've gone as far away as he could get."

"Running doesn't solve problems."

"That's true. Folks still hate you for starting that fire at the school. You caused a lot of trouble, burning up all the records for the senior class."

"It's an interesting theory. But I didn't start that fire."

"Oh, really? So why did you disappear afterward?"

"It wasn't too hard to see who would get blamed. I decided sticking around for a diploma wasn't worth getting jailed for arson."

"You just delayed the jail part, looks like. Got a little living done first?"

"Something like that."

Hayes looked at the file again. "Says here you slammed the guy into an iron radiator until his head broke open and brains spilled everywhere."

"That's pretty colorful language for a rap sheet. I was in a fight, yeah. The guy died. He had an equal opportunity to kill me. And would've, but I wasn't as drunk as he was."

"There was a woman involved?"

Noah refused to go there. "No. Just him and me."

"Ah." Wade looked at the file again, taking his time, keeping Noah waiting as long as possible. Footsteps sounded in the hallway outside the door, coming closer, stopping just behind Noah's back. The door squeaked open.

"Hey, son." That deep voice had never lost its rural accent, nor the ability to send a shiver down Noah's spine. "What's going on?"

"'Afternoon, Dad. I'm dealing with an old friend of ours. You remember Noah Blake?"

Noah got to his feet and turned around. "Hello, Sheriff Hayes."

A weathered, heavier version of his son, the sheriff looked Noah up and down. "You're just about the last person I expected to see in this town again." He looked beyond Noah to Wade. "You cross every *T* and dot every *I* on this one. If he so much as jaywalks, I want his butt in jail."

"Yes, sir."

"Give my best to your mother," the sheriff told Noah, then turned on his heel and left, closing the door behind him. Noah stayed on his feet but faced the desk again.

"Dad never did like you much," Wade commented. He completed the form he was filling out and pulled another from the folder. "Guess it's a good thing he dumped your mother. What a mess that would've been."

"Good for her, anyway."

Wade looked up, eyes narrowed. "What did you say?"

"I said, she's lucky she didn't stay involved with a bully like your dad."

In a quick move, Wade reached Noah's side of the desk and stood almost on top of him. "You always were a smart-mouthed bastard."

"And you always were the kind to whine about it."

The officer's big hands clenched on Noah's shoulders and shoved him backward, into the door. Noah ricocheted off the wood and launched himself at Wade, one hand grasping for a hold on the fleshy body, one fist drawn back for a punch.

"Hit me and I'll slam your ass back in prison so fast it'll make your head spin." Wade spoke through gritted teeth, holding Noah at arm's length. "I swear, I'll walk you through the middle of town in chains if you don't behave. That'll impress your rich friends, won't it? And I know old Marian will just love the idea. People think so highly of her in this town as it is."

The threat was real. His mother had a hard enough time without being harassed by the police and the sheriff's department. Noah jerked back, out of Wade's hold, and straightened his jacket.

"I'm here to play by the rules," he said. "I don't intend to cause trouble."

"Oh, please." Wade dropped into his chair again. "You were trouble from the day you were born. Why else do you think your old man was such a loser? The way I hear it, if not for you, he could've been a pro football player, way up in the big leagues. Instead, he dropped out of college to get married and raise a brat. And when he couldn't take it anymore, he ran off."

"You know everything, I guess."

"Don't forget that. Now, I'm gonna give you a run-down of the rules here in my town."

"Your town?"

"That's right. I'm just marking time in the police department. When my dad retires, I'm taking over as sheriff."

"I thought you had to be elected to be sheriff."

"And my dad's got the votes all in his pocket, no sweat. So listen up…"

Noah escaped, finally, when a call claimed Wade's attention. He wouldn't allow himself to run out of the building, but by the time he reached his bike, he was sweating and breathing hard.

Following his first impulse—leaving town—would only get him sent back to prison if he was caught. His second impulse—going to see Abby—wasn't any smarter.

He went back to his apartment, in the end, because he intended to give Rob the best work he could perform, and that meant understanding the technicalities of a security system. The winter afternoon waned into darkness as he studied the manuals. He warmed up Miss Daisy's leftovers for dinner, still reading and taking notes.

The sound of the garage door opening underneath him barely registered, but a knock on the door a few minutes later pulled him out of the books. Abby stood on his porch again, her long hair blowing in a cold wind.

"Well, come on," she said, motioning for him to step outside. "Let's get started."

"On what?" His first impulse was to pull her inside with him, shut out the cold and warm her up.

"The panel for the dance."

Oh. "Where are we doing this?"

"Dixon said we could use the half of his garage Miss Daisy's car doesn't occupy. Come on, Noah, get your jacket."

Surrendering to the inevitable, he did as she ordered, taking up his jacket from the arm of the sofa. "Don't we need supplies? Paint, brushes, pencils, rulers…the board itself?"

As soon as he put his right arm through the jacket sleeve, Abby grabbed his hand and started pulling him along toward the steps. Noah barely had time to close the door behind him.

"I bought paint," she said, leading the way down to the ground. "Dixon picked up a six-by-eight-foot panel for us and put it in the garage this morning." Abby led him through the open garage door. "See? All set. We're ready to decide what we want to paint. And how."

Noah shook his head. "Where do you get all this energy? It's after nine o'clock and you've been at work since dawn."

She shrugged. "I love Christmas. I'm excited about the dance. And…" She seemed to rethink the next explanation. "And I always loved art in school. So what should we draw?"

He turned to pull the garage door down, shutting out the wind if not the cold. "What's everybody else doing?"

"Um…Jacquie's doing something about horses and a stable. Maybe a sleigh ride. Phoebe and Adam said something about children and a Christmas tree. Rob and Valerie I'm not sure about—they'll probably let the three kids help decide. I saw one entry form that mentioned a manger scene, and somebody else wanted to do a menorah and symbols of Hanukkah. I can't remember all the others."

Crossing his arms, Noah leaned back against the fender of Miss Daisy's yellow New Yorker. "I'm sure you must have thought about this already. What do you want to do?"

She looked at him sheepishly. "Well, I did have an idea."

"Which is?"

"I thought about our Main Street, back in the old days, before it deteriorated, you know? Dad's told me all about it—Mabry's Department store was the place to shop, the Silver Screen Cinema showed movies, and there were restaurants and businesses all making a profit downtown. I looked it up—"

Noah chuckled. "Of course you did."

"—and there was a white Christmas in New Skye in 1954. Wouldn't that be just perfect? We could paint Christmas in 1954, with the cute cars and the great clothes and snow everywhere."

To his own surprise, Noah could see in his mind's eye exactly what she described—the energy and excitement of a small town in the recovery after a world war. Those old Packards and Fords and Chevys had sported great chrome details. "Can we include a vintage Harley?"

"Absolutely." Abby nodded. "What do you think?"

"Absolutely," Noah echoed, grinning. "Let's sharpen those pencils."

BY ELEVEN O'CLOCK THEY'D roughed in the outlines of their drawing—a diagonal view of Main Street with the cinema marquee in the foreground, Mabry's Department Store in the center and the courthouse in the horizon. Noah was a good draftsman, Abby had discovered, with a great eye for perspective.

"Considering the fact that neither of us took art lessons, or got any encouragement at all, I think this looks terrific," she told him, standing back to observe as he sketched in the Harley he'd parked in front of Leland's Restaurant and Grill. "I can't wait until we start putting the colors in."

Noah straightened up from a crouch to his full height, then stretched his arms high over his head. The long, lean length of him took her breath away. She bent to gather the rulers and pencils they'd left on the floor, giving herself an excuse for flushed cheeks.

"It'll be fun to paint in the decorations." He leaned backward, his body now a graceful arc. "Wreaths on the windows and garlands on the lampposts and little piles of snow against the curbs and walls." His grin, when he looked at her, was proud, but also a little shy. "I think we've got a winner on our hands."

"Wouldn't that be fun? The hardware store is donating a big, tall spruce tree and everybody who comes to the dance is supposed to bring an ornament. Then the winner of the panel contest gets to take the tree home."

She sighed. "Dad has an artificial tree we've put up every year since my mom got sick. I know he celebrated just for me those first few years, because I was still a teenager, and he needed a tree that didn't make too much trouble. But I've always wanted a fresh tree. Maybe this year will be the year."

Noah stared at her with a serious expression. "If you got your own place, you could have any kind of tree you wanted."

"But Dad would be by himself, and he'd hate that."

"What if you get married one day? What's he going to do then?"

She tried to laugh but doubted she carried it off. "That falls under the category of crossing a bridge when you get to it. The prospect of grandchildren would probably keep Dad satisfied."

As they finished cleaning up, a new tension entered the air. From Noah, maybe, who'd made it clear he didn't want anything approaching a real relationship. Or from herself, Abby thought, because she was trying so hard to keep things casual, which was almost impossible when she'd cared for such a long time.

"I'd better get going." She looked around as if she needed to bring something else home besides the car keys in her pocket. "Elvis will want to go out."

"Who is… That's what you call the dog?"

"He seems fairly comfortable with it."

Noah shook his head. "I'm completely missing his resemblance to the king."

"So come get him and bring him here to stay. Then you can call him Spot. Or whatever."

"*Whatever* might be a good name. But I don't want to impose on Dixon's hospitality with a half-trained mutt."

"He's very well trained, as a matter of fact. But that's okay. Elvis and I enjoy each other's company." Abby turned to lift up the overhead door. The rollers on the track made enough noise that she almost missed what Noah said next.

"I do, too."

The cold wind rushed into the garage as if it had been waiting all night at the door. She looked at Noah. "What did you say?"

He walked past her and waited until she'd stepped out onto the gravel drive before pulling the door down.

"I said, I do, too. I enjoy your company."

"Oh." She'd lost her breath again, but not because of the wind. "I'm glad." Gazing up at Noah in the dark, she thought she saw a debate going on in his eyes.

Maybe not, though, because in the next moment he stepped back. "Get into your car. And don't go anywhere else but straight home. There's some crazy running around robbing people."

"I heard about that. It's mostly businesses, though." She backed toward the Volvo. "I was glad to close up early tonight for that reason." Reaching the driver's door, she turned the lock and opened the panel. "Among others. 'Night, Noah."

He lifted a hand without saying anything else. The Volvo engine took a couple of tries to catch; Noah stepped forward just as the motor roared to life. For once, Abby wouldn't have minded car trouble. Instead, she waved and backed out to the circular drive in front of Magnolia Cottage.

A pretty successful evening, she decided on the trip home. Noah hadn't backed off, hadn't shut her out. If she managed to slip under his guard, she might still have a chance—a chance for the adventure that being with Noah Blake offered. She always felt alive with him, in ways she'd never known with anyone else. Not a single man in New Skye affected her the way he did. Plenty of dates and a reasonable number of kisses had assured her of one thing.

If she couldn't have Noah, she wouldn't settle for anyone less.

CHAPTER EIGHT

"YOU CAME IN AWFUL LATE last night," Charlie said when Abby hurried into the diner kitchen at six-thirty Tuesday morning.

"I was working on a backdrop for the reunion dance," she said breathlessly.

"I don't like you out by yourself so late."

"I know, I know." She patted him on the shoulder as she went by. "I was careful."

"Another bar got robbed last night," Billie commented as she stirred a big pot of grits. "Had a gun, the owner said, wore a Lone Ranger mask, emptied the register. Paper's started calling him 'The Lone Robber.'"

Abby tied on a clean apron. "Well, I wasn't at a bar. I was in Dixon Bell's garage, drawing pictures."

Charlie stared at her with lowered brows. "Dixon Bell's garage? That's where the Blake boy's staying, isn't it?"

"Yes." She went out to the front and checked the coffeemaker, hoping to avoid the rest of the conversation.

Her dad followed. "You're telling me you didn't see him?"

"No, I didn't tell you that." She sighed. "Noah and I worked on the backdrop together. No big deal."

"I'd say it must be a pretty big deal if you couldn't tell me about it."

"I just didn't want to argue. And I knew you wouldn't like me spending time with Noah."

"You got that right." He put a big hand on her shoulder and turned her to face him. "What are you trying to do, Abby girl? What else do I have to say?"

"Nothing. You don't have to say anything, because what I know about Noah and what you think you know about him are entirely different." She brushed by him and rounded the counter, crossed the dining room and unlocked the door. "It's time to open."

Tuesday's breakfast crowd was light, but Abby kept herself busy out front, away from her dad. She was cleaning up a table, with her back to the door, when a woman's fingers covered her eyes. "Guess who?"

Abby put up her own fingers and explored the left hand. "Hmm. Huge stone, square cut, embroidered band. Good morning, Sam."

The blindfold dropped from her eyes. "Do you know everybody's rings?"

"Probably." Abby turned and gave Samantha Crawford a hug. "Is Tommy here, or are you by yourself?"

"I'm meeting Phoebe and Jacquie for breakfast." The petite reporter grinned. "I've got news."

"Sounds like that's a capital *N*." Abby led the way to a booth on the wall. "What can I get you to drink while you're waiting?"

"Milk?"

"Oho. That kind of news, is it? One tall milk, coming right up."

When she returned with Sam's drink, Phoebe and Jacquie had arrived. The three women had become friends during Adam DeVries's run for mayor, when Tommy Crawford had worked as his campaign manager. "So, Miss Samantha," Abby said. "Are you going to make your announcement first, or should I get your orders?"

"I think I'll burst if I wait any longer." Sam gazed at each of them in turn. "I'm pregnant."

Phoebe and Jacquie didn't say anything for a second, then looked at each other. "Well, duh," Jacquie said.

"What?" Sam screeched.

They tortured her for one second longer, keeping their faces straight. And then they burst into laughter.

"Of course you are, sweetie." Phoebe reached across the table to capture Sam's hands. "And we're thrilled."

"You knew already?"

"We were talking just recently about how wonderful you look these days, a little rounder in your cheeks, and just so bright…and it occurred to us there might be a reason besides that cute husband of yours."

"So give us all the details," Jacquie ordered. "When are you due? What does Tommy think about it? Have you picked out names? What color will the nursery be?"

Abby listened long enough to find out the baby would be born in May, broke in to get their breakfast orders, and then went to the kitchen. She hit a run of customers at that point and couldn't get back to the conversation with Sam, as much as she wanted to. That was always the way, of course. She had a job to do, responsibilities to take care of.

Staring at her order book as she flipped through the pages, she walked up to a newly occupied table. "Can I help you?"

"I'd like a cup of coffee."

Only one man could claim that voice. "Noah!"

He smiled. "You're thinking about something serious this morning."

"No, not really." She could feel her cheeks flush. "I didn't see you come in."

"That's okay. All I need is coffee, when you get to it."

"Sure. Right away." She scanned the rest of the room, saw a couple of hands lifted for her attention, but ignored them in favor of getting Noah's drink.

"Milk and sugar are on the table," she told him. "But you probably know that."

"They're having fun." Noah nodded at Phoebe and Jacquie across the room, giggling with Sam.

"You've met Phoebe, Adam's wife. But Sam hasn't been at the dance meetings. She's married to Tommy Crawford, and she announced this morning that she's having a baby."

"Looks like good news." His grin softened to a smile.

"Babies are always good news."

In a moment, all the softness vanished. "Not always," he said in a hard voice. "Sometimes they're just in the way."

"What—"

"Hey, Abby!" A guy at a table near the door stood up and yelled in her direction. "I'm dying of thirst over here. Can I get some damn coffee?"

"Sure, sure. I'll be right there." She looked back at Noah. "Don't go away."

But when she came back to the other table with the coffeepot, Noah's seat was empty. Again, he'd left payment in exact change and a tip.

Abby snatched up the money and crushed it in her fist. How long was she going to be tied up in this place, always at the mercy of people who wanted something they thought she should provide?

When would she be free to have a life of her own?

NOAH GOT TO WORK at ten minutes before eight, just as he'd planned. He'd been tempted to stay and talk with Abby, but could only be grateful that he'd been given a chance to reconsider. Her life was complicated enough without her getting mixed up with him.

And Noah knew he couldn't afford more complications in his own existence. He'd always traveled alone, most of the time by choice. Before Abby, anyway.

He parked in back of Warren and Sons Locksmiths this time and went in through the rear entrance. Rob was already at the workbench. "'Morning, Noah. We're due at Mrs. O'Brien's house at eight-thirty. What do you know about installing security systems?"

"Lots of little wires running all over the place," Noah joked. "With bells attached so if somebody comes in, they'll trip and make a lot of noise."

Rob started laughing and shaking his head. "I'm in trouble now."

"You meant something else?" Noah grinned. "I guess I read the wrong chapters last night."

Together they reviewed the system they would install for Mrs. O'Brien, and the wiring diagram. Rob pointed out the equipment they needed and where he'd stowed it in the company van.

"Time to roll." He walked down the hallway to the main office. "Dad, we won't be back until quitting time. This is an all-day job."

"Yeah, sure." Mike Warren's voice rumbled all over the building. "I give you five minutes in Margie O'Brien's house with an ex-con. She'll have you out of there so fast, your eyes will be rolling around in your head like pinballs."

"Sorry about that," Rob said quietly as they climbed into the van. "He doesn't like anybody very much, if that helps."

"He could be right, you know." Noah watched traffic through the side window. "You're taking a big risk with your new business."

"Let's just see how things go. You and Dad may both be borrowing trouble."

Rob stopped the van at the curb in front of one of the houses on the Hill, the neighborhood on a slope above downtown New Skye where most of the biggest, nicest houses were located, occupied by the oldest, richest families. Kate and Mary Rose Bowdrey had grown up around here somewhere, along with Adam DeVries. Noah had never visited any of these homes, never hung around with the kids who lived here. He hadn't been considered good enough, back in high school, even to mow their lawns.

Was he good enough now to install their security systems?

Rob went up the slate sidewalk and rang the doorbell while Noah waited in the van. The front door opened to reveal an older lady with iron-gray curls, a lavender dress and matching shoes. A little dog wiggled in her arms, fighting to get down, but Mrs. O'Brien nodded and smiled as Rob talked to her. Maybe things would go more smoothly than expected.

Motioning for Noah to join him, Rob went around to the back of the van. "We're cleared for takeoff. The underground utilities are all marked and Trent came out yesterday to dig a trench for the new line to the street. She said she'd keep the dog out of the way. Good thing, since it snapped at me when I was here before. Let's get started."

Noah did a good deal of fetching and carrying for the first couple of hours as Rob planned out the work and set up the equipment. Wireless installations like this one were remarkably easy, with the only complicated portion being the connection of the control box to the street lines. Mrs. O'Brien fluttered around them as they worked, saying little but watching every move.

Just before noon, Rob sent Noah into the living room to retrieve a wire stripper. As he returned to the kitchen through the dining room, Noah heard Mrs. O'Brien's reedy voice.

"What did you say his name was?"

"Noah, ma'am. Noah Blake."

"Wasn't he in prison? For murder?"

"No, ma'am. Noah did serve some time for a man-slaughter charge. But he's explained the circum-stances to me and I'm willing to believe the incident was an unfortunate occurrence that will never happen again."

"But…he's been in my house. I'm all alone here since my husband passed away. With Fluffy, of course. But she's not a watchdog."

"Yes, ma'am."

"He'll know the codes."

"No, ma'am. The only people who will know your code are you and whoever you give it to."

"Surely there are some master formulas…."

"No, ma'am. Once we leave, we won't have access to your house in any way whatsoever. Even the police and the fire department will have to break in if the doors and windows are locked."

Noah thought of Wade Hayes and his dad, the sher-iff. If he were going to be afraid, those were the peo-ple who could scare him.

"You'll be completely safe," Rob continued. "Of course, as far as Noah is concerned, you'd be safe, any-way."

"I don't know…" Mrs. O'Brien clucked like a wor-ried chicken. "I just don't feel comfortable with him looking at my things. If you could send him away and finish the work yourself—"

"No, ma'am." Polite to the end, Rob's voice was as hard as Noah had ever heard it. "I can't do that. I stand behind Noah Blake just like I stand behind my brothers. I'm asking you to trust me on this."

In the silence that followed, Noah entered the kitchen. Mrs. O'Brien cast him a scared glance and left the room.

He handed Rob the tool. "Look, this is a bad idea. I'm going to clear out and let the poor lady relax."

His boss gave him a level look. "You'll give up that easily?"

Noah slapped a hand against the counter. "I'm trying to save the job for you, man. If I leave, you'll get the work done just as fast, she'll pay you and it'll be a good day. If I stay…she's gonna dither herself into asking us both to leave."

A door in the back of the house slammed. "Fluffy," Mrs. O'Brien called. "Fluffy, you come back here."

But Fluffy had reached the kitchen and announced her presence with a chain of high-pitched barks. Rob threw the moppy little dog a dirty look. "Don't come near me, mutt. I still have a scar on my hand."

With the courage of a lion, Fluffy did come nearer, but then detoured to Noah's feet. When Mrs. O'Brien reached the kitchen, Fluffy was making a thorough inspection of the scents on Noah's boots.

"Fluffy. Fluffy, come here." The old lady stood paralyzed across the room from Noah, afraid to approach him, desperate to get her dog.

Noah crouched down and put his hand near the dog's nose. "Hey, Fluffy. You like my boots? You're a good dog, aren't you? Taking care of Mrs. O'Brien?" Intent on snuffling, Fluffy dragged her nose over his hand.

After a couple of seconds, Noah ran his fingers over the streaked blond head and back, and then his whole hand. With just a little bit of coaxing, Fluffy trusted him enough to let him pick her up. When he walked over to give her back to Mrs. O'Brien, the dog was licking his face.

"Here you go." He cradled the dog in his hands until Mrs. O'Brien took hold. "She's cute."

The old lady stared at him as he backed away, and then at the dog. "Well. Thank you." She looked at Rob, and Noah, and Rob again. "I…I'll let you get on with your work," she said, and hurried toward the back of the house.

"Now, that's courage," Rob said, grinning. "I never would have put my hand close to that dog's teeth." He showed Noah a red crescent of bite marks on the side of his hand. "See what I mean?"

Noah couldn't help his own smile. "Guess I smell better than you do."

"Yeah, right. What's the name of your cologne?"

"Eau de Roast Beef."

They stopped briefly for lunch and then went back to work, finishing up the installation as daylight started to fade. Rob walked Mrs. O'Brien through her new security system while Noah put the tools and equipment in the van.

"If you drive, I can finish up this paperwork on the way back to the shop," Rob said. "Then we'll park the van and be ready to go home to supper."

Noah got behind the wheel and adjusted the seat, since Rob's six-four height left Noah about five inches short of the gas pedal. Once out of the neighborhood, he turned toward downtown and had just cleared the last traffic light when a siren sounded behind him. The rearview mirror showed him a police car on the tail of the van, lights flashing.

He knew, even without seeing the driver's face, what was coming. "Sorry," he said to Rob as he pulled the van over to the curb. "Supper's going to be a little later than we thought."

With the window rolled down, he reached for his wallet and brought out his driver's license. Rob took the van's registration out of the glove compartment and Noah held both at the ready when Wade Hayes came up beside him.

"I thought that was you, Blake." Wade jerked the registration and license out of his fingers. "And I wondered what the hell you were doing driving a van. Thought I'd better check it out." He leaned down and peered at Rob through the window. "Let me have your license, too, Warren. I don't want my man here driving a stolen vehicle."

Rob muttered something about what Wade could do with the license, the registration and the van. Noah swallowed a laugh and handed over Rob's ID as well. Then Wade walked back to his cruiser and stayed there for thirty minutes.

"I'm damn sure this is police harassment." Rob had already called home to let Valerie know he'd be late. "You should report him."

"They like to play these games. It's a power trip, but it doesn't mean anything."

"Pete doesn't play games. His work is serious."

"There are usually a few good apples in a rotten barrel."

Finally, Wade moseyed back to the window. "Sorry about the delay." He flipped the two licenses and the registration into the dark interior of the van, where they fell between the seats. "The computers were down and I had to wait for the system to come up again. You're free to go. Watch your step, Blake." With a slap on the roof of the vehicle, he walked back to the police car and turned off the flashing lights.

"So now I've got a headache the size of the county." Rob rubbed his eyes with the heels of his hands. "I hope you get to punch that guy out someday."

"Not half as much as I do," Noah told him. "And it had better be someday soon."

AFTER HIS SECOND SUCCESSFUL workday, Noah decided to stop by and see his mom before he went home. Just because she didn't want him living there didn't mean he couldn't at least visit.

As he waited at a traffic light on the far end of Boundary Street, he glanced at the car parked along the curb next to him and recognized the same beatup white Toyota he'd seen on his first day in town, with the same little kid in the back seat. Tonight, the child was asleep in his car seat. Through the window, Noah could tell that his face was dirty and tear-stained. Again. The jeans and shirt looked like the same ones he'd worn almost a week ago. Had anyone changed his clothes since then?

The Toyota sat in front of Chico's Fiesta Lounge. Judging by the music coming out the door, they had a real party going on inside. Noah was tempted to go in after the miserable excuse for a parent who would leave a little boy in a car outside a bar while he went in to get plastered.

When the light changed, he went so far as to turn the corner, instead of going straight, and parked in a no-parking zone nearby. But with his hand on the key, he stopped to think.

How many times had he rushed in to solve somebody else's problem, only to end up getting shafted himself? The last time, he'd spent three years in prison and had his life pretty much destroyed. Would this be simply one more example of Noah Blake setting himself up to take the fall? Just when he was trying to set up a new life?

He could call the police—and end up facing Wade Hayes again. Noah knew how that would turn out. Chances were good he'd be in jail before morning. Unless…

Putting the bike in gear, he drove on up the hill and parked in front of his mom's house. By the time he reached the porch, he felt almost confident. He had a reason to be here. She couldn't just throw him out.

The door opened a few inches and she peered out at him. "What do you want?"

Glad to see you, too. "Hey, Ma, I need to use your phone. Can I come in?"

"You get kicked out by the Bells already?" She grumbled, but she also stepped back and let him inside the house.

"Nope. But I need to report a kid left in a car outside a bar." He dialed 911.

"A kid in a car? So what?"

"A little boy, strapped in his car seat all by himself, outside a bar. And it's not the first time. I saw him the day I came into town."

The police dispatch station finally answered his call. "Yeah, I need to report an abandoned child." He explained the situation to the skeptical operator. "Chico's Fiesta Lounge, that's right."

When she pressed him for his name, he disconnected the call. "I guess they can get the records for the call if they really want to," he told his mother. "But as long as they take care of the kid, it'll be okay."

"So now you're leaving, I guess."

"I'd like to sit down and talk, if you've got time."

"Humph." She sat down in her chair again and picked up the remote, but only to turn down the volume.

"I was thinking," Noah said into the relative silence, "about doing some work on the house."

"What's wrong with the house? What kind of work?" He could hear her breath rasp in her chest.

So he tried to be gentle. "There's a shutter hanging loose. Screens torn. The fence is rusted and falling down in a few places. I can fix all that. I can even paint the house, when it gets a little warmer."

"Did you come back to town just to criticize the way I've taken care of the house? It's not like I'm rolling in money, you know. My social security barely covers food and electricity."

"I know, Ma. I'm not criticizing. Just trying to help."

She banged the remote control on the arm of the chair. "Well, I'm not paying for that kind of nonsense.

House stays warm and dry, that's all I care about. God knows nobody else ever cared even that much."

Noah stood up before the conversation could get worse. "I'll come over Saturday and see if I can get a few things done. If you think of something you want me to do, here's my new phone number." He set a card on the table by her elbow. "G'night."

"Humph," she said again, just as he shut the front door. But when Noah looked back into the house through the front window, he could see his mother sitting in her chair, staring at that card.

By now, any ambition he'd had to cook his own dinner had melted away. Heading toward the diner, he passed Chico's and got the satisfaction of seeing a couple of police cruisers parked out front with their lights flashing. In the next second, he realized that the white Toyota was missing from the picture.

He circled the block and came back to the corner across the street from Chico's. This time, he killed the motor, swung his leg over and left the bike parked. Joining the crowd gathered on the sidewalk in front of the bar, he started asking questions.

"What happened? What's going on?"

After a dozen I-don't-knows, he got hold of a guy who did. "Place was robbed, not fifteen minutes ago. Police showed up on time for once, but they didn't get the guy. He was long gone."

Shaking his head, Noah turned away. The police had come on his call and missed both the child abuser and the robber….

When the thought occurred to him, he nearly tripped

as he jolted off the sidewalk into the street. How likely was it that both the robber and the neglectful dad would be in the same bar at the same time?

Not nearly as likely as the idea that the robber left his kid in the car while he went inside to stick up the place.

By the time Noah finished giving the information to the police, his stomach had started roaring for food. He drove down to the diner, not sure if they'd even be open this late, or have anything left he could eat. He'd settle for a mug of hot chocolate, and one of Abby's smiles.

The lights were still shining inside the Carolina Diner, though, and he recognized Dixon Bell's truck in the parking lot. His stomach grumbling, he pulled open the door and heard the welcome jingle of the bell.

"Noah! You're just in time." Kate got up from her seat and came to meet him, caught his hand and led him back to a table where a crowd of people sat over the remains of a meal. Besides Dixon and Kate, Mary Rose and Pete Mitchell were seated, along with Adam and Phoebe DeVries. Abby was nowhere to be seen.

"Is this a meeting I was supposed to show up for?"

"No, but you're welcome to join the celebration." Dixon pulled back a chair beside him. "Have a seat. Abby is whipping up dessert. She'll be back in a minute."

"So what are you celebrating?" Noah dropped into the chair.

Kate held up a sheet of paper and fluttered it in the air. "This is it. I did it. I'm in."

He thought a second, then grinned. "Law school?"

"Yes, yes, yes!" She threw the paper into the air above her head and caught it as it drifted down. "Ten years later, I get to go."

"That's terrific, Kate. Congratulations."

"This will be handy," Pete said. "Having a lawyer in the family means we can get ourselves out of jail, sue whoever we want to, make our own wills…"

Mary Rose rolled her eyes. "Hush. What kind of law are you going to practice, Kate?"

She looked at them all for a long moment. "I'm thinking about going into the public defender's office."

Pete groaned and buried his face in his good arm, folded on the table. Mary Rose looked stunned. Baby Joey took advantage of the moment to pull her hair.

"Ow." Easing the golden strand from her son's chubby fingers, she pretended to frown. "Go to your father, rascal. I'd like five minutes alone."

Pete took over the little boy, whose dark hair and gray eyes made him the spitting image of his dad. "I don't have enough hair to pull, so what are you gonna do now?"

Joey closed a fist around Pete's nose and squeezed.

While they were all laughing, Abby came around the counter, carrying a cake flaming with candles. "I didn't have any decorations that looked right," she said, setting the creation in front of Kate on the table. "So I decided we'd just light up the night."

"It's beautiful. Do I get to blow them out?" Kate looked at her husband, who nodded.

"Damn right, you do."

Joey chose that moment to notice the candles. He

stretched his arms out, making an "ahahaha" sound. Before Pete could move, Abby swooped the little boy out of his dad's hold and walked to the other end of the table.

"We'll keep you safe down here," she crooned, "while your aunt Kate blows out her candles."

"Here I go," Kate said, drawing a huge breath. She gave a mighty whoosh and the flames disappeared, to applause and congratulatory shouts. Grinning, Noah clapped his hands with all the rest, then looked at the other end of the table, where Abby stood.

"Noah," she said as a surprised smile stole over her face. "I didn't know you'd come in."

She stared at him with an expression he'd never seen before. Yes, it was a smile, but at the same time something more than a smile, something warm and sweet and welcoming that seemed to move into him and take hold in the gentlest, softest way imaginable. For the first time in his life, he understood the word *transfixed*.

While he stared back, he had a chance to take in the picture Abby made with the little boy. Joey was pulling her long ponytail, playing with the curls in a way Noah longed to do. The sight of the two of them together—the baby happily resting on Abby's lush hip, with her right arm curled around his legs and her left hand resting on his waist—delivered a punch to the gut that robbed Noah of any breath at all.

The possibility of having a real life flashed through his brain—one that included babies and friends to celebrate with, a job he enjoyed, a chance to do some good for his town. For a second, he felt as if he could reach out and touch the future.

His future…his and Abby's.

CHAPTER NINE

The Diary of Abby Brannon

August 27, 1985
Dear Diary,
High school is very cool. The teachers don't treat us like babies anymore. We don't have to eat lunch if we don't want to. I'm not even taking gym class this year!

I saw the whole gang—Dixon and Rob have gotten tall. Adam's still cute and nice and Pete is still sports crazy. Mary Rose and Kate spent the summer at the beach and are tanned and beautiful. Jacquie rode every day and she's tanned, too. Beside them, I feel like a lump of biscuit dough. I don't eat much most days—being around food all the time kills my appetite. The magazines say exercise is important, and I walk every afternoon and all day Saturday and Sunday—between tables at the diner. I guess I'm just doomed to be pale and fat. Nobody's idea of a girlfriend.

Noah is in my homeroom, but no other classes. We're sitting in alphabetical order again, so he's right in front of me and he smiled as he walked in. It's such a nice smile, I can't believe he's as bad as they say. He's a lot

taller this year, too, and bigger somehow. Really tanned.
I didn't see him all summer, so I don't know what he
did. He walked to first period with Kim Curry, who
looks like Barbie, only better.

I think there are some doughnuts in the kitchen.
Maybe I do eat too much. I'll try to be better. Tomorrow.

November 12, 1985
Dear Diary,
I couldn't go to sleep if I wanted to. My heart's still
pounding and my hands are shaking. I want to cry, but
I keep smiling, too.

Dad let me off work at seven-thirty tonight so
Jacquie and I could go to the football game. We met
up with Kate and Mary Rose and Adam at the stadium. Dixon and Rob wandered up, as they usually do,
and we all sat together. Pete was out on the field, along
with Rob's brother Trent, and we were winning against
Southern Pines High. Yay.

In the third quarter, I decided to go to the bathroom,
behind the concession stand. When I came out, there
were three guys from Southern Pines hanging around
the men's room door. I turned the opposite way, but all
at once they were on either side of me, and one of them
moved to block my way. I tried to flirt my way out, and
when that didn't work (of course) I tried to be just nice,
then mean. All the time, they're backing me up against
the wall, brushing up against me. And, yeah, they
groped my chest and my rear end.

Then this voice came from behind them. "Back off. Now."

Two of the guys turned around and said something nasty. Noah said, "Make me."

And then there's this fight going on right in front of me, Noah against these three big guys, punching, kicking, swearing at one another. I just knew the security guards would show up with Mr. Floyd and Noah would be in so much trouble.

But nobody came. The game was tied at that point, Jacquie told me later, and so maybe they were all watching. Anyway, Noah laid those three creeps out on the ground like corpses. By the time he finished with them, they just lay there groaning.

Then he came over to me. "Are you okay? Did they hurt you?"

He touched me! He brushed back my hair, stroked my face with his fingertips, ran his hands up and down my arms. I thought I had died and gone to heaven. He smelled sweaty and clean at the same time. His eyes were worried. And from that close, his mouth is just amazing. I was hoping for a kiss.

Well, that didn't happen. But he took my hand and led me back to the bottom of the bleachers. "You shouldn't go back there by yourself," he said. "Take at least one friend with you. More would be better."

I couldn't say a word, but I nodded. He smiled again, patted my cheek and then walked away.

I don't care what anybody says—Noah Blake is a hero. I knew it in my heart, and now I've seen him in *action. I won't believe the gossip ever again. Noah is one of the good guys.*

April 17, 1986
Dear Diary,
Mom and Dad told me the news tonight. She's sick, something called primary pulmonary hypertension. Her lungs aren't working right. She'll be taking medicine, and she won't be at the diner anymore—she has to rest. They're putting her on the list for a lung transplant, in case the medicines don't work. But there's no guarantee a transplant would work either. She might die.
That's not the way it's supposed to be.

ONCE SHE GOT OVER the surprise of seeing Noah, Abby insisted on feeding him something besides cake and ice cream. He sat between Dixon and Adam, so she couldn't actually talk to him while everybody else was still there. But she kept an eye on him from her chair at the other end of the table and made sure he didn't have to ask for anything at all.

Joey started getting fussy about eight o'clock, so Pete and Mary Rose went home, followed shortly by Dixon and Kate.

"That little Joey is a handful," Phoebe commented, as she and Adam began to put on their coats. "Mary Rose was telling me he climbs everything in sight."

"Is that envy I hear in your voice?" Abby put her arm around Phoebe's shoulders and gave her friend a hug.

"Well, maybe. Adam and I have talked about it a little. But with so many kids already in the world needing good homes, I'm wondering if we should think about adoption. Or even fostering children."

"First horses, then children." Adam grinned at Noah, who looked confused. "Phoebe takes in problem cases. Abused horses, dogs, cats, a stuttering husband—" He dodged as his wife punched him in the shoulder. "And maybe a child or two. In the last couple of years, we've added three dogs, two cats and three horses to the menagerie she had before we got married."

"Several of those were your choice," Phoebe reminded him. "You brought Bo home, and Sandy Cat. He rescued a snake from the side of the road one day and wanted me to take care of it."

Noah gave her his adorable grin. "You didn't?"

"I have to draw the line somewhere, actually. No mice, rats, hamsters, guinea pigs, Komodo dragons or black snakes. I let the snake loose and he does a lovely job keeping the mice out of the barn."

"How is your panel for the dance coming?" Abby walked with Phoebe and Adam to the door. Noah followed, and she was afraid that meant he would be leaving, too.

"We were supposed to work on it tonight, after we had dinner here," Adam said. "But then the Bells and the Mitchells came in, and now it's probably too late." He looked at his wife, who confirmed his decision with a nod. "Tomorrow, though, I think we can get started. No meetings for me. Phoebe?"

She winced. "I do have a staff meeting, but I can be done by five. Really, I can." They bickered lovingly on the way to their separate vehicles—Phoebe drove a lime-green VW bug and Adam drove a truck with his company name on the door. Each honked as they left the parking lot. Abby waved, and then backed inside…only to bump into Noah, standing right behind her.

"Oh." His hands grasped her shoulders, and didn't let go when she turned around. "I'm sorry. I didn't realize you were there." She wouldn't have changed anything if she had known.

"It's okay."

He loosened his hands slowly and took a step back. "Are you ready to close up?"

"I think so. It's after nine." She began to clear the table but stopped when Noah started picking up dishes. "You don't have to do that."

He frowned at her. "I don't think I'll just stand here watching while you work."

She wasn't going to suggest that he leave. "Okay. How was work today?"

"Pretty good." He told her about the mop dog who'd bitten Rob but left Noah alone. "Once the dog accepted us, Mrs. O'Brien settled down."

Abby, hearing what he didn't say, hurried to reassure him. "Mrs. O'Brien is the really nervous type. She depended on her husband totally, and when he passed away, she didn't have any idea what to do. Mary Rose spent some time helping her with the finances, and still checks up to be sure everything is running smoothly. Rob's mom is hoping to convince Mrs. O'Brien to take a trip one day, just up to Raleigh, or maybe Asheville, to get her out of the house and into the mainstream of life again. It hasn't worked so far."

"She doesn't have kids to take care of her?"

"No. It was just the two of them."

"I'm sorry." Again, she thought she understood more than just the words.

"You're here now." She patted his hand as he extended a plate for her to load in the dishwasher. "You'll do right by your mom."

He sighed. "It's about time."

They finished up in silence. Abby played no games putting on her coat tonight, and waited until Noah joined her at the front door before turning out the lights.

"Thanks," he said with a grin. "I've still got a bruise on my hip from the last time."

"You deserve it." He went out ahead of her and Abby locked the door. The weather had warmed up this week, with nighttime temperatures in the mid-fifties, almost too warm for a coat. "At least you won't freeze riding home."

"Nope. It's colder in Atlanta than here. I forgot how warm December can be."

"And we're painting a snow scene. Can we work on it tomorrow night?"

"I don't see why not." He faced her across a wide expanse of gravel. "I'll expect to see you about nine o'clock."

"I'll be there." The idea of Noah expecting her was just about the most thrilling, exciting thing that had ever happened to her.

Except for Noah kissing her.

"Stay safe," he said, lifting his hand.

"You, too." She shut herself in the car, tempted to sit

and just enjoy the moment. But Noah was waiting for her to leave, so she drove herself home with a smile hovering on her face.

She actually understood for the first time what it felt like to have your heart sing.

WHEN NOAH CAME TO WORK on Wednesday, Rob had not arrived. "Ginny's got a doctor's appointment this morning," Trent told him. "He'll be here as soon as he gets her back home. Dad's out on a call—somebody locked their keys in the car."

"No problem. I can spend the time studying, unless you've got a job for me around here. Want me to do some cleanup?"

Trent looked around the work area. "I guess things are a pretty big mess, aren't they? It drives Rob crazy, but the old man and I are sloppy. Yeah, some organization might be a good thing. Yell if you've got any questions."

Noah worked for more than an hour, setting tools back in their places, filling several plastic bags with rubbish, using a broom and dust cloth to get the shelves cleaned off. Trent turned on the radio and they worked with a comfortable background of country music and traffic reports.

"Hard to believe they call this rush hour," Noah commented as he walked by the bench where Trent was assembling a computerized lock. "Atlanta at five o'clock, with six lanes of bumper-to-bumper cars stretched for ten miles—now that's rush hour."

"Yeah, New Skye's not exactly a metropolis. At least

we do have traffic lights, even if we don't need them much. I remember when I went to school in Chapel Hill, the traffic there seemed incredible, especially on game days." Trent shook his head. "Man, I was the proverbial yokel from the country, come to visit the bright lights. I learned to handle myself in the city eventually, for all the good it did me."

"You were headed for professional ball, last I heard. Did you change your mind?"

"In a manner of speaking. I planted a foot wrong, felt this explosion in my knee…and that was it for the NFL."

"That's too bad."

Trent heaved a sigh. "Yeah, it was. I wish I'd at least seen a big-time stadium before I lost it all. You ever go to a game in Atlanta?"

"A couple. Now, there's a team that could use a decent quarterback. Maybe you'd still qualify."

"Twenty years and twenty extra pounds later? Doubtful."

The 9:00 a.m. news came on in the silence following their conversation, including a report on last night's robbery. The announcer mentioned that a bystander had reported seeing a child left unsupervised in a white Toyota outside the bar, but police had not been able to find the vehicle or connect the car with the robbery.

Mike Warren walked in through the back door and crossed the room. "Now, that's interesting, don't you think?"

Trent looked up from his work. "What are you talking about, Dad?"

"An ex-con shows up in town, and suddenly we start having this rash of robberies. Kind of a funny coincidence, if you ask me."

Noah didn't try to defend himself, because it wouldn't do any good. The oldest Warren heard what he wanted to hear and ignored the rest.

But Mr. Warren didn't want to *be* ignored. "What have you got to say for yourself, Blake? Isn't that a coincidence?"

"I guess so. I know I'm the guy who saw the car with the kid locked inside."

"Or maybe you're just the guy who wants people to think there's somebody else doing these crimes to divert attention away from yourself. This wouldn't be the first time a criminal lied in self-protection."

"Cut it out, Dad." Rob strolled in, his long, lanky body silhouetted against the light coming through the door from outside. "Noah's not a thief. You know it and I know it."

"I don't know anything of the sort. We'll be lucky if he doesn't rob us blind by the end of the week."

"No, sir," Noah said. "I don't steal. Just kill."

Rob cuffed him on the shoulder as he walked by. "Don't encourage him," he said. "The two of you should leave each other alone. We've got an estimate to do this afternoon—go read up on the system again and we can talk about what you learn as I'm writing up the bid."

Noah followed Rob into the office, but not before he heard Mike Warren mutter to Trent, "Damn convict thinks he runs the place." Trent just rolled his eyes and gave Noah a scornful grin.

After lunch, Noah headed out with Rob to work on the estimate for a recently completed home in one of the town's newest neighborhoods. The area was being developed by L. T. LaRue—Kate Bell's ex-husband, Rob told him, and Trace and Kelsey's dad.

"He's a jerk, but sometimes you have to work with that kind. Adam's already agreed to let us install security systems in all his new construction, so we're not taking anything away from him by hoping to get LaRue business, too."

Noah looked around as they turned in between fancy brick walls at the front of the development. "I remember this was all farmland. Tobacco, mostly." The new streets were lined with large houses fronted by small trees. "It's gonna take a long time to get any shade in these yards."

Rob stopped the van in the driveway of the biggest house Noah had seen so far. The doors of the three-car garage stood open, revealing a Mercedes sedan, a Cadillac SUV and a big Harley cruiser. "How do you suppose he decides what to drive each day?" Rob murmured as they waited for someone to answer the ring of the doorbell.

When the door swung open, they confronted a very short, very pudgy man, with heavy black brows and a balding head. "Can I help you?"

Rob extended a card. "You asked for an estimate on a security system, Mr. Marino. I'm Rob Warren, and this is my associate Noah Blake."

Those black brows drew together. "Yeah, that's right. Come on in." His accent was not Southern, unless it was southern New Jersey. He left the door open and walked down the entry hall ahead of them. Noah shut the door and followed, gazing around with a strong urge to laugh. The house resembled pictures he'd seen of Italian villas—columns in the openings between rooms, fountains in the corners, and niches containing painted statues on the walls. The main room Marino led them to looked like the set for a Roman orgy, with lots of armless couches, big pillows and low tables scattered around. Grapevine garlands were draped on the walls. The man must have a Caesar complex.

"When you called, we talked about what kind of security you're looking for," Rob said. Marino had gone to stand by the floor-to-ceiling marble fireplace. He didn't ask them to sit down. "So today we'll survey the house and yard, take measurements and figure out just what we need. Then we can come back as early as next week to install the system. Does that sound good?"

Marino had fixed his gaze on Noah. "You said his name is Blake? Noah Blake?"

Rob's easy stance stiffened. "Yes, sir."

"He's that ex-con who just came into town. A killer."

"That won't be a problem, Mr. Marino. I stand behind every one of my employees and Noah is no exception. You don't have to worry a single second."

"So you say." The short man clenched his fists at his sides. "But I've got daughters. A beautiful wife. The last thing I want is some reprobate prowling through their bedrooms, casing the place for a break-in." He dragged in a breath and glanced at Noah. "Or rape."

"You little—" Noah felt Rob's grip on his arm before he realized he'd moved.

"That's completely uncalled for," Rob said. "You know there's no question of anything like that."

"The hell I do. I'm not having an ex-con work on my house. Get him out of here, and we'll talk."

Rob stood still for a second, staring at Marino. Noah ignored the twist in his gut and stepped back. "I'll wait outside."

"Not necessary." Rob walked across to Marino and jerked his business card out of the other man's fingers. "We're both finished here. Let's go."

"What about my security system?" Marino followed them to the front door. "You're the only business in town. How am I going to protect my house?"

"Get a Rottweiler," Rob said, without looking back. He chuckled as the door slammed shut behind them. "Or a sign that reads Beware of Human." He characterized Marino with a foul word Noah had never heard him use.

In the van, Noah tackled the real issue. "This isn't going to work, Rob."

"What are you talking about?"

"Don't play innocent. Having me on the job will lose you more business than you can afford. I quit."

"Not an option." As they sat at a red light, though, Rob turned to look at him. "I can't make you show up for work."

"Right."

"I can't pay you if you don't."

Noah waved the issue away. "No problem."

"But I would like to know one thing." The light changed. Rob turned his gaze to the road ahead and stepped on the gas. "When will you get tired of running away?"

Noah had no idea how to answer that question.

So he said nothing at all.

As soon as she walked into the garage Wednesday evening, Abby could tell something had happened. Noah's eyes were shadowed, and his face had lost the open expression she'd loved last night.

She unwrapped her scarf with one hand. "What's wrong?"

He glanced up from the paint he was stirring, but his gaze didn't linger long. "Nothing. Ready to get started?"

"Sure. I brought some smaller brushes for the tiny details. And…" She held up a can. "Silver paint."

Finally, he smiled. "Terrific. I didn't want to paint all the nice chrome on the cars plain gray."

"I didn't think you would." Hands on her hips, she surveyed the big panel. "Where do we start?"

Noah came to stand beside her. "I could start on one end while you take the other. Then we won't get in each other's way until we're almost finished."

Abby looked up at him. "You've really planned this job out, haven't you?"

"I like to know what's happening ahead of time."

"I'm the opposite—I like surprises." She took a risk. "Like the surprise of you coming back home."

From the side, she saw the corner of his mouth lift.

"Believe me, I'd been planning the trip for a long time. It takes more than a year to get the paperwork done for parole transfers." The smile faded and he shrugged. "But then, I didn't have much else to worry about."

"Are you sure you're okay?"

"Yeah. Let's paint."

They worked for two solid hours, collaborating on colors and brushstrokes, admiring each other's accomplishments. Noah was clearly the better artist, and when he added a new dimension to a ribbon she'd painted with a single stroke of his black-tipped brush, Abby stomped her foot.

"Why didn't you do something with this talent of yours? Didn't anybody in school realize how good you are? Who was that art teacher…Mr.—Mr…"

"Delaney," Noah supplied.

"Right. Why didn't Mr. Delaney snap you up for art classes?"

"I don't think I was interested in art. Besides, who would have wanted a troublemaker like me in a free-form class like art?"

"Would you have been such a troublemaker if you'd been doing something you really enjoyed?"

Crouched at the bottom of the panel to paint in some snow, Noah rested his elbows on his knees to consider. "Yeah, probably. I liked school okay—hell, I got a meal there, and a quiet place to sit sometimes. But—"

Finally, they were getting to the question she wanted to ask. "Then why burn up the senior class records?"

He looked up at her. "Good question."

"In other words, you didn't."

"No, I didn't."

"But you left town a day later."

Resuming his effort with the snow, Noah didn't say anything.

Abby came closer and put a hand on his shoulder. "Why did you run away?"

"I could see where the future would lie. I wasn't going to take the rap for something I didn't do."

"Even if it meant losing your diploma?"

"I got along without it. Construction workers, mechanics, carpenters, landscape hands...none of them need high school diplomas."

"You could have come home a long time ago. Before..."

"Before I got arrested for manslaughter?" He stretched to his full height. "Maybe."

As he straightened, her hand slid along his arm. Abby closed her fingers around the strong column of his wrist. "It's definitely a case of 'Better late than never.'"

For once, he didn't flinch as she gazed at him. A light began to dawn in his dark face, from a small glimmer in his eyes all the way to the smiling curve of his lips. His free hand came up between them, and he brushed his fingers over her cheek before slipping them underneath her hair to touch the nape of her neck. Their mouths were now just a whisper apart.

"Abby, I—"

The rumble of the garage door track above them provided the second's warning they needed. As the big panel swung up, Abby jumped to her side of the painting and Noah to his. When Dixon and Kate stepped into the garage, they found two people painting furiously and no sign of the battle that had been fought and almost…*almost*…won.

But Abby knew. And she would remember.

THURSDAY, ROB TOOK CALLS for the locksmith service and Noah stayed at the shop all day, reading manuals, talking with Trent and avoiding Mike Warren's verbal potshots. He avoided Abby, too, with a call to say that he couldn't meet her that night at Dixon's garage.

"You have a hot date?" A thread of strain ran through her light tone.

"I do." The silence vibrated like an anvil struck by a hammer. "With a really lusty security-system manual. Rob wants me to take a practice test tomorrow, getting ready to be a certified installer. Aren't you impressed? I'll be certified."

"Or certifiable." Her voice had relaxed. "I guess I'll give you to your work. I might drive over and work on the painting a little bit. If you get bored, come down."

Noah spent several painful hours Thursday night acutely aware of Abby just below him, alone, painting. He wanted to go to her. He wanted her to come to him. He wished electronic-surveillance systems had never been invented.

Friday, in addition to taking the practice test, he went with Rob on another installment job. The resistance wasn't as fierce as Marino's or as fearful as Mrs. O'Brien's, but the homeowner hovered over them every minute they were in the house. The wiring in the house was a convoluted mess—compliments of L. T. LaRue, whose company built the place—and darkness had long since arrived when they finally got the system put together.

"I want my dinner," Rob groaned. "And a long night's sleep."

"That's two of us." They parted in the parking lot of the locksmith shop. Noah got all the way home before acknowledging that he didn't want to make his own dinner from odds and ends in the refrigerator. He wanted a decent meal, the kind Abby would make. Seeing her in the crowd at the diner wouldn't cause too many problems. They'd had a close call the other night, and he considered it lucky Dixon and Kate had come in, preventing him from doing something Abby would regret. The same would be true at the diner—they'd just talk. And he'd get another chance to see her smile.

After spending an afternoon crawling around underneath the house, he had to get cleaned up before he could go anywhere. Then, as he drove down Boundary Street, he realized he should have thought to check in with his mother first. He planned to be at her house early tomorrow, to make as many repairs as he could get done. Still, it wouldn't hurt to stop by tonight.

Through the front window, he could see that the lights and TV were on in the living room, but she didn't answer his knock. His throat closed as he tried the doorknob and found it unlocked. Sweating, breathing fast, Noah pushed quickly into the house and strode into the living room.

He stopped short at the sight of his mother in her

chair, cocooned from chin to toe in a quilt he remembered from the old days, with her head turned to the side and her eyes closed. Over the TV noise, he could hear her gentle snores.

Asleep. That was all. He hadn't lost his chance.

The house felt cold, he realized as he relaxed. The thermostat was set at sixty degrees—no wonder she'd wrapped herself up in the quilt. A week ago, she'd had the heat on unbearably high, now she seemed set on freezing to death. Why?

Noah didn't wake her up to ask. Questions could wait until tomorrow. And his mother didn't stir while he was in the house. He locked the door as he left.

The bank clock he passed on the way down Boundary Street read nine-fifteen—Abby should have closed the diner by now, if not earlier. Chances were good that she'd be gone by the time he got there. Chances were good he'd be settling for odds and ends, after all. The thought of missing her depressed him, and the cold air chilling the sweat on his body made him feel sick. Maybe he'd go to bed without any dinner at all.

Across the highway from the school, he could see the diner lights still shining. Only one car sat along the outer edge of the front parking lot, with Abby's Volvo parked near the back door. There wouldn't be a crowd around to protect her, after all. He'd just have to behave himself.

Noah parked the Harley near the Volvo and got off to walk around to the front. Again he glanced at the car across the parking lot—a white Toyota. From here, he could see the child's seat in the back. And without the noise of the bike, he could hear the kid screaming.

A glance through the window to his left showed him Abby standing at the cash register. Beside her, a man wearing a ski mask and a padded vest held a gun in one hand and an open paper sack in the other.

The barrel of the gun was jammed into the vulnerable flesh just beneath Abby's jaw.

CHAPTER TEN

"HURRY UP." HE EMPHASIZED HIS point by pushing the gun farther into Abby's jaw, making her wince.

"I can't do anything like this." Talking hurt. But she hoped if she kept him here long enough, somebody would come along. Surely somebody would come.

"Get that cash in the bag."

"If you'd back off—"

The gun poked her again. "Do it."

Her hands shook so much, she didn't have to fake fumbling with the bills. This guy hadn't killed anybody so far. She prayed that she wouldn't be his first. She'd never been out of North Carolina....

The bell on the front door jingled and Noah stepped into the diner. Abby's sob of relief was choked off as the man beside her wrapped his arm around her neck and pulled her back against him. The paper bag bounced against her breast. The gun drilled harder than ever into her throat.

"Let her go," Noah said calmly. He didn't have any kind of weapon to enforce the order. He held a little boy in one arm. A sniffle broke the tense silence.

Her captor jerked her even closer. "Put the kid down. I'll kill her."

"Here's a better idea. You let her go, I put the kid down and you leave with the cash."

"Hell, you already called the cops." The guy dragged Abby backward, out from behind the counter. "Come on, Tyler. Get down and come to Daddy."

The little boy looked across the room but didn't make a move to get down.

"Tyler, get over here." He tried to moderate his voice. "Come on, Tyler. You come to me and we'll go get some ice cream."

"Tandy," the little boy said. "Tandy."

"Jeez…candy. Fine. We'll go get candy. Just come here."

"Uh, he's trying to tell you he already got his candy," Noah said. He held up the wrapper of a chocolate bar. "You should feed him before you pull these jobs. Now…" He took a couple of steps forward. "You send her here, and then you get the boy."

Indecision—desperation—thumped into Abby's back with each beat of the heart behind her. Mostly the guy just wanted money and a getaway. When would he realize he could shoot both Noah and her and have everything he wanted?

He withdrew the gun from her neck, and she knew he'd discovered his power. Extending his arm, he pointed the pistol at Noah. "I'll kill you and her. Put the kid down."

Noah stood motionless for a second. "Sure. Okay." He took another three steps, bringing him a table's width away from her. Bending low, keeping his eyes on the gun, he set the little boy's feet on the floor. The child began to cry and reached for Noah. "Wannaaaaa…"

"Abby, move!" At the instant of his shout, Noah grabbed the edge of the table between them and shoved. Abby jerked hard to the side and found herself suddenly free. As she fell, the table screeched by, skidding across the floor, then slammed into Tyler's dad with a thud. Gun and paper bag went flying. Noah put his head down and drove the table all the way to the wall. Pinned between the heavy tabletop and concrete block, the robber slumped over the table and was still.

And then Noah was on his knees beside her. "Are you okay?"

She nodded but couldn't make a sound.

"Are you sure?" He looked her up and down. "Wait—there's blood. What's wrong?"

A throbbing pain separated itself from the rest of her aches. "My foot," she whispered.

Noah turned to look. "Aw, man." The table leg must have raked over her foot. Her shoe was gone, her sock ripped, and a big gash opened over her instep. "I'm sorry, Abby. God, I'm sorry I hurt you."

Before she could reassure him, he was tackled from behind by an anxious toddler. "Tandy?"

With a laugh that sounded like a sob, Noah turned to pick up the little boy. "How about cookies? Do you like cookies?"

"Tookies" was the grinning reply.

"I've got to call the police," Noah told her. "Just sit there and don't move. I'll find him something to eat and then help you off the floor."

But while he was in the kitchen rummaging through

the pantry for cookies, Abby decided she could get herself to her feet—a concept that worked better in theory than in practice. She used a stool at the counter for leverage and actually stood up, only to find she couldn't put any weight on the hurt foot. As the pain escalated, she began to wonder if something was broken.

"Do you ever follow orders?" Noah stared at her from the kitchen door. Tyler perched happily on his hip, holding a box of vanilla wafers. Several were already smeared on the little boy's thin face.

"I follow orders all day long, day in and day out, for fifty weeks a year," Abby said, irritated. "There was no reason I couldn't stand up by myself."

"Oh, sure. So why don't you just walk over and sit down somewhere? The police will be here in a couple of minutes."

Her bravado faded. "Um, well, walking could be a problem."

"You think?" Noah set Tyler down on the seat of a nearby booth with the box of cookies. Then he came toward Abby. Without another word, he put an arm around her shoulders and another under her knees and swept her up against his chest. She was still gasping when he gently set her down across the table from Tyler.

"Scoot back against the wall so you can rest your legs on the seat." This time she did as she was told, and Noah nodded. "That's better."

He sat down next to Tyler and said. "I also called your dad. So all we have to do is wait." Holding out a wafer, he smiled. "Want a cookie?"

THE NEXT TWO HOURS were ones Abby would be happy to forget. The police arrived and wanted to arrest Noah, until she made them look at the man behind the table. Her dad's entrance created chaos all over again. He yelled. He stomped around in his uneven way. He insulted Noah, didn't so much as say thank you.

And every time he looked at Abby, he had tears in his eyes.

She answered the questions she was asked and tried to listen in as Noah answered questions, most of them hostile and suspicious. A social services representative took charge of Tyler, but couldn't leave without taking the vanilla wafer box along. That little boy knew what he wanted and how to get it.

An ambulance arrived, and Abby was actually relieved to let them take her to the hospital for X-rays, away from her dad and the mess of the dining room. But then, propped up on a gurney in an emergency-room cubicle, she found herself suddenly shaking, teeth chattering, freezing cold—though they'd covered her from chin to ankles with blankets—and on the verge of tears.

"What's this?"

Almost afraid to believe in that voice, she looked to see Noah standing at the foot of her bed.

"Noah," she whispered.

Whatever he read in her face was enough. The next thing she knew, he was sitting beside her on the bed, and his arms came between her and the pillow. He cradled her against his chest, rocking a little, making soothing noises and pressing kisses on the top of her head. Abby relaxed for the first time in what felt like forever. She didn't need to cry anymore.

"What have we here?"

Noah turned his head to look over his shoulder. A doctor dressed in green surgical clothes stood at the entrance to the cubicle, smiling. That probably meant *he* should let Abby go.

Easier said than done, but he did manage to lay her back against the pillow and stand up. She wouldn't let go of his hand.

"Hi, Ian," Abby whispered.

"I heard you had been brought in and thought I'd better come down and see what the fuss was." He looked at Noah and extended a hand. "I'm Ian Baker."

"Noah Blake."

"Ian's married to Cass," Abby explained. "You remember her from high school? Ian came from Atlanta to work and they were practically an instant couple. Cass's Sugar and Spice catering company will be making the food for the dance." She coughed after this long speech. Noah found a cup of water by the bed and offered her a drink.

"So what happened?" Ian came to the other side of the bed and smoothed Abby's bangs back from her forehead. "You look a little beat up."

Noah didn't miss the hint of suspicion edging the glance the doctor cast in his direction.

"That guy who's been robbing businesses came into the diner." Abby coughed again. "Noah turned the tables on him, literally. If he hadn't, I'd probably be dead."

Until that moment, Noah hadn't let himself think that far. Bile rose into his throat. He forced himself to swallow it down.

Ian looked at him with an entirely different expression. "Then we all owe you a debt of gratitude," he said. "We wouldn't know what to do without Abby to take care of us."

Abby waved the idea away. "Anyway, I'm just a little sore. The table caught my foot, which might or might not be broken. So here I am."

"And here I am," a nurse said, pushing a wheelchair to Ian's side of the bed. "You're going to X-ray."

The nurse and the doctor got Abby into the chair without fuss. "Can Noah come with me?" she asked. Her scarred voice twisted his heart.

"Sorry. Patients and staff only, except with children."

Abby looked back at him as they wheeled her away. "Stay."

Noah nodded. No way would he leave her here by herself.

After about twenty minutes, he heard the sound he should have expected all along. Somehow, as he'd followed the ambulance on the drive to the hospital, he'd completely forgotten about Charlie Brannon.

But the voice booming out in the waiting area was certainly Abby's dad. The sound came closer, and then the curtain on the cubicle was jerked aside.

"Where is she?" Charlie limped up to the bed. "Where's my girl?"

"They took her for X-rays. She'll be back anytime now."

"God, I hate hospitals." The older man looked as if he could spit thunderbolts. "Too much time spent in them." He saw the chair by the head of the bed and dropped heavily onto the seat. "My place is a wreck. I'm closed tomorrow. I'll be losing thousands."

Noah didn't have an answer.

"I guess I owe you," the gruff voice went on. "You were there to take care of my girl. There's nothing in my life that matters more than Abby."

Noah got to his feet. "You don't owe me anything. I did what I could for her." *And for me.* "Since you're here now, I'll hit the road."

For a second, he thought Charlie would object. But then he simply nodded. "Good idea."

"Tell her…I'll be thinking about her. And to take it easy."

"Sure." From the lack of enthusiasm in the word, Noah doubted his message would get through to Abby.

Back on the bike again, he shivered in the cold night air. Somewhere a church bell rang midnight. Stars glittered in the black sky like…well, like the glitter Abby loved, used sparsely on velvet.

Abby's injury might be enough to keep her from finishing the panel with him. And that might not be such a bad thing. Each time he saw her turned out to be more of a disaster. He touched, he kissed—he couldn't seem to stop and Abby showed no inclination to exert control. Taking their relationship any further in this direction would be downright wrong.

For once in his life, though, Noah really wanted to do the right thing.

NO BROKEN BONES, just a deep cut, now stitched. Scrapes and scratches. A badly bruised throat.

And a sense of abandonment, to find Noah gone. She loved her dad. But she wanted Noah. To leave without a word...

Abby tried not to pout on the way home, tried to respond to her dad's real efforts to take care of her. She smiled at Elvis's feverish welcome, his willingness to curl up next to her good foot and leave the injured one alone. Choking down a grilled cheese sandwich, she listened to Charlie vent about the nerve of a guy who thought he could rip off the Carolina Diner.

"I wish I'd been there," he declared. "I would've showed him what happens to people who steal from me and threaten my little girl."

She shuddered, imagining that scenario. If the diner had to be robbed, she was glad it had happened this way. Noah had handled the situation with a cool head and quick thinking.

And then he'd run away.

So she'd let him run a little, like a fish on the line. He wouldn't get far, wouldn't escape for long. A man didn't comfort a woman like Noah had comforted her unless there were real, strong feelings involved. Abby was sure of her own feelings. And she thought she understood Noah's.

All she had to do was reveal them to the man himself.

The Diary of Abby Brannon

March 15, 1987

Dear Diary,

Today is the best day of my life. I don't believe I'll ever be happier.

Noah kissed me.

It was totally unexpected. I hadn't seen him since homeroom that morning. I stayed after school for an Honor Society meeting, then went to my locker before I walked to the diner.

I heard footsteps coming down the hall, which scared me a little, because everybody else had left. But when I peeked around my locker door, I saw Noah and relaxed.

I even got up the courage to say hello first. "What are you doing here?" I called while he was still halfway down the hall.

"Detention," he said. "What else?"

He came closer, walked behind me, and I thought he would just go on. But then he leaned his shoulder against the locker beside mine. I was caught, kinda, between my locker door and him. I didn't even consider trying to get away.

"What did you do?" I wasn't even nervous anymore. It was like somebody else—somebody experienced and sophisticated and pretty—had taken over my body.

Noah shrugged. "According to Floyd, I'm the source of all evil. If something goes wrong, he pins it on me and gives me detention. In this case, I believe there's some graffiti on the parking lot he associates with me."

"I saw that. Did you do it?"

"Let's just say I didn't stop the people who did."

"What's the point of graffiti?"

"What's the point of anything? Why do you work so hard for good grades when you know you're going to be waiting tables across the street for the rest of your life?"

I stared up at him, then had to look away because I thought I was going to cry.

"Abby, I'm sorry." His voice was gentle. He put a hand on my shoulder. "I didn't mean to hurt your feelings."

"No," I said. "It's okay. I know that's the truth...but I keep hoping something will change." I looked up at him again. "You know?"

He looked at me for a while without saying anything. "I know," he said at last. "I do know."

And then he kissed me.

I can't describe it. Like velvet and fire all at the same time. My heart pounded and I couldn't breathe. He moved his mouth against mine, which surprised me, but, oh, it felt so wonderful. No gross stuff with his tongue or anything. Just the sweetest, nicest, most exciting minute I've ever known.

Then he straightened up. "You make me think of sunshine and wildflowers," he said. "Stay just the way you are."

Before I could say a word, he turned and walked away.

If I died tonight in an earthquake, I know I would die content.

M arian woke up S aturday morning from a dream that included the sound of a hammer. When she tried to straighten up, the crick in her neck from sleeping in the chair sent her falling back with a groan.

Why get up, anyway? The quilt had kept her toasty warm all night, the TV was showing a morning cooking show, and she wasn't hungry. She had nowhere to be, nothing to do, nobody to care for. Or to care.

Then she heard the hammer again, only this time it was no dream. At seven-thirty on a Saturday morning, some idiot neighbor of hers had decided to start pounding nails, showing no consideration for folks who might still be asleep.

Gathering the quilt around her, she stomped to the front door, turned the lock and stormed out onto the porch. "Hey, jerk—"

The sound, she realized at that moment, wasn't across the street, or even next door. Noah—her son, Noah—sat on a ladder just outside her front porch, nailing the crooked shutter into place.

She couldn't believe her eyes. "What the hell are you doing?"

He looked over and grinned. "'Morning, Ma. I'm nailing this shutter back."

She hadn't thought he would show up and didn't know what to say. A strange truck sat out by the curb, the back piled with rolls of wire and screening and who knew what else. "Whose truck is that?"

"Dixon Bell traded with me for the day, so I could haul supplies." He tapped a few more times at the top corners of the shutter, then climbed off the ladder. "He's coming by later this morning to help me put new wire on the fence." Setting a nail in place at the bottom of the shutter, Noah drove it home.

"I guess you expect breakfast," she said. She wasn't sure she had anything in the house besides bran cereal.

"No, thanks. I ate before I left my place."

"Your rich friends are really taking care of you."

He stepped back from the shutter and turned to face her. "They are helping me out, the rich ones and the not-so-rich ones. I've got a job with Rob Warren, working on security systems. I'm trying to make this work, Ma."

Marian grunted and went back into the house, slamming the door behind her. She changed out of the clothes she'd slept in and made coffee, all the while hearing the sounds of work going on outside the house. He'd been a stubborn little boy, too. If he wanted something—like that motorcycle he'd reconstructed from a bushel basket of parts when he was fourteen—he worked until he got it. A year of late nights had gone into rebuilding that bike, fixing what he could, finding the money to buy a new part when he had to.

She'd known back then that he didn't always acquire the cash by legal means. He probably stole some of those parts he needed. As long as he didn't get caught, she looked the other way. Those years right after Jonah left had been her real bad spell. By the time she'd pulled herself back together, Noah was a lost cause.

And now he was a murderer.

Would he be different if she'd…what? What else could she have done? She'd worked her job at the tool plant to support the two of them as best she could. She hadn't run around like other women, had had no boy-friends coming in and out.

Well, except for Chet—Sheriff Chester Hayes—who'd insisted on keeping their relationship a secret even from their sons. Noah realized, of course—some-how he always knew what was going on. And when Chet discovered Noah had found them out, he'd dropped her like a dead bug. Shortly afterward came the fire. And Noah vanished.

Carrying a second cup of coffee, Marian went to the living room window. Noah was taking the bent and rusted wire down from the fence frame. She could tell he was being extra careful not to step on the plants in her garden. They'd worked out there in the afternoons, the two of them, happy enough until Jonah came home and chased them into the house. Jonah, Chet, Noah…deserters, all of them.

What had she done to deserve that?

Beside her, the TV weatherman announced the cur-rent temperature—thirty-five degrees. She could take out some coffee, warm Noah up a little.

Had she asked him to get out there? Had she wanted him to fix up the house? He thought he could come in without even a word of notice and straighten out her life…after messing up his own so bad?

Marian sat down in the same chair she'd slept in, picked up the remote and found herself a movie.

As far as she was concerned, her son was still gone.

ABBY STAYED HOME on Saturday, curled up on the couch with Elvis on the floor at her feet. They'd been lucky, she and Charlie—no major illnesses had kept them from opening the diner three-hundred-fifty mornings a year, more or less. They'd shut down for a week when her mom died. And the occasional hurricane or ice storm cut off the electricity for several days at a time, making cooking impossible. Otherwise, three meals a day were always available.

But today, the Carolina Diner was officially closed for business. Where would Dixon and the guys eat breakfast after the basketball game? Would they settle for fast-food biscuits at the local burger place?

Would Noah be playing with them?

When the telephone rang, she thought it might be him. Wrong.

"Hey, Abby, it's Samantha."

Abby stifled a sigh. "How are you and baby Crawford doing?"

"Great, just great. I heard you had some trouble last night. I wish I'd been called to the scene. I would have liked to be in on the first article."

"I'll put you at the top of my 'names to be called in case of a crime' list."

Sam laughed. "Sounds good. You know reporters are ghouls at heart. Listen, I've been a little out of the loop on Noah Blake. Tommy hasn't mentioned him all that much. But the article states that he's on parole from the Georgia prison system after a manslaughter conviction."

"That's right."

"And he's working for Rob Warren's security business."

"Yes."

"Well, I may be wrong, but my reporter's instincts have gone on full alert. There's something about the whole situation that strikes my funny bone. Only instead of getting that weird pain, I'm getting the urge to snoop around."

"I don't think Noah would be interested in being snooped around."

"Is anybody? But since he's a public figure now, coming in to rescue you with a little kid on his hip, he's fair game. I want to do a follow-up on what's going on in his life."

Warning bells sounded in Abby's head. "Sam, that's really not fair. Leave Noah alone."

As if she hadn't heard, the reporter said, "I was hoping you'd give me some help."

"No, I can't."

"From what I gather, you've seen Noah Blake more than just about anybody in town. You probably know him best. I know for a fact there are people with really negative reactions to Noah," Samantha went on when Abby didn't answer. "I thought the article needed some balance, and you seemed like a good person to present his positive side."

Abby had no doubt she was the best person to speak in Noah's favor. She was the woman in love with him. So it was her responsibility to say, "He'd hate being in the paper."

"If I turn up information that would make things

worse for him in any way, I'll ditch the whole concept. I promise."

Veto power. That seemed safe enough. "What do you want to know?"

NOAH WORKED LIKE A DEMON all Saturday morning and afternoon, including the three hours Dixon joined him in stringing up the new chain-link fence and gate. By dark, the house looked less like a tenement and more like the home of a woman somebody cared about.

With his tools and supplies loaded into Dixon's truck, Noah stepped onto the porch and knocked on the new screen door he'd installed barely an hour ago.

His mother answered after a couple of minutes. "Well?"

"I wanted to let you know I'm finished for the day."

She looked beyond him at the fence, glanced at the shutter he'd hung straight and the porch rails he'd fixed. "Okay." The door closed almost all the way. As he started to turn, though, it opened again.

"Thanks," his mother said.

Noah turned back. "Sure." He gave her a smile, then left the porch as fast as he could without running. He wasn't trying to create a debt.

He was just trying to pay the ones he owed.

When he drove by the Carolina Diner, he found it closed. Dread gripped him for a second, until he forced himself to remember his encounter with Charlie at the hospital last night. Later, he'd talked to Ian Baker, too, who agreed to share the general news about Abby's injuries. No broken bones, he'd reported, just scrapes, bruises and the one deep cut. She would be fine in a couple of days, completely healed in two to three weeks.

The Brannons had taken time off just to recover. He hoped they'd take off the whole next week. Both of them needed some serious rest.

At home, once he'd showered and put on a clean T-shirt and flannel pajama bottoms, Noah fell asleep on the couch. He woke up slowly, aware that something had changed in the apartment. With his eyes still closed, he investigated the difference. Surely the smell of bacon and hot bread was imaginary.

"Wake up, sleepyhead. It's breakfast time."

Abby? He opened his eyes just as she sat down on the couch beside his hip.

"I brought you orange juice as a temptation," she said. "Fresh squeezed, I might add, by my own little hands."

Noah propped himself on an elbow and took the glass. "Then I wouldn't dare refuse."

"Smart man." She took the glass back when he had drained it. "I've got eggs and bacon, toast, grits and more juice. Come and eat."

When she started to rise, he put a hand on her knee. "Abby, what are you doing here?"

"Fixing you breakfast, for starters. I thought we might work on the panel later."

"Your dad let you walk out—" he glanced down at her bandaged foot in an untied sneaker "—limp out to come here?"

Her cheeks flushed. "Well, actually, he's gone to church. I…played sick."

He sat up all the way, scrubbing his hands over his

face. "Terrific. He'll be here with a shotgun a few minutes after noon."

She put a hand on his arm. "No, no, he won't. He decided to take advantage of the unscheduled day off. He's driving up to Raleigh to have lunch with a couple of his buddies from the marines. They'll drink beer, go back to somebody's place and fall asleep watching a football game. It's his traditional vacation routine. I don't expect him home until nine o'clock, if then."

Twelve hours? Twelve unchaperoned hours?

Noah dropped his hands to stare at the woman right in front of him, only inches away. For the first time since he'd come back, she wore her hair loose—soft curls framing her face, covering her shoulders almost to her elbows. In place of the usual white shirt and khaki slacks were a pale gold sweater and a long, dark green skirt.

A soft whistle escaped him. "You look different."

"So do you." She pinched up a fold of his red-and-green-plaid flannel pajama bottoms. "Not what one pictures the BBD wearing to bed."

"BBD?"

"Bad-boy drifter."

"You're saying I'm—"

She nodded. "A BBD. Definitely."

Genuinely curious, he asked, "How did I qualify?"

"Leather jacket, biker boots and the Harley, not to mention leaving home and staying gone for fifteen years."

He digested her assessment. "So, what do BBDs wear to bed?"

Her gaze wavered, but then she shrugged. "Nothing."

After a second, he said, "Does that mean you've given extensive thought to the subject?"

Again, she blushed. "Um…"

"And just in general or…" He smiled, still teasing. "Did you get specific?"

He'd intended to turn the subject with a joke. But Abby opened her gold-green eyes wide. Then she put her palm squarely in the middle of his chest.

"I," she said, touching the tip of her tongue to her top lip, then the bottom one, "have a *very* active—and specific—imagination."

CHAPTER ELEVEN

ABBY COULDN'T BELIEVE she was doing this. But she had no intention of stopping.

"So, the answer is yes. I've thought about what a bad-boy drifter wears to bed. What *this*—" she tapped his chest with her finger "—bad-boy drifter wears to bed."

Noah's eyes had darkened. "Now you know." His voice rumbled against her palm, resting over his breast-bone.

She moved her hand in a small circle. "Did I mention I'm a very curious kind of person?"

He settled back against the arm of the couch, which took him farther away. But then he cupped his hands over her shoulders. "Nice sweater. Feels good." His palms stroked down her arms and up again.

"Nobody in town would believe it, but I do actually own something besides work clothes."

"They all take you for granted."

"I like being needed." Bringing her other hand to his chest for balance, she leaned forward. Her hair fell over Noah's arms.

He took a quick breath. "Your hair is…"

"Mmm?"

"Unbelievable. Like melted copper, but soft." He lifted her curls with the back of his wrist. "Sexy as hell."

"I like the sound of that. What shall we do about it?"

His smile disappeared. "You already said it. 'Nothing.'" He let his hands drop from her shoulders, out from underneath her hair.

"How can I change your mind?"

"You can't. I've told you before—this is a bad idea. You'll be glad I had the good sense to stop before we made a big mistake." He slid down the couch and shifted to put his feet on the floor.

Abby turned to face him. "I'm sorry, Noah. But I'm not playing by the rules anymore." She slipped the bottom button on her sweater free of its hole. "I'm not going to take no for an answer."

His gaze dropped to her fingers, working the next button, and came back to her face. "What are you doing?"

"Making you an offer you can't refuse." Or so she hoped. She didn't really think she could force Noah into making love. But she could force him to break her heart.

"Abby—" He put out a hand to stop her. Quick as lightning, she placed his palm on her bare skin, underneath the sweater. His breath hissed between his teeth. His fingers trembled. "Please don't."

Second-to-last button. "Please don't love you? Too late. I've loved you for most of my life. Please don't want you? How can I stop? Even when I thought you would never come back, when I thought you might be dead, I wanted you. Now that you're here—all I can think about is being with you. Like this."

Noah watched in disbelief as Abby undid the last button on her sweater. The two halves immediately drew apart, even before she slipped the sweater backward, off her shoulders, over her elbows, her wrists.

"Dear God," he whispered, and it was a prayer. Her creamy white skin, smooth and slightly flushed, was partly cloaked by those rich, reddish curls. A lacy pink bra confined the most beautiful breasts he'd ever seen. He looked into Abby's face. "You're incredible."

"I'm yours. Please, Noah." She stared down at his hand. A single warm teardrop fell on his knuckle. "Don't make me beg."

"I'm the one who should beg," he muttered. Then he pulled her into his arms.

In seconds, it seemed, they lay against each other skin to skin, his hands roaming freely across the sweet roundness of her hips, the bounty of her breasts. Abby's palm dragged over his back, his bony shoulders, the sharp arches of his ribs.

"You need to gain some weight," she whispered. "I should feed you more."

At that moment, Noah took the peak of her breast into his mouth.

Words stopped. Thought ended. They entered a refuge in which they touched each other in every possible way, simply seeking *more*.

At the last possible moment, Noah reared back on his knees. "Wait, wait." He held her wandering hands tight in his own. "I don't have anything for—for... We can't—"

Her smile made him think of Eve in the Garden. "I do." She felt around on the floor beside the sofa for her skirt and drew a box of condoms from the pocket. "I'm desperate, but I'm not dumb."

He didn't laugh. "I'm clean, Abby. They left me alone in prison. I got tested every three months. And I've always been careful."

"Shh." She pressed her fingers against his lips. "I trust you."

Noah squeezed his eyes shut. Nobody had ever said that before. He wanted to cry.

Instead, he slipped on protection and slipped into Abby's welcoming embrace. There was a moment of resistance, a bolt of surprise.

Then the tide swept over them, in roaring waves of sensation that tumbled their bodies like shells on the beach. Noah stiffened, felt Abby shudder beneath him. With a sigh, he finally put his head down on her shoulder and allowed himself to drown.

"YOU SHOULD HAVE TOLD ME, you know."

Lying tucked between Noah's body and the back of the couch, with his arms around her and his face in her hair, Abby drew a breath of pure happiness. "Told you what?"

"That this was your first time."

She frowned. "I didn't want to be treated like a virgin."

"You deserved more consideration than you got."

"Do you hear me complaining?"

Noah's answer was a deep sigh.

Abby pulled away enough to see his face. "Are you sorry?"

He tightened his hold on her but didn't open his eyes. "I couldn't be sorry if I tried. I just don't see…"

She waited, but he didn't continue. "Where we're going?" she finished for him.

"Yeah."

"I can tell you that. In a few minutes, we'll get up and eat cold eggs and bacon and make new toast, drink warm orange juice."

Noah grinned. "Now, there's a tempting prospect."

"And then we're going to climb into your bed together and discover all the ways to enjoy a rainy Sunday morning."

"I have a suggestion." He rolled to his feet, giving her a moment to appreciate the lean, balanced beauty of his body before he bent and picked her up off the couch.

"What are you doing?" She laughed and blushed at the same time. "Noah, I'm too heavy to carry. Put me down."

Her protests were ignored as he went down the short hallway to the bedroom. As she clung with her arms around his shoulders, Noah pulled the covers back with one hand. Then he lowered her to the cool sheet. In another second, he was beside her.

"I suggest we skip the cold eggs and bacon part," he said softly, as he skimmed his mouth over her cheek, her eyelids, her mouth. "And go straight to the rainy Sunday morning in bed."

Abby smiled and sighed. "I always knew you were a very smart man."

THEY WOKE AGAIN ABOUT two o'clock, cooked new eggs and toast, warmed the bacon and grits, and poured the orange juice over ice while they talked about nothing that really mattered. Noah tried to focus, to concentrate hard so that he could keep the memories of Abby and this morning strong.

Because, of course, it couldn't last. Rainy Sunday mornings gave way to partly cloudy afternoons. Dixon and Kate came out to the garage about four o'clock, arriving at exactly the same time Noah and Abby wandered downstairs to start painting.

The four of them stared at one another for a few seconds, trying to think of what to say. Noah knew Abby was blushing, knew she looked like a woman who had spent the morning with her lover.

"We thought we'd see how far you'd gone," Kate said. Dixon choked and she stared at him, eyes wide. "I mean—"

"I came to make Noah breakfast," Abby explained, "and time just slipped away."

"It happens," Dixon said, controlling his grin. "We also wanted to know how you were after Friday night."

"A cut on my foot is the worst of the damage."

Kate nodded. "I hate that you had to go through such an ordeal. And we're so glad you were there, Noah. We can't thank you enough for taking care of Abby."

Another awkward silence fell. Dixon put his arm around his wife. "Kate, honey, I think we ought to go back to the house before you step in it with both feet instead of just one."

Red-faced, Kate agreed and said goodbye. When they were alone again, Abby laughed. "We'll only have to go through that about, oh, a hundred more times before everybody in town has figured it out."

Noah flipped the bristles of a paintbrush against his hand. "Figured what out?"

"Us."

"I think it would be better if there wasn't any 'us.'"

"What does that mean?"

"I don't think anybody else should know about this. And I'll ask Dixon and Kate to keep it quiet."

"You're ashamed to be with me?"

"I'm ashamed for you to be with me." Before she could ask the question, he answered. "I'm a felon. An ex-con. A killer. And that's only the most recent of my crimes. I didn't live a clean, tidy life before I killed a man. I made trouble here, and I didn't stop just because I left. Women, alcohol, gambling—"

"Drugs?"

He gave a bitter laugh. "Illegal drugs are about the only sin I haven't committed. Oh, and adultery. I never slept with another man's wife."

She started toward him, but he held up a hand. "I can't—wouldn't—give up what we shared today. But at the very least, we've got to go slow. Until I've made some kind of progress, I don't want you too involved with me. It just wouldn't be smart."

She was staring at her hands, twisted together at her waist. "Does that mean…you don't want to see me again?" Tears thickened her voice.

And he almost broke down, himself. "Of course I do. But:..not like this. Not so private, so…dangerous."

Abby lifted her chin. "You know, yesterday, I would have assumed that you just didn't want me anymore, that I wasn't good enough to satisfy you."

"That's bull—"

"Exactly. Because I know what happened between us this morning. I know how strong it is, how right, how…how eternal. But you, apparently, missed the point. So I'll just wait around until you get the message. If hell freezes over first, I guess that'll just be too bad for both of us." She turned and marched to the garage door. "And you can finish the damn panel all by yourself—since *alone* is what you think you do best."

She stomped up the steps to the apartment and stomped down again. The Volvo engine coughed, sputtered and caught. Noah reflected that he really ought to give that car a tune-up. Engines, he understood.

Relationships?

Forget it.

BY THE TIME CHARLIE GOT home Sunday night, Abby was pretty much back to normal. She'd showered, washing away the scent of Noah she imagined clung to her skin, and changed into regular clothes, putting her hair in its usual ponytail. She ate too much for dinner from a noodle casserole she'd frozen back in September, and made matters worse with ice cream for dessert. Who said she couldn't solve her problems with food?

Charlie was full of jokes and stories from his buddies, but the drive had tired him out, so he went to bed soon enough. Abby stared at the TV for an hour or so, barely comprehending the program, and finally went to her own room. She'd been up early this morning. Surely she could fall asleep fast. If not, those painkillers the doctor had given her might help.

On the point of turning out the light, though, she picked up the phone instead, and dialed Marian Blake's number.

"You're calling awful late."

"Yes, ma'am, but I thought I'd let you know about Noah."

"He was here yesterday. Spent hours working on the house. Even put up a new fence."

"I'm happy he had a chance to do that. I know he wants to make things easier for you."

"He'd have done better to just stay away."

"I think he needed to come home."

Marian didn't say anything for a long time. "So what did you want to tell me?"

"I wasn't sure if you had a chance to talk with Noah. But he's got a good job with Rob Warren and he's working terribly hard to put his life together. I think if people in this town will just give him a chance, he'll succeed."

"I hear he got you out of trouble Friday night."

"Yes, he did. I might have died if Noah hadn't shown up when he did."

The idea of losing Abby was not something Marian wanted to consider. If she'd had a daughter, she would have wanted someone like this girl, with spirit and strength. She'd been pregnant with a little girl once, but Jonah knocked her down one too many times.

"So I guess he's sticking around for a while."

"I hope so." Behind the girl's words was a feeling Marian recognized. Did Jonah's son deserve that kind of love? Jonah certainly had not.

"You be careful, missy. He'll break your heart—and that'll be all, if you're lucky. His dad was a bully and a drunk." She hung up before Abby could protest.

Marian hated to see Abby wreck herself on Noah. He'd left just like his dad, hadn't he? He'd been a gentle boy but grown up violent, like Jonah. Maybe Abby would be smarter than Marian, though. Maybe she'd avoid getting knocked up, so she wouldn't have to tie herself to a man she already feared.

And maybe Santa Claus would show up on Christmas Eve.

IF GREAT SEX GUARANTEED a good night's sleep, Sunday night proved the rule as far as Noah was concerned. But he was up and dressed by 6:00 a.m. on Monday morning. The diner would be open as usual, and he needed as few witnesses as possible for what he was about to do.

The parking lot was empty and the inside lights on when he arrived in the dark before dawn. He pushed the door gently, hoping to keep the bell quiet, but he couldn't repress a small jingle. Well, that would bring somebody to see him, anyway.

Charlie came out of the kitchen but stopped behind the counter when he saw Noah. "What do you want?"

"Is Abby here?"

"No. She's staying home this morning. So move on."

"I will." Noah walked up to the counter. "But I wanted to give you something first." He pulled his hand out of his jacket pocket and put a roll of bills on the counter beside the cash register. "One hundred dollars," he said. "I owe you."

Charlie came close enough to pick up the bills. "I don't get it."

"You know I stole it, fifteen years ago." The older man nodded. "So, I'm giving it back."

"Why?"

"Why'd I steal it?" Charlie nodded. "I wanted new mirrors for my bike. Extended arms, chrome finish, really cool. I'd seen them on another guy's bike and I was jealous. You left me alone with the cash that morning. The temptation was more than I could resist."

"So why pay it back now?"

"I want to be square. I want to pay my debts. Then, when I walk away, I'll be free. Really and truly free."

Charlie put the cash in the register. "Sit down. I'll pour you a cup of coffee. On the house."

He poured himself one as well, and they sipped in silence for a minute or two.

Finally, Charlie set his mug down. "I knew your dad."

Noah shrugged. "My condolences. Or apologies, whichever works."

"You look like him."

"Which explains a lot about my mother."

Charlie raised a critical eyebrow. "As a matter of fact, it does."

Noah felt his cheeks heat up.

"You're tall like him, but not as beefy. He played football, you know."

"So I heard." And he wasn't sure he needed to know anything else. "Thanks for the—"

"You're not going anywhere." Charlie refilled Noah's mug. "Jonah Blake was a big deal, his senior year. I was a few years ahead of him, but I remember. Scouts from colleges all over the country came to watch him play, and even from the pros. The only way he'd be able to go to school was on a football scholarship, and he had several lined up. All he had to do was choose."

"But there was a baby."

"Yeah. Your mother refused to get an abortion, as much as Jonah pressured her. So they got married—that's the way things were done back then. The scholarships dried up. The scouts disappeared. No college for Jonah—just a dead-end job at the tool plant. He didn't handle the disappointment very well."

"No, he didn't." The little kid who only wanted to follow his dad around had usually been kicked away like a bothersome puppy. "I was glad when he didn't come home again."

"The whole town was. He'd managed to get on just about everybody's bad side."

Noah looked up from his coffee and tried out a grin. "Like father, like son."

"Not exactly." He left to seat a couple of customers, brought them coffee and water, then took their orders to Billie in the kitchen. "You came back, first of all. And I'm beginning to believe your intentions are good."

Would he feel that way if he knew Noah had spent yesterday in bed with his daughter? "Thanks."

"You're starting over, something your dad never even tried. Hard work was a foreign idea for Jonah—

he wanted to play ball, make big money and live high on the hog."

After refilling his own coffee cup, Charlie settled behind the counter again. "The main thing is, you're taking responsibility for your life. You paid your debt for what happened in Atlanta. You're accepting the penalties and working through them. That's a man's job, to be the master of his own life, whatever he does with it. Jonah never understood, not while he was here, anyway." Charlie extended his right hand. "I'm glad to see his son's got guts."

Noah couldn't refuse to shake that hand. He looked Abby's dad straight in the eye with as much confidence as he could muster. And he left the diner as soon as Charlie turned his back.

At least he'd made amends to the man he'd wronged. And in return Charlie had given him food for thought. His dad had pretty much been a jerk all along, even before the baby—Noah—put an end to his dreams. So maybe Jonah Blake would have been the same kind of dad, even if everything had gone his way. Maybe he would have victimized any woman he married. Maybe there was nothing Noah could have done, as a child or an adult, to earn his father's love.

Riding toward the locksmith shop, Noah laughed aloud. He'd made plenty of his own mistakes, in this town and others. But he didn't have to keep paying for something he hadn't done. His dad—and, to be honest, his mother—had tried to blame him for a situation he hadn't created and couldn't change, no matter how hard he tried. He felt as if he'd had a fifty-pound weight taken off each shoulder, and another off his chest.

He thought of Abby, and what he'd said to her yesterday. Could he—should he—take it back? She'd said she would wait until he understood the truth of their relationship, even if hell froze over.

Noah really didn't want to wait that long to make love to her again.

For the length of a red light he considered going to her house to tell her what a jackass he'd been. But the bank clock gave him only fifteen minutes to get to work. If he went to see Abby, he might never get there at all, which would not make a good impression on his new boss. So he kept the bike headed in the direction of downtown, promising himself some time with Abby tonight.

A police cruiser sat in the front parking lot of Warren and Sons. With the hair on the back of his neck standing straight up, Noah wheeled around to the back, parked the bike and walked into the work area, swinging his helmet from one hand.

Mike Warren, Rob and Trent stood together at the far end of the workroom, talking with a police officer who was all too recognizable, even from the back. As Noah reached the group, though, the cop turned around.

"It's about time," Wade Hayes told him. "A good employee gets to work ahead of time."

"I'll remember that." Noah looked at Rob. "What's going on?"

But Mike Warren answered. "Just what I said would happen. There's been a robbery."

"Here? At the shop?"

"Nope." Wade flipped the pages of his palm-size notebook. "At 390 Hampton Court. Sound familiar?"

Noah shook his head. "Never heard of it."

"That's funny." Wade grinned at him but didn't explain.

"So tell me the joke and I'll laugh, too."

"Three-ninety Hampton Court is John Clement's house," Rob said. "He spent Sunday with his mother in Aberdeen and came home that evening to find his whole house trashed."

"I still don't get it."

"He's on our client list." There was no easy grin on Rob's face this morning. "We were supposed to install his security system tomorrow."

"Convenient, ain't it?" Wade tried on an innocent look. "Man with no security system gets robbed just before he installs an alarm. A suspicious person—say, me—might begin to think the coincidence was too strong. That an employee with the security firm might very well have access to the addresses of people who wanted a security system but didn't yet have one."

He wrote something in the notebook. "So tell me, Mr. Noah Blake—just what were you doing Sunday afternoon about three o'clock?"

WADE HAYES STROLLED into the diner in the middle of Monday afternoon and slid into a booth. Charlie was taking a nap in the recliner in the office, so Abby limped over to ask the policeman what he would have.

"A slice of you would be a nice treat." He smacked his lips. "Yum, yum."

He'd be lucky if she didn't throw up on him. "Not on the menu, Wade. How about pecan pie and ice cream?"

"Okay, I'll settle for second best. With coffee."

When she brought the pie, he scooted farther to the inside of the booth. "Why don't you sit down and talk to me? Nobody else is here."

She did need to sit down. Her foot throbbed and her back ached. "Thanks." Instead of taking the seat next to him, she sat across the table. Wade frowned but kept shoveling in the pie.

"I saw a friend of yours this morning."

"Who would that be?"

"Noah Blake, mystery man."

Her heart froze in her chest. "What's the mystery?"

"Well, how about where's he been for the last fifteen years? With who? Why did he come back to North Carolina when parole in Georgia would have been so much easier and so much less embarrassing?"

"I couldn't tell you."

"Anyway, I had to run him down this morning. We had a question or two he needed to answer."

"Wade, stop stringing me along and tell me what you want me to know."

"John Clement got home last night to find that his house had been trashed and burglarized."

"What did that have to do with Noah?"

"Turns out Mr. Clement is due to have a security system installed. By Rob Warren."

"I don't see the connection." But she did, of course.

"I thought it was interesting that our man Noah should ride into town and within ten days we start having robberies at homes he might reasonably be expected to know were not secure."

"But—" Noah wasn't anywhere near Hampton Court. He'd been with her, in bed.

"Yep, it looked mighty suspicious. And Mr. Blake wasn't much in the mood for providing an alibi."

The idiot. "I think—"

Wade shook his head. "In the end, though, I had to let him go."

Her heart fluttered back to life. "Why?"

"He suggested I talk to Dixon Bell. And Dixon swears Blake's Harley sat in one place within sight of his living room windows the entire day. He even talked to Noah, along about four o'clock. He could be lying for his friend, of course. But I doubt I could get him to admit it, not without stronger evidence of Blake's presence in the house." Wade sighed. "The SOB was smart enough to wear gloves and shoe covers, so we don't have much to go on."

"That's too bad. I'm sure it would have made your week to arrest Noah." She slid from the booth and stood up without remembering to favor her hurt foot. Before she completely lost her balance, Wade had caught her, holding her with one arm around her waist and a hand under her arm, near her breast.

"Watch yourself." He didn't let go when she took her own weight back. "Would have been nice if Blake could have managed the rescue without hurting you in the process." His hand slipped a little more forward.

Abby pushed him away. "Or he could have driven on by and I'd be dead. I'll take a cut on the foot any day." She tore his check from her pad and put it on the table. "Thanks for stopping by. Have a nice day."

She got into the kitchen before giving into the

shakes. The idea of Noah in prison again, at the mercy of Wade Hayes's venom... She could scarcely keep from being sick. Maybe she should go back and give him Noah's real alibi. She was the only person who knew exactly where he'd been all day Sunday.

"What's wrong, Abby girl?" Charlie came out of the office, stretching and yawning. "Are you okay?"

"Good enough." She smiled, for his sake. "Just tired."

He nodded. "I'm tempted to close down for the night. To hell with the dinner crowd."

She stared at him, surprised. "I never heard you say anything like that before."

"I guess I'm getting old. I just...don't have the energy I used to." His hand landed on her shoulder, heavy, warm, comforting. "It's good to know I've got you, and that you'll be here, carrying on, even when I can't anymore. This place meant everything to your mother, and to me. At least I'll be able to pass our legacy on, knowing you care every bit as much as we did. That's a real blessing."

He went out to the front of the diner, and she heard him talking with Wade, ringing up the pie. The doorbell jingled as Wade left, and again almost immediately. Dinnertime.

But she sat for a moment more, head bowed, shoulders slumped. Her dad trusted her to take care of the Carolina Diner. He pictured her here, every day, for the rest of her life. She supposed her children should be here, too. If she ever had children.

When she closed her eyes, though, Abby didn't see

a long stretch of years behind the counter of the diner. She saw herself seated on the Harley with Noah in front of her, a strong wind in her face as they raced down a coastal highway, or crossed a desert in winter. She felt snowflakes on her face in the Rocky Mountains, sand beneath her feet in Mexico. And always there was Noah beside her, to share, to laugh, to love.

Opening her eyes, she saw the kitchen, smelled beef stew on the stove and roast beef in the oven, heard the chatter of customers and her dad's deep voice. This was her world, the life she lived. The world, the life, Noah had run away from fifteen years ago.

And as far as she could tell, he was running still.

CHAPTER TWELVE

TUESDAY'S BREAKFAST crowd kept Abby hopping—literally—until almost eleven o'clock. Three separate groups of senior citizens came in to celebrate birthdays. Each group required four or five tables shoved together and separate checks for every couple, plus sweet tea, unsweet tea, decaf and regular coffee, water with and without lemon, and food orders. Everybody smiled, everybody was nice when she forgot to bring the biscuits, when she had to be asked twice to refill coffees, when she had trouble hearing what they said over the noise in the rest of the room.

With the last of the seniors standing at the register to pay their checks, Abby loaded a tableful of dirty dishes onto her tray and started toward the kitchen. Just as she reached the counter, a little boy she didn't recognize came around her from behind and cut across her path, heading for the bathroom. Startled, she stepped sideways onto the hurt foot, which gave under her weight. The tray and its contents cascaded to the floor.

All conversation stopped, so everyone heard the swearword Abby said. Several of the old ladies at the register gasped.

"Sorry," Abby muttered. She got down on her hands and knees to clean up the mess. As she gathered up shards of plates and mugs, another pair of hands joined her, and then another.

Kate Bell used a napkin to collect the smaller pieces. "Are you all right? You didn't get cut, did you?"

Abby shook her head. "I can't believe this. I haven't dropped a tray, even an empty one, since I was ten years old."

"Luckily, they all cleaned their plates," Mary Rose Mitchell said. "There's not much food to pick up, except for a couple of pieces of toast."

Charlie came over with a pile of towels. "I'll take the tray back." He stood for a moment, staring at her. "What's got into you? I haven't known you to drop a tray since you were six or seven years old."

The Bowdrey sisters, their delicate eyebrows lifted in question, turned back to Abby when Charlie went into the kitchen.

"I didn't tell him about the time when I was ten," she explained with a small smile. "I didn't want to get yelled at."

With the floor swept and mopped, Mary Rose and Kate went back to their booth. The dining room had cleared out almost magically, so Abby had a chance to get her breath back. She brought her friends their usual drinks—black coffee for Kate and sweet tea for Mary Rose.

Kate pushed the coffee away. "I'm sorry, Abby. The smell of coffee really bothers me these days. Could I have some water? With lemon?"

"Sure." She brought the water and coffee for herself, then sat down next to Kate to enjoy a free second or two.

"Where's Joey?" she asked Mary Rose.

"My mother wanted to keep him for a few hours. She loves just sitting and rocking him. I never imagined she'd be such a baby person."

"Your dad, too, I bet."

Mary Rose nodded, laughing at the same time. "He's already bought wooden trains and a set of miniature golf clubs and he can't wait until Joey walks by himself. Given the way the kid is already climbing, I'd like to put off that challenge as long as possible."

Abby glanced at Kate, noticing her pale cheeks and lips. "Are you feeling okay?"

"A little sick to my stomach. It'll pass."

"There's a flu going around. Maybe you've caught it."

A meaningful look passed between the sisters. "It's not the flu," Mary Rose said. "It's a baby."

"You're going to have a baby?"

Kate nodded, but didn't smile.

"Dixon must be over the moon," Abby suggested carefully.

The other woman sighed. "I haven't told him."

"Because…"

She put her head in her hand. "I guess I'm just not ready to face it myself."

Abby looked to Mary Rose for an explanation. "We celebrated her law school admission last week, remember? But she didn't count on having a baby *and* going to school."

With everything else going on, Abby had completely forgotten the law school acceptance. What kind of thoughtless friend was she, anyway?

"I'm sorry you're unhappy." Abby reached over to cover Kate's fingers with her own. "You've been waiting a long time for the chance to get your law degree."

"I have." She drew a deep breath and straightened, like a drooping flower after being watered. "I love the thought of giving Dixon a child. It's just…"

"One thing at a time?"

"Right. And as if this weren't enough…"

"What else?"

"Kelsey's been admitted to Vanderbilt. She's thrilled, and she wants Sal to go with her to Nashville."

Abby groaned. "I was hoping maybe she'd let you talk her out of it."

Mary Rose gave an unladylike snort. "Not in this century."

They sat silent for another minute, until Abby said, "Well, have you eaten something today?"

Kate shook her head. "I can't face breakfast."

"Then you're definitely due for some food. You, too," she told Mary Rose as she slid out of the booth. "You're always too thin. I'll bring something light, not too greasy or spicy. And more water. Maybe some crackers."

When she returned with freshly made chicken salad garnished with white grapes, the dining room was filling up again. The lunch rush. Great.

After Mary Rose and Kate left, the hamburger crowd

poured in, and she answered questions about the robbery with every order she took. People meant well. It wasn't their fault she was feeling ornery and tired.

Wade Hayes came in around three o'clock, as he'd done too often lately. "I thought about your pecan pie, Miss Abby, and I just had to have a piece."

"Coffee? Ice cream?"

"You know me too well, darlin'."

She cringed and went to the kitchen. "I'm not going back out there," she told her dad in a low voice. "I can't take any more from him." Shoving the tray with the pie on top into his hands, she pushed him toward the dining room door.

Without protesting, Charlie took the tray to Wade's table. "Here you go," she heard him say.

"Where's that pretty daughter of yours? She always makes the food taste better."

"She's taking a break." His tone discouraged any protest or argument. "I see you got that motorcycle of yours out of the shop."

"Yeah, took them long enough, didn't it? All I asked for was a paint job like the original my dad bought back in '87. They waited three months to get the right color."

"It's a nice bike."

"I love driving it. I'll have to take Miss Abby out for a ride sometime."

"Have you always had those long-armed mirrors?" Abby couldn't help chuckling. Trust her dad to remember the vehicle of every kid who'd graduated from New Skye High in the last thirty years.

"Yep. First thing I changed on the bike was getting rid of the dinky ones and putting on extended-arm mirrors. The shop refinished all the chrome for me, too."

"Must've cost a lot."

Wade laughed. "I'm a single man. I can spend my money however I want to."

"Right. Want anything else?"

"To say goodbye to Miss Abby."

"She's busy," Charlie said, and limped back to the kitchen.

"Thanks," Abby said, but her dad walked past her without even a nod. "Dad? Hey, Dad."

He jumped, then looked at her as if he hadn't known she was there. "Is something wrong?"

"I said thanks for helping me dodge Wade."

Charlie nodded. "Sure thing. Anytime." He went inside the office and shut the door.

In the next second he opened the door and came out again. "Did I tell you Noah Blake paid me back the money?"

She nearly dropped the bowl of potatoes she'd just peeled. "The hundred dollars?"

"That's right. Walked in here first thing Monday morning and handed over the cash. I couldn't believe my eyes."

Abby wanted to smile and cry at the same time. "So what do you think of him now?"

Her dad stared at her for a minute. "He might just make it. But…"

When he didn't go on, she prompted, "But?"

"But I wish he'd chosen somewhere else to try."

AROUND MIDNIGHT ON Tuesday, Noah finished the Christmas scene. While the white paint was still wet, he laid the panel flat on the floor of the garage and sprinkled clear glitter on the piles of snow painted in the corners of doorways, under the trees and on the street. He hoped Abby would approve.

And he hoped she wasn't suffering the way he was, trying to stay away from her, to keep her safe…from himself.

Wednesday morning, Rob sent him out to do a simple installation on his own. The neighborhood was nice, without being rich, and the house was all on one level. Piece of cake.

He rang the doorbell and waited. The appointment had been set up for nine o'clock, and he was right on time. After five minutes, he rang again.

The door creaked open, and a woman peered out at him over the chain lock. "What is it?"

"I'm Noah Blake, Mrs. Schultz." He extended his card, which she snatched between her clawlike fingernails. "I'm here from Warren Security Monitoring to install an alarm system."

"You're him."

"I beg your pardon?" He knew what was coming. Should've expected it.

"You're that murderer."

"I—"

"Go away!" She screeched like a parrot. "Go away, before I call the cops! Go away, go away." The door slammed in his face. From the other side came the sound of furniture sliding across a bare floor. "Go away," she yelled again.

Noah drove back to the locksmith shop and parked the van in its space near the door. He found his boss at his workbench, checking out the circuits in a faulty signal box.

Rob glanced up as Noah approached. "That was fast." And then, as he looked closer, he asked, "What happened?"

"You can guess." Noah put the van keys down on the bench. "I'm quitting. I won't do this to your business. I appreciate everything you tried to do. Some plans just don't work, and this is one of them." He turned around to leave. "I brought all the manuals in this morning. They're on the office shelf."

"Noah." Rob caught up with him before he reached the door. "Wait a minute. Let's regroup. So maybe the public isn't ready to accept you in their homes. If you stay, we'll—"

"You'll what? Conjure up a job so I can get paid for doing basically nothing? Thanks, Rob. You are one of the real good guys. But your business can't afford that kind of charity. And I can't take it."

"Let him go," Mike Warren advised as he came up to them. "We don't need any more liabilities in this company. If we're going to survive with the economy the way it is, we ought to be cutting costs. Not making up jobs."

Hands on his hips, Rob faced his father. "Warren Security Monitoring is not 'our' company. It's mine. And I'll hire whoever I damn well please to work for me. Shut up, Dad. And butt out."

"Now, you listen here—"

The two men, father and son, continued to argue as Noah walked out to his bike. Yet another place he'd managed to create conflict.

You can't go home again. Noah wasn't sure where the quote came from. Thomas Wolfe? That sounded right.

The man sure as hell knew what he was talking about.

THE NEWS THAT NOAH HAD quit his job came to Abby through a phone call from Valerie Warren. Abby checked with Kate, who said she hadn't seen the Harley parked out by the garage since early morning. A call to Mrs. Blake produced a fifteen-minute indictment of just about everybody in town, but no real news.

Noah had vanished. For good?

By only the fiercest of struggles did Abby resist the temptation to drive to his apartment and wait there until he returned home. She'd chased him and pursued him and seduced him. The next step had to be his.

Every minute of Wednesday night seemed to last an hour. The hours were days. She'd never been so glad to hear her alarm at five-thirty, so she could get up, get moving and stop thinking.

She left the house before her dad, and arrived at the diner in the cold dark of night. But the streetlights showed her a vehicle already parked next to the front door. Noah's Harley.

He came around the corner of the building as she got out of her car. "It's me, Abby. Don't be afraid."

"I'm not sure those two statements don't contradict

each other." Keys in hand, she marched to the back entrance and unlocked the door. She palmed the switches on the wall, and the fluorescent lights in the kitchen flickered to life, harsh and painful to her eyes. Noah followed her inside and closed the door behind him.

He caught her arm as she started out into the dining room and turned her to face him. "Wait a minute."

Abby couldn't meet his gaze with her own. "What? What's there to say?"

"I love you."

Her heart stopped, then pounded in her throat like a freight-train engine. "Good try. Too late."

"And I want you to come with me."

Finally, she looked up at him. "Come where?"

"Atlanta, first. I have to go back to meet the parole requirements. But after that, we're free. We can go anywhere in the world. Just the two of us."

She could practically feel the wind in her face. A knock on the back door announced Billie's arrival. Abby pretended not to hear. "Say the first part again."

His mouth lifted into the smile she adored. "I love you."

"Hey, there," Billie yelled through the door. "Let me in." She pounded on the heavy panel.

"Go sit out front." Abby pushed Noah toward the dining room door. "I'll be there in a minute."

Once he'd left the kitchen, she let Billie in. "Took you long enough," the cook grumbled. "What do you think you're doing, making me stand out in the cold that way? My arthritis is acting up bad enough as it is."

"I'm sorry, Billie. I—"

"I saw that devil machine out front. I know exactly what you were doing." Her face set in lines of anger, Billie walked straight past Abby and pulled out the bowl she used for making biscuits. "I'm about ready to get me another job. Too much work here, no consideration…" She continued to mumble as she sifted flour into the bowl.

Whipped by guilt, Abby went to join Noah in the dining room. He hadn't turned on any lights, but the glow of the street lamps in the parking lot shone through the windows, creating a black-and-white image of the room. Noah sat in a booth, hands folded on the table as he waited.

She sat down across from him. "What's going on?"

He stared at her for a few seconds, his face unreadable. "You probably know I quit my job." When she nodded, he continued. "I don't want to destroy Rob's business. And my mother doesn't want me in her life."

"Noah—"

"No, it's okay. She has a right to the way she feels. But I don't have to stick around being punished because she made bad choices."

"That's true."

"So it's better if I go back to Georgia and finish the parole there." He reached across the table to fold his hands over hers. "And I want you to come with me. I've made my own mistakes. I don't have to punish myself, though, by leaving you behind. We could be happy together, Abigail." He lifted her hands to his mouth and kissed her knuckles. "I love you."

Abby blinked back tears. "I almost believe you." She heard Charlie's voice in the kitchen, responding to Billie. *No time,* she thought. *No time.*

"How can I convince you?" Noah's fingers on her cheek wiped up tears. "What will it take?"

Charlie strode into the space behind the counter. "Abby?" The lights came on with a glare that felt like a cymbal clash. "Abby, what the hell are you doing?" He limped up and down the galley, inspecting his territory. "No coffee made, the door locked…and what's he doing here? Why are you sitting in the dark? What in the name of God is going on?"

"Dad, I—"

"You think I can run this place by myself? Billie's talking about quitting and you're sitting out here holding hands with…him."

The first of the breakfast crowd knocked on the front door. "Hey, Charlie, we're starved. Let us in."

Her dad headed for the door. "I might as well have a heart attack and we'll just close the place down altogether. Will that make you happy?"

She couldn't look at Noah. Pulling her hands away, she stared at the vinyl top of the table. She could leave all of this. With one word to Noah, she could have the life she'd dreamed about for fifteen years.

The change of tone in her dad's voice caught her attention. "What are you talking about?" Arms folded over his broad chest, Charlie stood across the room with the two older men who had just come in. "That's ridiculous."

One of them held up a newspaper. "Says here he didn't really murder the guy at all."

Noah turned his head sharply, focusing on the conversation across the room. He must be getting paranoid. Surely he hadn't heard…

Charlie Brannon stood for a minute with the paper in front of his face. When he lowered his hand to his side, he looked straight at Noah and started walking their way.

He stopped at the end of the table, stiff and accusing in his drill-sergeant stance. "Is this some kind of novel? Some tale you made up thinking folks in town would take you back?" The other two guys—the ones who had caused the problem to begin with—crowded at Charlie's back.

"I don't know what you're talking about." He was aware of Abby's complete confusion. If he reached for her hand, though, her dad would probably punch him out.

Charlie held up the newspaper. "This is what I'm talking about."

Below the fold on the front page, the headline read Portrait of a Hometown Hero. His picture—the one on his driver's license—filled part of the first column.

"Dad?" Abby took the paper and flattened it on the table top. Noah couldn't read upside down, but Abby saved him the trouble by reading aloud.

"When a local man rescued a waitress at the Carolina Diner last Friday night, it wasn't the first time he'd stepped forward to play the hero.

"Noah Blake, 33, interrupted a robbery in progress. Joe Cates, 26, took waitress Abby Brannon hostage, holding a gun to her throat. Blake distracted the thief and then knocked him unconscious, ending the standoff without serious injury to Brannon or Cates's two-year-old son, Tyler, who was also on the premises."

Abby glanced in his direction, then cleared her throat.

"Blake, a former student at New Skye High School, returned to town several weeks ago. He was recently paroled by the state of Georgia after serving two and a half years of a seven-year sentence for involuntary manslaughter. The incident that landed him in prison is, oddly enough, further proof of his heroism.

"On the night of April 20, 2000, Blake was having dinner with a woman named in an Atlanta apartment complex. Wanda Harrison's estranged husband, Hubert "Bull" Harrison, ignored a restraining order and broke into the apartment, threatening Wanda, the Harrisons' two-year old son Mac and Blake.

"Bull assaulted Wanda and inflicted multiple injuries, including a broken arm. He had just turned on his child when Blake hit Bull. During the ensuing fight, Bull fell and hit his head on an iron radiator, dying instantly."

Noah felt as if his face was on fire. Across the table, Abby stared at him with the biggest, roundest eyes he'd ever seen. "I knew it," she whispered. "I knew it."

When he looked around, he saw that other people had entered the diner. Many of them carried newspapers. Billie stood behind the counter, her arms crossed at her waist. Nobody said a word.

"Former New Skye H.S. students report that Blake was a difficult student during his years there. 'He was a wild one,' said Wade Hayes of the New Skye police force, now Blake's parole officer. Hayes alleges that Blake set a fire at New Skye H.S. in May 1989, destroying the senior class's school records. Blake was a suspect in the incident, but there was insufficient evidence to lay charges. The case remains unsolved.

"Not all of Blake's former classmates agree with Hayes. 'I never believed Noah was guilty,' says Brannon, the woman he saved at the Carolina Diner. 'I thought he was treated unfairly by most of the teachers and by Principal Floyd.'

"She added that Blake's background—an alcoholic father who abandoned Blake's mother, leaving the family with only a marginal income—spurred him to struggle against authority. 'He needed guidance, not guilt. Someone to listen to him and to understand. He didn't run away. He was driven off.'"

To the heat in his face, Noah added a deeper burn in his gut. His whole life laid out in the newspaper—his dad's flaws, his mother's failings. He sounded like a charity case, a sob story practically begging for pity.

Thanks to Abby.

More customers came in as Charlie finished the article.

> "Several other former classmates share Brannon's opinion of Blake. One of them, Robert Warren of Warren Security Systems, recently hired Blake to install home alarms. Warren says that some customers have been worried about having an ex-con in their homes, but Warren is not concerned. 'I trust Noah completely,' he says. 'I would put my life in his hands.'
>
> "'I trusted Noah to take care of me, and he did,' Brannon says, echoing Warren's words. 'Isn't that the definition of a hero?'"

Charlie looked up from the newspaper. "Hell, son, why didn't you explain? We wouldn't have given you such a hard time."

The men and women standing around them nodded. Somebody said, "Sounds to me like that guy—Bull Harrison—deserved what he got. You did a good thing, taking him off the planet."

Other voices agreed. "I'll buy your breakfast, Noah," somebody else said.

"The coffee's on me," came from someone else. "For everybody."

The folks moved to their tables, though some made sure they clapped him on the shoulder first. Sunshine had started to creep in through the windows, and the diner finally settled down into a new day.

Noah started to slide out of the booth, but Abby caught him by the hand.

"Where are you going?"

He sat back down to avoid drawing more attention. "Atlanta," he said.

"But—" He couldn't look at her, so he didn't know what her face revealed. "But this article makes such a difference."

"Does it?"

"People know the truth now, Noah. They understand that you didn't just kill a man—you rescued a woman and a child from a cruel, miserable excuse for a human being."

"It's a good story, I'll give you that." He twisted his hand in her hold until she let go. "A good story that doesn't mention I was drinking that night, or that I worked for Bull, and we had fought a couple of rounds in the past, just for the hell of it. I think that's what the politicians call 'spin.'"

"You can't turn this into something sordid. You are a hero, a man who makes sacrifices for other people."

"What I am," he said, finally meeting her gaze, "is everybody's latest trick pony. That article was a seasonal fluff piece, designed to make everybody feel good about human nature so they'll go out and spend more money."

"That's not true. Sam's a good reporter and she thought your truth should be told. She did you a favor."

"With your help." He shook his head. "Damn, Abby—did you think I wanted all of that in the paper? Did you think the town needed to be reminded about my dad the drunk, my mom the bitch? How's she going to feel? You practically blamed all my sins on her."

"I did not say that."

Noah leaned forward over the table. "You might as well have. But nothing could be further from the truth. Yeah, I had it rough as a kid. My dad had reasons to re-sent me, and so did my mom. She had some reasons of her own to hate her life. But I'm the one who made my destiny. I take full responsibility for the man I am. I don't make apologies or excuses. And if you think I need them, then…" He struggled to get the words out. "Then what was between us isn't worth fighting for."

This time he stood up and headed for the door. He stepped out into a cold wind, with Abby following.

"You're going back to Atlanta?" She stood beside the bike as he got on, wrapping her arms around her body for warmth.

"That's right."

"Alone?"

Noah closed his eyes, took a deep breath. "Yeah."

Kicking the engine to life, he eased past Abby, turned sharply by the diner's front door and rumbled out of the parking lot, into the rest of his life.

Alone.

CHAPTER THIRTEEN

The Diary of Abby Brannon

January 24, 1989
Dear Diary,
Today was my mom's funeral. All my friends came, and really just about everybody in town who ever ate at the diner. Dad was strong. He went straight to his room once they all left.

They were all nice and said the right things. Doesn't help, but they tried. Noah came to the service, and then he came to the back door for a minute during the reception. When I went outside with him, he didn't speak, just folded his arms around me. Then he kissed the top of my head, walked me back to the kitchen door and went away again.

I wonder if he loves his mother as much as I loved mine.

THE LAST MEETING OF the dance committee took place Thursday night. No one had seen Noah since he'd left the diner that morning. He was, however, the first topic of discussion.

"I'm not surprised by Sam's article in the least," Kate said. "The bad-boy image was just that. An image."

Dixon shook his head. "You're being a little optimistic, there, sweetheart. I remember some of the rougher times in high school. Noah wasn't acting. He was serious about making trouble."

"Sometimes," Rob countered. Dixon lifted an eyebrow. "Okay, a lot of the time," he said with a smile. "But he's always had his good side."

Phoebe looked in Abby's direction. "Will he be here tonight?"

"I don't know." He could be back in Atlanta by now. Or in Washington, D.C. Or right here in town. The distance between them was insurmountable, wherever he'd gone.

"Has everybody got their panels finished?" Kate picked up a piece of paper covered with her neat handwriting. "A couple of teams have dropped out, but I think we still have enough panels for a lovely backdrop."

The couples who had volunteered confirmed that their panels were completed. "I don't know," Abby said again, when asked.

"It's finished," Dixon confirmed. "Noah got it done Tuesday night. Looks terrific."

They went through the rest of the agenda, talking about food and drink and tickets and balloons.

"I've got gag gifts as awards for the painters," Phoebe announced. "Adam volunteered to present them with appropriate humor."

"I did?" He grinned when his wife frowned at him. "I don't do jokes. I'm the one who st-st-stutters, re-member?"

"No, as a matter of fact, I don't." Phoebe had been Adam's speech therapist, before the mayoral campaign. These days, Adam rarely hesitated over his words, and few of his constituents remembered that he ever had.

Abby had thought tonight's meeting might last for-ever, but Kate proved her wrong and pronounced them ready for the dance at a few minutes after nine. Clean-ing up involved only coffee cups—Abby hadn't had the energy to put together treats for the crowd.

Valerie helped her load the dishwasher. "What hap-pened? Where is he?" After Abby's brief explanation, she shook her head. "Men—you gotta love them. I guess you hurt his manly pride."

"How sad." Throwing a sponge in the sink just didn't release enough tension, so she tried again with a plas-tic bowl. Better. "Chasing after him, waiting on him, dragging him out of his splendid isolation didn't have any effect on my pride, of course." Deciding crockery would be best, she picked up a ceramic bowl. "Move back."

"Abby—" But the protest came too late. The bowl hit the stainless-steel sink with a satisfying crash.

"Now I'm going home." She locked the back door, dragged on her coat and went to the front. "Rob left you here? Do you need a ride?"

"We came in separate cars—I had to work late."

That got her attention. "You haven't had dinner, have you?" Her best friend shook her head. "Why didn't you say something? I could have fed you. Damn it, I can't do anything right these days." For the first time all day, tears threatened to escape her control.

Valerie folded her into a hug. "I'm not going to starve," she promised. "Rob said he'd rustle up some macaroni and cheese. He does a great job."

Abby rested her head on Valerie's shoulder for a second, letting herself be loved. She didn't often experience a woman's touch. In the beginning, she'd hoped that Noah's mother could fill the void her own mother's death had left. That maybe, once Noah left, they could help each other. But Mrs. Blake's personal wounds were too serious for that kind of effort.

Loving Noah—being loved by him—had filled the emptiness. But only for a moment. Now she was alone again.

She drew a deep breath and straightened up. "I'm okay. Really, I am," she insisted, in the face of Valerie's doubting expression. "Limping around all week has been tough. But it'll give me a good excuse for not dancing."

"Why wouldn't you want to dance?"

Because the man she wanted to hold wouldn't be there. "This afternoon I told Wade I'd be his date."

"You did what?" Valerie stared at her, dismay written all over her face. "Why? Oh, Abby, why?"

"I—" She shrugged. "I might as well. Maybe he'll stop coming in all the time. I just couldn't think of a reason to refuse."

"How about the fact that he's a...a creep? That he's been torturing Noah? That you don't like him?"

"It's just one night." And she had a whole lifetime of nights to get through without Noah.

Valerie gazed at her for a few seconds, then shook her head. "I'm not looking forward to this anymore. Maybe Rob and I will just stay home with the kids."

"No, you won't." She pushed Valerie out the door and turned the key in the lock. "You'll show up and give me a chance to talk to you. We can go to the bathroom to check our makeup every thirty minutes."

"I guess." After a quick hug, Valerie ran through a drizzle of rain to her own SUV, but waited until the Volvo engine started before pulling away.

Abby drove home without the radio or a tape, trying to sort out the mess of her life in ten minutes. She wouldn't be going away with Noah, that was definite. But she had her friends to take care of, her dad, her customers. Would she want to leave and miss Kate's baby and Samantha's, miss seeing Joey grow up to be just like his dad? She worked with Valerie's Girls Outdoors! troop most weeks—what would she do without them? Adam and Rob, Tommy and Dixon and Pete were her weekend warriors. She cared about their basketball games as much as they did. How would she feel if she lost touch?

The very idea of leaving her dad was almost too painful to examine.

She pulled into the driveway, resolved to make the best of the blessings she'd received. Sex with Noah had been beautiful. If it never happened again, she would still be grateful. If she never saw him again, at least she'd kissed him, held him. Loved him with all she had to give.

The house was silent when she let herself inside. She turned on the TV but kept the volume low so she wouldn't wake Charlie. He needed his rest.

And she needed food—she wasn't sure she'd eaten today at all. In the kitchen, she was halfway through the construction of a peanut butter and banana sandwich when she realized Elvis hadn't scratched at the door. He must be sound asleep, too.

But she wanted help boosting her shaky mood, so she opened the door. "Elvis? Hey, buddy, wake up. Elvis?"

Out on the dark sunporch, nothing moved. Was he sick? She flipped the light switch, afraid of what she would find.

Worse than a sick dog was no dog at all. The sunporch was empty.

Elvis had left the building.

LOST—ONE JOB, ONE WOMAN, one hometown. Found—the misery of regrets.

After spending the day riding the back roads of North Carolina's farmlands, Noah sat on the couch in the apartment above Dixon's garage, legs stretched long, hands behind his head, as he considered the rest of his life. He could go back to the old ways in Atlanta, walking a line between honesty and deceit, right and wrong. Or…

Before he had figured out what his alternative might be, he heard someone coming up the outside stairs. Not Abby's light steps, but heavy, deliberate, uneven thumps. The knock on the door matched the sound—powerful, ruthless. Angry?

With the door open, he could only stare. His voice had deserted him.

"Don't leave me standing out here in the rain." Charlie Brannon stepped inside. "The dog here hates rain." He bent with a groan and put Elvis down on the carpet. "Close the damn door, why don't you?" Instead of waiting for him, Charlie did that, too.

Once on the floor, Elvis started celebrating. He hopped and skipped and jumped up at Noah's knees, eager to greet and be greeted. When Noah picked the dog up, he got the licking of a lifetime all over his face.

"Yuck." He found his voice, with the dog, anyway. "That's enough. Come on, stop." Setting Elvis on the floor, he looked at Charlie. "Have a seat."

"'Bout time." The older man lowered his bulk onto the couch. "You probably wonder why I'm here."

Noah rested his hip on a bar stool. "To dump the dog, I guess."

Charlie shrugged. "Incidental. I have something to tell you. Something you need to know."

"What would that be?"

"You remember that Harley you had in high school? The one you put together from parts you bought in a box at a garage sale?"

"The Sportster XLS, 1983. Sure."

"You told me you stole the hundred bucks to buy long-arm mirrors. Did you get them?"

"No. That money was all I had to live on when I left town."

Abby's dad nodded. "Yeah, that's what I thought."

"Where is this going?"

Charlie took a deep breath. "The night of the fire, I was in the dining room cleaning up. I glanced out the window, across the street to the school, and saw a motorcycle parked near the wall. A Harley Sportster."

"Yeah, and you told the police."

"Right. I knew you had one, knew that's what I saw, and put the two together. But somebody else had a similar bike. Sheriff Hayes bought one for Wade, as a graduation present. Wade talked his dad into letting him use it early."

"I remember." He remembered the sheriff telling his mother how Wade had begged for a bike after seeing Noah's. "So?"

"Wade had those mirrors you wanted. He still has them, and he just got the bike repainted. When I saw it the other day, I realized…"

Noah waited.

"The bike I saw that night wasn't yours. It was Wade's." He opened his hands, as if presenting a gift. "Wade must have started the fire."

Could there be such a simple explanation? "Why would he do that?"

"I don't know. I thought you might. What reason would he have to destroy grades?"

Elvis went up on his hind legs, bracing his front paws on Noah's boot. Noah picked him up and the dog immediately curled into a ball in his arms. "I don't remember that his grades were so bad. But then, we didn't exactly share secrets."

"Besides the bike, what did the police have that connected you to the fire?"

"My reputation. And the argument I had with Floyd the day before."

"You argued with the principal?"

"He took exception to my Grateful Dead T-shirt. I took exception to his face."

"Smart." Charlie shook his head. "I guess lots of kids at school heard this argument."

"Probably."

"And somebody who wanted to hurt you might take advantage of that argument to get you in serious trouble."

"I suppose. There was definitely no love lost between Wade and me. Still isn't." He thought Charlie might ask for details and he braced himself to deflect the attempt.

But the older man just nodded. "So you need to let people know about this. You've been wrongly judged all these years. Wade Hayes deserves to be punished."

Noah shook his head. "I think the statute of limitations has run out on that fire. And I don't believe another newspaper article is called for."

"You'll just let him get away with it?"

"Does what happened fifteen years ago really matter anymore?"

"You tell me." Charlie struggled to his feet. "This afternoon, Abby told Wade she'd go to the dance with him."

He felt as if he'd been drenched with ice water. "That's…her choice."

"No, it's her last resort." His limp more pronounced than usual, Abby's dad went to the door. "You think about that. Then decide what's the right thing to do."

SEATED AT THE KITCHEN table, a mug of cold tea between her hands, Abby looked up as Charlie came through the back door.

"What did you do with my dog?"

He stopped for a couple of seconds, then shut the door behind him and shrugged off his jacket. "Took him where he belonged."

"Where, in your opinion, was that?"

"I took him over to Noah Blake. He brought the dog with him. He should keep it."

That meant Noah was still in town. Until tomorrow, anyway. "Why? Why tonight, at nine o'clock, did you suddenly decide this was an errand that had to be done before you went to bed?"

Charlie turned away from her to get a glass of water. "I saw how mad he was about the newspaper article. I thought he might try leaving town without the mutt. I wanted to make sure that didn't happen."

"It wasn't your decision to make!" Her temper exploded into fury. "He's my dog now. I want him here, with me."

Her dad didn't turn to face her. "He needs a fenced yard, somebody around most of the day. We talked about this before. And I figured Blake would take the dog when he left town." He finished off his water. "He seemed happy enough to be there."

"Why don't you want a dog?"

"We don't have time for a dog."

"What kind of life is it when you don't even have the time to enjoy a dog?"

At that, he turned to face her. "A damn good one. You've been happy with it all these years."

"Comfortable, maybe. Happy?" Abby shook her head. "I wouldn't use that word."

She'd never seen her dad look so surprised, so confused. "You're not happy?"

"I love you. I love New Skye and my friends, I love being needed. But when I think about what's out there, the places I could experience, all the unique and wonderful people I could meet…" She shook her head. "When I think I might never even cross the North Carolina state line, I regret how much I'm missing in my life."

"You would leave?"

"If I got the chance."

"What would I do without you?"

That was the big question. Abby got up and went to put her arms around him. "It's not a problem, is it? Noah will take the dog with him when he leaves and everything will go back to normal. We'll have our vacation, like we always do, and we'll start the New Year at the Carolina Diner with hoppin' john and collards for good luck and more money."

With his arms around her, Charlie took a deep breath and blew it out again. "You're a terrific daughter."

"You're a great dad."

And Noah Blake was just a stranger she'd have to learn to forget.

THE PHONE RANG AT MIDNIGHT. Abby had barely struggled awake when her dad knocked on her door. "It's for you."

"Who is it?" He didn't answer—all she heard was

his footsteps in the hallway, heading toward the kitchen. With fear settling in her stomach, she picked up the phone. "Hello?"

"It's Noah."

At the words, she started to cry.

"Abby, are you there?"

She struggled to control her voice. "Yes."

"I apologize for calling so late, but—"

"Why don't you just say goodbye and hang up?"

"I... There's something you need to know, first." When she didn't say anything, he cleared his throat. "Are you there?"

"Yes."

"I thought you might have hung up on me."

"You deserve it."

"Probably." She thought she heard a hint of a smile in his voice. "Listen, your dad told me you're going to the dance with Wade."

Would the man leave her no pride at all? "It's none of your business. But...yes."

He was quiet for a second. "Wade set the fire in the school office."

For a moment, the words made no sense. "Say that again." He did, and she listened carefully. "How do you know?"

"Your dad figured it out." He explained the motor-cycle details.

"But—"

"I think he thought I would want to tell you."

She could—and would—take that up with her dad later. "Why would Wade set fire to the records?"

"Good question. I don't know the answer. I thought maybe you would have an idea."

"Me?"

"You always know everything that's going on. You listen and remember. What did you hear about Wade Hayes?"

"That was—"

"Fifteen years ago. Think hard."

Abby closed her eyes, trying to travel back to those last months of school. Her mom's death always came to mind first. Friends arrived in class every day with college acceptance letters. The prom—she'd gone alone because Noah didn't ask her. Wade had come alone, too. And bugged her until she danced with him.

"Wade didn't have a date for the prom," she told Noah. "I thought that was strange, since he was the sheriff's son and a basketball star. Some girl should have snapped him up. You, of course, didn't go at all."

"No tux, no car, no cash. So Wade didn't have a girlfriend?"

"I don't think so. But there was talk…" She rubbed her temples, picturing the crowded hallways, the lunch tables, the gossip during those last few weeks of high school. "I heard he was seeing somebody. Heard he'd been bragging."

Noah listened to Abby thinking and tried not to push her. "Bragging?"

"About the sex." He could almost hear her blush. "And with somebody older."

Before he could ask, she gasped. "That's it. I can't believe I remembered. I can't believe I forgot!"

"Abby, I'm going crazy on this end. What are you talking about?"

"The secretary," she said in an excited voice. "Ms. Lacey. She was Mr. Floyd's secretary, she took care of the important paperwork for transcripts, report cards, stuff like that."

"She was involved with Wade? How old was she?"

"Not very—maybe twenty-five. She was pretty, too. Very blond, blue eyes, cute figure. Cheerleader material. Oh, yes, I can see she was just Wade's type."

"But why would he set fire to the records, just because he was…uh…"

"Screwing the secretary?" She was laughing at him. "I don't know. Maybe you should ask Ms. Lacey."

"If I could find her."

"Oh, she's still right here in New Skye. She got married about ten years ago, to a farmer. Kenny Riddle, that's his name. I bet their address is in the phone book."

HE FOUND THE ADDRESS just as Abby had predicted he would, and rode out there early Friday morning. The white farmhouse sprawled under tall old trees. A separate garage in the rear housed a minivan and a small barn huddled farther back. Several horses grazed the fenced pasture and a child's swing set sat within sight of the front porch.

When he rang the bell, a woman holding a baby on her shoulder faced him from the opposite side of the screen door. "Can I help you?" Then she recognized him. "It—it's Noah Blake, right?"

"Yes, ma'am. How are you?"

"F-fine. Just fine. What can I do for you?"

"I wondered if we could talk for a minute."

"Well, I'm kind of busy right now. My eight-year-old has the chicken pox and the baby's ready for a nap...."

He smiled as gently as he knew how. "Looks to me like the baby's already asleep." The little face was turned out on her shoulder, eyes closed, mouth relaxed into a soft kiss.

"But my son—"

"I don't hear a sound. Could it be he's asleep, too?"

She threw him an irritated glance. "What do you want?"

"I want to talk to you about the fire."

THEY FACED EACH OTHER across the kitchen table, a mug of tea in front of each of them. Pamela Lacey, now Pamela Riddle, had put the baby to bed and checked on her son.

"I don't know anything about that fire," she told Noah. "I didn't do it. I didn't have any reason to—to burn those records."

"I'm sure of that. I'm sure I didn't, either."

"The police said you did."

"That's what they said, whether they believed it or not." He took a sip of tea and realized how long it had been since he ate. "I think you *know* who set that fire, though. I think you've known for fifteen years."

"No." She looked away from him, but her cheeks turned bright red.

"I can give you a name, or you can give me one."

"I don't know what you're talking about."

"Wade Hayes."

She jumped, and that was all Noah needed. "Why? Why did he burn those records?"

He waited a long time before she finally spoke. "He…wanted his grades changed. He'd goofed off in biology and failed the last grading period. He wanted me to make a new transcript. And I wouldn't." Pam curled forward onto the table, covering her head with her folded arms. "I argued with him and he went crazy, started pulling the drawers out, dumping the files on the floor. He found his transcript and lit it up while he still held it. Then he threw it onto the pile. And everything just blazed up. I ran," she sobbed. "I was afraid he would kill me."

"Why didn't you tell the police?"

"W-Wade said he would t-tell them about us. I would have lost my job. Everybody would know."

Another long pause. "A-and then you were gone, and it was easier just to let them blame you. I never dreamed…"

"What?"

"That you'd come back."

WHEN NOAH WENT TO HIS mother's house on Friday afternoon to get more work done, he thought for a second that someone else had opened the door. She'd had her hair cut the way she used to wear it, just below her ears, and now it curled, as he remembered. Her outfit looked new—soft black pants, a white turtleneck and a red sweater. He thought she might even have put some makeup on. Lipstick, at least.

"Wow, Ma. You look really good."

She waved the comment away. "What are you here for?"

He held up the box he carried. "I thought I'd replace your shower nozzle, improve the spray. You've got faucet leaks and a drip under the bathroom sink."

Taking a step back, she held the door for him to come in. "Want some coffee?"

He hadn't gotten much sleep. "Sure."

"About four different people made sure I saw the paper yesterday," she said, handing him a steaming mug as they stood together in the kitchen. They sipped in silence for a minute. "Why didn't you explain to anybody?"

"The basic facts are the same, whatever the reason."

"You really think the world is that simple?"

Her eyes held his, and Noah couldn't look away. "Maybe not."

"You don't have much reason to trust anybody around here." Marian turned to refill her mug. "But if you give…us…a chance, maybe we'll surprise you." After a pause, she added, "The way you've surprised us."

"Don't make a hero out of me," he warned.

She turned, and for the first time in—twenty years?—he saw her smile. "You're not a villain, either, son. You're just a man."

By nightfall, he'd fixed her plumbing, changed the filters in her heating system and repaired the attic fan. As he washed his hands at the kitchen sink, his mother came into the kitchen. "I could fix some dinner."

"Or I could take you somewhere to eat." He saw the pleasure in her eyes before she stifled it. "I've got Dixon's truck—you wouldn't have to ride the Harley."

Another first—Marian Blake actually laughed. "But wouldn't you like to see Charlie Brannon's face if I did?"

NOAH AND HIS MOTHER were the talk of the diner during the dinner rush. Abby could scarcely keep her eyes off them—she'd never seen Marian Blake so content, never seen Noah so relaxed. Well, except for the time she'd spent with him in his bed.

She took their orders, brought their food and drinks, cleared their dishes. No dessert—Noah didn't ask for any and Mrs. Blake couldn't eat the sugary cakes and pies. And although Charlie usually manned the cash register, Abby managed to be standing there when Noah came up to pay the bill.

"Good food," he said, handing over a twenty. "As usual."

"Thanks." She made change, handing back a five and three ones. "I'm glad to see your mom out of the house."

He glanced over his shoulder at the table where Mrs. Blake was finishing her coffee. "Yeah." When he looked her way again, Abby searched his eyes. "Did you find the person you were looking for?"

"I did."

"And did she tell you what you needed to know?"

"Oh, yes."

"So what are you going to do?"

"First, I'm going to make sure you don't go anywhere near the guy. Especially tomorrow night."

"So he really did it?"

Noah nodded. "I've talked with Dixon, Pete, Rob and Adam. Told them what I know. We're going to take care of this. But you have to promise to be somewhere else. Go to a movie, shopping, wherever."

"You're saying I can't come to the dance?"

"Right."

"You're crazy!" She spoke too loudly, and everyone in the diner looked in their direction.

"I'm coming to the dance," she whispered. "Especially if you're planning something to do with Wade."

He braced his hands on the counter and leaned closer. "I can't trust him, Abby. And I don't want you hurt."

"Wade won't hurt me. Besides, if I back out, he might not show up. Then what would you do?"

From the look on his face, that was an angle the would-be heroes hadn't considered. "Right," she said triumphantly. "Think about it. All your plots won't count for anything if Wade doesn't come to the dance.

"And I," she pointed out with a superior smile, "can guarantee he'll be there. You need me, Mr. Noah Blake, whether you like it or not."

Noah stood up straight, shaking his head. "You're right, Ms. Abigail Brannon." His smile turned her warm and shivery at the same time. "I most definitely do."

CHAPTER FOURTEEN

WAITING FOR WADE TO ARRIVE on Saturday night was a little like waiting to be electrocuted. Or, maybe, hanged by the neck until dead.

Abby sat on one chair in the living room, hoping she didn't crush her velvet skirt too badly. Charlie had closed the diner early and come home to wait with her. "There's no way I'm letting you go off with that reprobate all alone. I wish you'd said you'd meet him at the school."

"I should have done that," she admitted, now that the moment had arrived. "But what can happen between here and the school? He has no idea we're on to him, so he'll just drive straight to the dance."

Her dad gave her a glum look. "I hope so. If he tries anything, you kick him where it counts and get out of the car."

She had to laugh. "I can't quite visualize that kind of kick in the front seat of a Corvette."

"Don't visualize. Just do it."

But Wade, when he showed up, was on his best behavior. "Good evening, Charlie." He shook her dad's hand at the door, then turned to look at Abby. "You're

a sight for sore eyes tonight, Miss Abby. Beautiful."
Drawing his left hand from behind his back, he offered
her a florist's box. "I hope you'll wear this for me."

She opened the box with trembling fingers. "Talk
about beautiful." The wrist corsage was exquisite—a
pristine white gardenia set against dark green leaves,
tied with a red bow. Wade slipped the band on her wrist
and she lifted the flower to her face. "I love the scent
of gardenias. Thank you, Wade."

"You're most welcome. Shall we go?" He held out
his arm for her and walked her down the sidewalk to
his car by the curb.

"Have a good time," Charlie called from the front
porch. "Be careful."

Abby rolled her eyes, afraid her dad had given something away.

Wade just laughed as he cranked the engine. "Dads
never want to let their little girls grow up, do they?"

She tried to relax against the leather seat. "I guess
not. This is a great car."

The distraction worked perfectly, and he filled the
minutes of the drive to New Skye High School with a
monologue detailing all the fine points of his pride and
joy. The dance committee had hired Sal Torres and some
of his responsible friends to park cars for the attendees,
but Wade made it to Abby's door before Sal did.

"You scratch this car," he told Sal, "and I'll pull your
license until you're fifty years old, at least."

Sal winked at Abby. "Yes, sir. I'll be extra careful,
sir, and park it all the way at the far end of the lot. Sir."

Wade glowered at him but soon recovered his good humor as he escorted Abby into the lobby of the gym.

Rob and Valerie had just arrived, as well. "You look terrific," Abby said as she gave Rob a kiss on the cheek. "And you, woman, are gorgeous." She hugged Valerie, careful not to crush her friend's midnight-blue silk dress.

"Are you okay?" Valerie whispered in her ear. "I'm so scared."

"Just wonderful. Really." Drawing back, she found Rob chatting with Wade about a recent pro football game, as if they were casual friends. Only someone who knew Rob very well would have detected the unfamiliar glint of anger in his blue eyes.

Abby decided to separate the spark from the fuse in this explosive situation. "I haven't seen the gym yet. Let's go inside." All she wanted was to keep Wade away from her friends until the right moment.

When they stepped inside the gymnasium itself, though, she stopped with a gasp. "Oh, how wonderful!"

Most of the dance committee had worked on decorations since dawn, and the effect they'd created was stunning. Shiny silver snowflakes hung on black wires from the ceiling, and with the lights dimmed, they did look as if they were falling from the sky. A revolving "disco ball" over the dance floor cast sparkles of light onto the snowflakes and the crowd below. At the far end of the big space, the band was warming up on a portable stage. The Christmas tree to be awarded for the best Christmas panel stood just to the side of the stage, filled with glittering ornaments of every description and at least a thousand twinkling lights.

The panels themselves had been erected along both sidelines of the basketball court. Though every scene had been created individually, they were arranged so that the pictures seemed to flow into one another. Abby recognized Jacquie and Rhys's horse-drawn sleigh, Phoebe and Adam's outdoor scene—a longleaf pine tree being decorated by birds and beasts—and the Warrens' portrait of Santa Claus putting gifts around a beautiful indoor tree. Along the other side, the Hanukkah panel was a lovely blue-and-gold celebration full of candlelight and family love. There was an ice-skating scene, as well as a picture of children lined up to sit on Santa's lap and whisper their wishes in his ear.

On the end nearest her was a nostalgic view of 1954 New Skye itself, filled with happy shoppers in their best clothes, busy storefronts and the wonderful old courthouse on its snow-covered circular lawn. The snow sparkled with diamonds, and Abby realized that Noah had sprinkled glitter on her picture. She blinked back tears, just as the band struck up "We Wish You a Merry Christmas."

With the start of the music, the reunion dance took off. Wade seemed content to follow Abby around as she sought out the people she wanted to talk to. He didn't push an agenda of his own, didn't indicate anyone he particularly wanted to see, but he brought her punch and some of the delicious food, then stood beside her quietly while she visited with friends.

"I'm beginning to wonder if we're all wrong," she confided to Valerie as they visited the rest room together. "I mean, he's being a real gentleman. Do you suppose…?"

Valerie shook her head. "You're forgetting Ms. Lacey…Mrs. Riddle…the secretary. She confirmed what your dad guessed, because she was there that night." Moving closer, Valerie lowered her voice. "Pete checked the phone company records. There have been calls made from Wade's office and his home number in the last couple of weeks to the secretary's home. Pete went out there this morning and she confessed that Wade threatened her with exposure if she talked to Noah."

Abby actually felt deflated, sad that Wade wasn't the person he pretended to be. "I'll try to remember this is all a sham." Then she asked the important question. "Where is Noah? He will be here, won't he?"

But her friend shook her head. "I don't know. He wasn't here today while we set up. And Rob doesn't know what the exact plan is—whether Noah intends to confront Wade during the dance or afterward." She squeezed Abby's hand. "I'm sorry."

Weaving through the crush of people to rejoin her "date" at the punch table, Abby surveyed the crowd yet again, hoping to find the one face she'd been missing. She reached Wade, however, without seeing Noah at all.

Wade turned when she tapped him on the shoulder. "Welcome back! Would you like to dance?"

She hadn't intended to let him get that close. But if Noah wasn't here…didn't care enough to tell her what was going on…

"Sure." She smiled up at the dishonest, untrustworthy police officer. "Let's dance."

FROM THE SHADOWS in the corner, Noah watched as Wade and Abby moved onto the dance floor between the Christmas panels. He clenched his jaw as he saw Hayes's arms go around her. When she put her hands on the guy's shoulders, he forced himself to stay where he was, instead of going out to yank them apart before pounding the jerk into the floor.

Abby looked gorgeous, of course, with her hair piled in curls on back of her head, wearing a dress he would never have expected to see on her in a hundred years. Rich gold velvet clung to her hips but flared a little at her knees, leaving a long length of leg, in gold glitter stockings, for him to enjoy. The top of the dress draped in folds over her breasts but revealed her silky arms and dropped low in the back…where Wade Hayes had taken full advantage of the lovely skin left exposed.

"Relax," Dixon said, leaning against the wall beside him. "She knows it's a game, if he doesn't. She's just providing a smoke screen."

"Sure," Noah said, though he had to admit the word sounded more like a growl. "I'm relaxed."

"And I'm Santa Claus."

Kate joined them as he spoke, wrapping both her hands around Dixon's elbow. "Oh, good. Can I have a baby for Christmas, Santa?"

Dixon's grin shone like a megawatt searchlight. "I do believe that can be arranged, Mrs. Claus."

Noah looked from one glowing face to the other. "Are you saying…?"

"We are definitely saying Kate's pregnant." Dixon

picked up one of her hands and kissed the knuckles. "I'm an incredibly lucky guy."

"Well, congratulations. But—" He stopped, realizing he was about to ask a less-than-diplomatic question.

"But…what about law school?" Kate gave him her serene and beautiful smile. "I've asked for a deferment of my acceptance and I believe I'll get it. So the baby will be born in July and we'll have a year together before I start school. Fortunately, I have a built-in baby-sitter."

Dixon nodded. "Otherwise known as Dad. I figure I can write songs and rock a baby at the same time."

Out on the floor, the dancers stopped to applaud the end of the song. Noah figured Wade would bring Abby off the floor for a drink, and tensed up all over again when the cop simply took her into his arms and began swaying with the next tune.

"I think I'll take a walk," he told the Bells, and made his way out of the gym. He hadn't known what he was asking for, watching from the sidelines as Abby danced with somebody else. Anybody else, but especially Wade Hayes.

Standing outside in the cold, with his hands in his pockets, he stared up at the black sky and wondered if he would make it through the evening without losing his temper. He planned to accuse Hayes calmly, present the truth without mentioning Pam Lacey Riddle at all, using Charlie's name only as a last resort. He didn't want Hayes in jail, didn't need to see him punished. Noah only wanted Wade to admit the truth in front of the people who mattered—Noah's friends…and the woman he loved.

"Well, well, well, who have we here?" A big man in a tan uniform windbreaker strolled into the light.

"Sheriff." Noah nodded, hoping Chet Hayes would go about his business without pausing to chat. Then Principal Floyd came up on his other side.

"I thought I'd come by and see how things are going at the big dance." Hayes turned to face in the same direction as Noah. "Are folks having a good time?"

"They seem to be." Just standing next to the man gave him the creeps—how bad would it have been to live in the same house?

"You shouldn't even be here," Floyd said. "You didn't graduate from my school."

Noah faced him directly. "Do you want to try throwing me out?"

The sheriff clicked his tongue. "Now, now, let's all keep our tempers. How's your mom, Noah?"

"Good."

"I've always had a soft spot in my heart for Marian Blake. She was nice to me and my son, after my wife died."

Noah had no intention of engaging in that conversation.

"I thought about making her a part of my life on a full-time basis, you know." When Noah turned on his heel to head back inside, the sheriff clamped a hand on his shoulder. "But she held out on me. Said her boy wasn't ready, wasn't supportive." He made the word sound ugly. "He didn't like me, she said, or my son. We'd have to take some time to get him used to the idea.

"Then there was the fire, and I had to tell her this son

she was so concerned about was a criminal. A fugitive. I swear, boy, I wanted to hunt you down with dogs. But the D.A. said there just wasn't enough evidence for a warrant."

Noah turned back to face the big man, shaking off his heavy grip. "And all the time, the real arsonist was right under your nose."

The sheriff's eyebrows drew together in genuine confusion. "What are you talking about?"

"Everybody knows you set that fire," Floyd sputtered, standing in the sheriff's shadow.

Noah stared. Did they not know the truth? Oh, man. "Never mind." He walked toward the door to the gym lobby.

Hayes came after him. "You answer me, boy. Who is this real arsonist?"

"You'll find out soon enough," Noah promised him. "I hope you're sitting down at the time."

THE AWARDS WERE TO BE given out at eleven o'clock, while the band took a break before their last hour of music. Adam climbed onto the stage and claimed the microphone, with Phoebe beside him holding a stack of small gift boxes.

"Good evening," Adam said, and the crowd quieted down right away. "As mayor of New Skye and a member of the NSHS class of 1989, I'd like to welcome all of you to this reunion dance. I hope everyone is having as much fun as I am." The audience answered with a round of applause.

"What we'd like to do now is present awards to the

talented people who created these lovely walls surrounding our dance floor. We have a lot of artistic talent in this town of ours, and I'm proud to see it demonstrated tonight."

The prizes ranged from the sublime to the ridiculous—a crystal snowflake ornament for the panel representing the true meaning of Christmas, given to Kate and Dixon for their nativity scene, a bagful of chocolate coins for the picture of a Christmas dinner table. Rob and Valerie received a sprig of mistletoe.

"Not that they need it," Adam commented, as the couple kissed in celebration.

One by one, each panel was recognized with humor and with appreciation for its contribution to the festivities.

Abby realized soon enough that the scene she'd painted with Noah was being saved for last. The Christmas tree, in all its glory, would be theirs… his?…hers?

"Finally," Adam said, "the grand prize of the night will be awarded to the panel that expresses a very special sentiment—the love we all share for this place we call home. The town of New Skye has sheltered its citizens for more than two hundred years now, through war and peace, prosperity and depression, sadness and joy. Tonight, we award this wonderful living symbol of the season to the painters of 'New Skye Retro'—Abby Brannon and Noah Blake!"

As had all the other artists, Abby started across the dance floor toward the stage. She was sure she must be beet-red from her hairline to her collarbones, and probably all the way to her toes. Did she have to say more than thank you? Did she have to do this all by herself?

As she reached the stage, a shadow detached itself from the darkness behind the nearest panel and Noah walked across the floor to meet her.

He took her breath away, in a simple black tux that skimmed his great shoulders, his lean waist and long legs. His shirt was blinding white, his bow tie perfect. In the two weeks since he'd arrived his hair had grown enough to make a decent haircut.

He looked like the man she'd always loved.

Taking her hand, he steadied her as she stepped up onto the platform, and then he joined her.

"Congratulations." Adam grinned at them, shook Noah's hand and kissed Abby on the cheek, then turned to the crowd once more. "The reunion dance committee would like to thank Noah and Abby and all of you who contributed to this beautiful setting and a terrific holiday party. I suggest that our panel painters step out on the floor to begin our next dance. Everyone else, feel free to join in."

The band started up "Silver Bells" as the artists, most of them husbands and wives, moved into each other's arms.

"Do you know how to waltz?" Noah asked Abby as he helped her off the stage.

"Three beats," she said. "That's about the extent of my experience."

"Good. I won't be embarrassed." As if they danced every day, he drew her into his arms. "We'll do what feels good," he murmured just above her ear. "Nobody will notice in this crowd."

As far as Abby was concerned, what felt good was merely standing close together, so close that the slightest breeze couldn't have slipped between them. Noah's hand was warm on her bare back. Hot, in fact. Or perhaps that was her skin, reacting to his touch. Somehow her right arm was twined with his, resting snugly against his chest, while her left hand was free—free to stroke his hair, smooth the fabric over his shoulder, set her palm along the line of his jaw.

Noah turned his head and pressed a kiss into the center of that palm. Abby's knees buckled underneath her.

"Sorry," he said, keeping her on her feet. "I haven't danced much. Does your foot hurt? We can stop anytime."

"No, oh, no. I'm fine." Her deep breath shook. "I'm just not very good at this, myself."

He drew back a little and smiled at her. "I don't have a single complaint."

All at once, staring into his dark eyes, she felt completely at ease. "Me, neither."

Smiling up at Noah, humming along with the music, Abby didn't notice disaster approaching until a long finger tapped on the shoulder right in front of her nose. She jumped, startled, and Noah stopped moving for a moment to glance back at the man behind him.

"Cutting in," Wade said. The smile he'd worn all night was conspicuously absent.

"Sorry," Noah replied. He turned to Abby and began to dance again.

This time, Wade grabbed Noah's shoulder and jerked him backward and around, away from Abby. "I brought the lady. I want to dance with her."

Noah didn't raise his voice. "You've confused me with somebody who gives a damn about what you want." Around them, the dancers slowed, stopped, stared.

Surely he didn't mean to stage a confrontation now, in front of everybody. Abby put a hand on Noah's arm. "It's okay. I'll—"

He glanced at her. "You're not letting this creep put his hands on you ever again."

Wade said a foul word and shoved at Noah's shoulders with the heels of both hands. Noah staggered a few steps but recovered quickly and surged forward with fists clenched and eyes flaming.

Suddenly, Adam and Dixon were there between them, with Pete grabbing Wade's arms from behind while Rob gripped Noah's shoulders.

"Take it outside, gentlemen," Adam ordered. "This is a party, not a wrestling match."

"I don't want to fight," Wade insisted. "I just want to dance with my date."

"Not an option anymore," Noah told him.

"Out of here," Pete said in his fiercest trooper voice, and practically frog-marched Wade off the dance floor. Principal Floyd followed, complaining and getting in the way.

Rob kept a hand on Noah's shoulder as they followed, while Abby brought up the rear with Adam and Dixon. She wasn't about to be left behind now.

The procession came to a halt in the lobby. A few interested onlookers started to join them, but Tommy Crawford and Rhys Lewellyn closed the double doors in their faces, standing guard so that no one else came in. While the party continued inside the gym, Abby realized that the moment she'd been dreading had arrived.

"Let go of me." Wade shook off Pete's hold, but only because the trooper allowed him to. "What do you think you're doing, manhandling a fellow officer?" He glared at Noah. "You're screwed, Blake. Totally screwed. I'm sending you back to prison."

"Doubtful." Noah stepped away from Rob's hold. "I believe you'll reconsider that threat before too many minutes have passed."

"Sure. You're about to stage some grandstand move, I guess. For a convicted felon, you're pretty cocky, you know that? You think you've got something on me? Go ahead, put it out."

Noah folded his arms across his chest. "Arson, for starters."

"Oh, for heaven's sake." Mr. Floyd crossed his arms and stared at Noah with contempt. "Are you ever going to let this go?"

Wade looked around, pretending to be confused. "Did we have a fire here in town, recently? I must've missed it."

"Don't be a smart-ass, Wade." Pete cuffed him in the shoulder. "You know what fire he's talking about."

"You mean the one *he* started, fifteen years ago?"

"Good try." Noah nodded. "But now we know it was your bike outside the school that night. You're the one who burned the school records."

"Uh-huh. What did you have to do to convince ol' Charlie to change his story? Agree to take his bitch of a daughter off his hands?"

Noah exploded across the space between them, closing his hands around Wade's throat. Though the policeman was heavier and taller, size didn't seem to matter as Noah knocked him to the floor.

"I'm going to gag you with your own tongue," Noah promised. "You've made the last lewd comment of your life."

"Stop him!" The principal flapped his hands. "Somebody stop him."

Rob and Dixon were already dragging Noah back again. Pete pulled Wade to his feet. "I'd watch your mouth, if I were you." He made a pretense of dusting off Wade's jacket and slacks. "Next time, we won't get involved."

The threat actually seemed to make Wade hesitate. "Look, the arson is no big deal, okay? I'll let the subject alone if you will."

"Okay," Noah said, to Abby's surprise. "We'll let the arson charge drop. Let's move on…to blackmail."

She expected Wade to laugh, make another denial, throw out one of his sarcastic comments.

But he looked nervous now. "I don't know what you're talking about."

"I'm talking about threatening phone calls, with

promises to use the legal authority of your job to harass a private citizen."

"You're crazy."

"If you're not interested in dealing with blackmail, how about breaking and entering? Vandalism? Or maybe charges of tampering with an election?"

Wade seemed to shrink where he stood. "I'm getting out of here." He glanced at Abby. "I guess you can find your own ride home." When he turned toward the doors, though, Pete stood like a rock in front of one set.

Sheriff Hayes stood in front of the other pair of doors, his face as rigid as stone. "Election tampering?" he said, as if the idea had never occurred to him. "Son, what the hell have you been talking about?"

In a matter of seconds, Wade had disappeared, followed by his father. Principal Floyd looked at Noah, and then the rest of them, with his mouth working as if he wanted to say something. In the end, he just threw his hands up and walked back into the dance.

"Well," Dixon commented to no one in particular. "That was exciting." He caught Kate's hand and turned toward the gym again, gripping Noah's shoulder for a moment as he went by. "Welcome home. We're glad to have you back." Rhys and Tommy opened the doors again, letting out the music and the noise of the crowd.

Rob and Valerie, Phoebe and Adam, Jacquie and Rhys all had something equally nice to say. Tommy and Sam Crawford took a moment to congratulate Noah.

"I understand you didn't like my article," Sam said.

Noah shook his head, frowning a little. "I didn't want my problems, my family's problems, spread all over the front page. But," he said, lightening up, "things have turned out better than I expected. Just don't use me for any more stories. I'm really not all that interesting."

Sam winked at Abby. "I know somebody who thinks differently."

When Abby looked around, she realized that everyone else had gone into the gym to eat and to celebrate. She and Noah stood alone in the lobby.

"Want to finish our dance?" he asked, holding out a hand.

"Oh, yes," she said, starting toward the gym door.

But Noah pulled her back, all the way into his arms. "It's crowded in there. Let's stay where we are."

The music came through a little muted, but the tune was easy to place. Mel Tormé's "The Christmas Song" surrounded them as they fell once more into each other's rhythm. This time Abby wrapped both her arms around Noah's shoulders. She could feel his palms on her back, one above the other, his fingers spread wide as if to absorb every inch he could touch.

"Where should we tell them to deliver the Christmas tree?" she murmured, closing her eyes to block out the overhead lights as she focused on soaking up all the sensations of Noah she could collect.

"How about my mom's house? She doesn't have any kind of decorations, and I think she might actually want to think about Christmas this year."

"What a lovely idea." She rested her head on his shoulder. "You are a kind and gentle man. Well, except when you're threatening to gag someone with his own tongue."

"I plead extenuating circumstances. Not guilty by reason of temporary insanity."

Abby didn't have to ask for further explanation. "Thank you for the glitter. It was perfect."

"My pleasure."

She lost track of time as the song wove its wistful melody around them, creating a moment she would remember all her life. When the end came, she drew back to look at the man holding her. He was everything she'd ever wanted. And tonight, she thought he'd finally come to believe in tomorrow.

"How about a drink?" he asked, and they turned toward the gym doors together. Inside, the lights had been dimmed for the final dance—"I'll Be Home for Christmas." Abby sipped the glass of punch Noah brought her, staring out over the crowd, enjoying the pleasure of being with her friends, the delight of being with the man she loved. His hand on her shoulder was all the warmth she would ever need.

"This will be a big cleanup job," Abby commented, turning her face a little to the side so Noah could hear. "I'm glad we can wait until tomorrow to do the bulk of the work."

He started to answer but stopped to glance at the new arrival coming through the gym door. The dim light glinted on a badge on a law enforcement uniform. As he stared, the marshal's gaze met his. The man nodded, and beckoned Noah to follow him out the door.

Though his breath was stuck in his chest, Noah managed to squeeze Abby's shoulders. "Be right back."

When he joined the marshal in the lobby, he found

himself facing a very tall, stern-faced officer. "What's going on?"

The guy handed over a paper written in legalese. "I've been detailed to escort you back to Atlanta, Georgia."

"Why?"

"There are proceedings under way with reference to your parole."

"What kind of proceedings?"

"I'm not at liberty to say. Come with me." He pivoted toward the outside doors.

Noah stood his ground. "Can't this wait until tomorrow? I'm in the middle of a party here. Come in and have some punch."

"Now," the marshal said firmly. "I've got a car outside."

"Okay, then, let me say goodbye—"

When Noah turned toward the gym entrance, the officer grabbed his arm. "I have orders to bring you back to Atlanta without delay. Now, are we going to do this the hard way or the easy way?"

One thing he'd learned in prison—don't argue with the people in power. They always got you back.

"Whatever you say," Noah conceded. "Just lead the way."

CHAPTER FIFTEEN

The Diary of Abby Brannon

May 3, 1989
Dear Diary,
Noah is gone. Kate asked one of the teachers who knew the facts, and it's true. The police are blaming the fire in the principal's office on Noah—thanks to my father, of course—and I guess that was as much as he could take. I didn't get a goodbye. I wonder if any of his girlfriends did.

I don't think he'll come back. There's so much world out there, and now he has the chance to see it all. I'd give anything to be with him right now.

I wonder...if I ran away, could I find him somewhere? Would he let me stay?

THERE TURNED OUT TO BE very little talk around town about the confrontation between Noah Blake and Wade Hayes during the reunion dance, mostly because the witnesses refused to discuss it. Though Abby felt as if time had stopped with Noah's disappearance, the days of the week rushed past. By Thursday, Christmas Eve,

Wade had dropped off the radar altogether. Pete Mitchell heard that he'd taken a leave of absence from the police force and gone to Florida.

"I also caught wind of a rumor that the sheriff is hinting he's ready to retire and move to the beach." Pete and Mary Rose had come into the diner for breakfast before doing some last-minute shopping for Joey. "Nobody knows for sure whether Wade's boast about fixing elections was just his big mouth or actual fact."

Abby set down two plates of pancakes and sausage. "Isn't the sheriff coming up for election this very next year? Who'll run in his place?"

Pete glanced at his wife, then concentrated on pouring syrup over his pancakes. "I'm thinking about it."

"Seriously?"

He nodded, and Mary Rose's smile confirmed the good news. "I'm a little young, maybe, but I've got almost fifteen years of law-enforcement experience. And I guess it is time I thought about protecting my own skin. Let the younger guys chase the villains. I'll be glad to sign their paychecks."

"You've got my vote," Abby told him, with a pat on the shoulder. "We'll even put up a sign in the window of the diner. Vote Pete Mitchell for Sheriff."

He grinned. "I like the sound of that."

A few hours later, Kate and Dixon Bell came in for lunch, bringing Kelsey and Sal and Trace along with them. "We're celebrating again," Kate announced as Abby served their drinks.

Abby wasn't sure whether to mention the baby or not. "What's the news?"

Kelsey gave two thumbs-up. "I got in. Vanderbilt wants me!"

"Oh, terrific, honey." Abby gave her a hug. "I'm so happy for you." She noticed Sal was looking fairly happy himself. "You've got a very talented, intelligent girlfriend."

He put an arm around Kelsey's shoulders. "I know it. I'm a lucky man. I just hope she won't forget about me when she's so far away."

Abby looked a question at Kate. "Sal's got a new job," Kate said. "He's going to be the manager at that QuickChange auto-repair shop they're building south of town."

"Congratulations to you, too, then."

"The salary is too good to pass up," he said. "If Kelsey and I want to get married after she graduates, I need to save as much money as possible."

"You're engaged?"

"Unofficially," Kelsey explained. "We're being cool about everything. We're too young to make irreversible decisions about the rest of our lives."

"Here's an irreversible decision," Trace said. "I'm starved. Can we order some food?"

Laughing, Abby took their orders and served up the meal fast enough that Trace didn't faint from hunger. The flow of customers was steady, but not too rushed. By two, the diner was empty of everyone but Abby. Charlie had taped a sign to the front door—"The Carolina Diner will be closed from 2:00 p.m. December 24 until 6:00 a.m. January 2. Happy Holidays!" Once Abby had assured him she could get the place cleaned up and closed for vacation, he'd left for home. Valerie and Rob had invited them to Christmas Day dinner and Charlie had volunteered to make desserts. That meant a lot of pies and two cakes to bake before noon tomorrow.

With the last of the day's dishes loaded and washing, Abby swept and mopped the floors, cleaned the tables, scoured the bathrooms and dusted and closed the blinds on all the windows. The hungry folks of New Skye would have to make their own breakfasts for a week. She planned to sleep until noon and only eat what someone else had cooked.

As she took her coat out of the closet in the kitchen, though, she thought she heard the doorbell jingle. Somebody evidently couldn't read—Charlie's sign was right in front of their face. Tired, sad, lonely, Abby ignored the instinct to open the door. Instead, she punched her right arm into and through her coat sleeve.

Unbelievably, the jingle sounded again, this time with a long series of knocks.

Abby shook her head. "Too bad," she said aloud. "If you're not Santa Claus, I'm not opening the door. And if you're Santa, you can come down the chimney. Try the roof."

After a moment's pause, the knock started again. Loud, insistent, shaking the door so hard that the bell danced on its rope, sounding like sleigh bells in the night sky.

Though she knew she shouldn't, Abby left the kitchen and crossed the dark dining room. Some people just wouldn't take no for an answer. When she reached the door, she bent over, grabbed the cord of the blind and jerked sharply, snapping the metal strips up to the very top of the window.

"Can't you read—" she started, then stopped. Her throat closed up completely.

Noah stood on the other side of the glass.

It had been five days since she'd seen him or heard from him. He'd abandoned her at the dance without even saying goodbye. No one in town knew where he'd gone. And now, out of the blue, he wanted in?

Her first impulse was to let the blind drop and then hide in her windowless office with all the doors locked until he went away again and she could sneak home. So tempting….

She tightened her fingers on the draw rope.

But, then again, why should she let him off so easily? Why shouldn't she tell him exactly what a jerk he'd been, how miserable he'd made her, how much she'd come to hate him—

Abby dragged the key out of her pocket, unlocked the door and yanked it open. "Well, well, if it isn't Kris Kringle. Or maybe the Devil himself. I get them confused sometimes."

"Merry Christmas." He held out a tiny silver box, tied with a red ribbon. The small size was suspicious…a ring?

She looked into his face again. "No, thank you," she said, and started to close the door.

But he slipped inside with her. Then it was Noah who shut the door and Noah who pulled the blind down. They were alone in the dark.

He didn't touch her, but he stood very close. "I can't blame you for being mad at me. But I didn't have a choice. I had to go."

"Oh, of course. Somebody kidnapped you from the gym? Why didn't I think of that?"

"That's pretty close to the truth. Not a criminal, though. A U.S. Marshal."

Her knees started to shake. "Why? What did he want? Your parole was legitimate—"

Noah put a finger against her lips. "Shh. It's okay. I had to go back to Atlanta. The governor—God bless his soul—wanted to give me a pardon."

"Pardon?"

"Yeah. He'd decided to play Santa Claus and review some of the parole cases from the past year. Turns out Wanda Harrison—the wife of the guy I killed—has written him repeatedly since I was convicted, trying to explain what happened, trying to get me a pardon. And, finally, it worked."

"Oh, Noah! So you're free?"

"Yeah. I'm still in shock."

"You could go anywhere now. You don't have to stay in New Skye if you don't want to."

He grinned. "That's true."

She didn't want to know the rest. But she had to ask. "Then why did you come back?"

Stepping away, he took a chair off the table and eased her down onto the seat, then set another one on the floor for himself. Their knees touched.

"I talked with Wanda for a while. She stayed in Atlanta, got a job. Her son Mac is in school, and they have a decent place to live. I think maybe she believed there were some sparks between us that could be revived."

Abby couldn't say a word.

"I appreciate what she did," Noah continued, "and she's a good woman. But for the first time it occurred to me that maybe she played me a little, back when she was married to Bull. I saw the bruises and the broken bones he gave her. But she didn't leave him. She allowed—encouraged?—me to solve her problem, instead."

"That's why you came back?"

Noah took her hands, and she let them lie motionless in his. During the past five days, she had imagined giving him a blistering with her tongue and then kicking him out of her life. She had imagined him sweeping her into his arms and carrying her away.

She had no idea how to deal with what was happening now.

"I came back," he said, "because I finally realized what kind of man I want to be. And there's only one place I can become that kind of man."

"I don't understand."

"I want to be dependable," Noah told her, watching her pale face. She didn't look as if she'd slept much since Saturday night. He knew he hadn't. "I want the people I care about to know they can count on me."

"That means—"

He nodded. "That means not running away. Ever again. I want to be able to face whatever comes in life. I'm not dodging the truth about myself or anyone else, ever again."

Abby's mouth had relaxed into an almost-smile. "That's a hard one."

"I want to be strong." He put his hands together, with hers between them. "I want to be strong for my friends, helping and supporting them the way they all supported me these last few weeks. I want to be strong for my mother, make her life a little easier, a lot more secure."

Noah slipped out of his chair to kneel on the floor, looking up into her lovely face. "Most of all, Abigail, I want to be good. I want to be a good man, as my dad wasn't. I intend to be a good husband, like Rob, a good father…like yours. And I came back because the only place I can do those things is here. With you."

She started to say something, but he interrupted. "I should have said, first, that I'm sorry I left. I'm sorry I hurt you, worried you, angered you. I'll spend the rest of my life making you happy…." He stopped when she slipped one hand free to put a finger against his mouth.

"Hush." She was smiling for real now, and crying at the same time. "Just stop talking and kiss me. And then give me the ring."

"It's snowing!" Kelsey turned from the window, her face shining with delight. "Abby, it's snowing for your wedding!"

The women in the room—nine of them, and the bride's chamber at New Skye Baptist Church barely held them all—clustered at the two tall windows. "Look at that," Phoebe said. "I've never seen such huge snow-flakes in my life. And falling so thick and fast!"

"Two years in a row, we've had snow on New Year's Day," Kate declared. "This is amazing!"

Or maybe just a miracle. Abby smiled, and went back to stand in front of the full-length mirror for a last-minute inspection. "Is it ten o'clock yet? Is my hem straight?"

"Ten minutes," Valerie said. As matron of honor, she wore a crimson velvet dress and carried white mums in her bouquet. "And you are beautiful."

"We're all beautiful." She'd asked her friends to wear Christmas colors and they'd obliged, filling the room with a tapestry done in deep greens and reds, the gold of Jacquie's silk suit, the purple velvet of Kate's first maternity dress.

Noah's mother wore the soft pink of a Christmas rose. As everyone but Valerie left to find their seats in the chapel, Abby held Marian Blake back a moment.

"I just wanted to say thank you," she told her soon-to-be mother-in-law. "And to promise I'll take care of him."

Mrs. Blake shook her head. "Then you'll be doing better than I ever did." She took a deep breath and straightened her shoulders. "But maybe you can keep him from getting into trouble from now on. The whole town will thank you for it." Hesitating, she reached up to touch Abby's cheek with her fingertips. "I will, too."

Charlie stepped up to the open doorway as the older woman hurried across the hall to take Dixon's arm and let him escort her to her pew.

"Are you about ready, Abby girl?"

"I am." She faced him across the threshold. "You look good in a tux, Dad."

He tugged at his tie. "Haven't worn one of these for at least thirty-five years."

"Since your own wedding?"

"That's right." He looked at her sadly. "I wish your mama could have been here today."

"Me, too." Abby kissed his cheek. "But you're here, and that's the most important part." She stepped out of the bride's chamber and closed the door behind her. Side by side, they walked to the center of the entry hall and waited for the music to start.

"I'm gonna miss you," Charlie whispered in her ear.

She slipped her hand into the crook of his elbow. "I love you, Daddy. Always."

He put his palm over her fingers and squeezed, gave a big sniff, cleared his throat, then nodded at Dixon. "Let's march."

NOAH HAD NEVER ATTENDED a church wedding in his life, and wasn't sure he would survive this one.

He almost jumped out of his clammy skin when the music changed from a soft medley of carols to a bright trumpet call. Before he realized what was happening, the organ started playing a song he couldn't help but recognize. *Da-da-tee-da...*

What have I gotten myself into?

When he glanced at Rob for help, his best man was staring down the center aisle of the church, and Noah followed his gaze to see Valerie approaching, carrying white flowers and looking beautiful in a dark red dress. As she neared the place where they stood at the front of the church, the smile she gave her husband was like sunshine on a cloudless summer day. Noah only hoped his wife would look at him like that in a year's time…or fifty years' time. He intended with everything in him to deserve that kind of love.

Da-da-tee-da started over again, even louder. The people in the pews got to their feet—the church was practically standing-room-only, anyway. A movement at the very back drew his attention. He looked, and his breath deserted him.

Abby glided down the aisle like a princess, graceful, elegant, and so lovely he wanted to cry. No veil hid her face from him, but she wore an ivory fedora, with a white rose tucked into the band, over her shining curls. She'd told him her wedding suit was made of ivory brocade, whatever that meant besides gorgeous. Kate had helped him choose the bouquet—more white roses tied up with red-berried holly leaves and sweet-smelling herbs. Surrounded by the smiles of her friends, and with snowflakes falling outside the church windows like blessings from heaven, she came to him with her gaze fixed on his face.

Charlie shook his hand, then gave him Abby's fingers to hold. From that moment on, all Noah could see was his beautiful bride, his wife. Suddenly, a wedding was no reason to be nervous. Instead, it was the perfect place to promise Abby and all their friends and family that he would take care of her every day he lived on this earth.

For the first time in his life, he understood what *cherish* really meant.

THOUGH THEY COULD HAVE held the reception in the diner, Abby had not wanted her dad to work on her wedding day, so they partied in the church fellowship hall, instead—a good thing, since otherwise they'd all have had to drive through the several inches of snow now lying on the streets to go anywhere else. Marian filled a plate and picked up a glass of punch, then found a quiet corner of the room to sit down in. She didn't need to socialize. She just wanted to watch.

A goodly number of the town's rich people had shown up for the wedding. All the Bells and Crawfords—Daisy Crawford must be almost ninety, but she looked every bit as pretty as she had at thirty. Her grandson kept an eye on his wife as if she was an egg about to hatch—Abby said she was expecting in the summer. Marian wondered if…when…she might become a grandmother herself.

Old Jonah, miserable sot that he was, would never have believed the town's mayor would show up at his son's wedding.

But Adam and Phoebe DeVries stood there big as life, laughing at something Noah had said. They'd brought a little boy with them, and took turns holding him—Marian understood they were keeping the toddler Noah had rescued that night at the diner during the robbery attempt. Tyler, his name was. Would Abby and Noah have such a cute little boy?

Would she manage to be a better grandmother than she'd been a mother?

As she sighed, not wanting to face the question, Charlie Brannon sat down in the chair next to her. "You found a place to relax, I see. This wedding stuff has me worn out."

"That's why folks get married when they're younger and have the energy."

"I think you're right."

They both watched the party for a while, without talking. Then Charlie shifted in his chair. "I don't know how I'm gonna manage, having my girl married and living somewhere else."

"You manage," Marian told him, from experience. "You don't get a choice."

"I figured they'd be off on their adventures as soon as they got back from the honeymoon," Charlie said. "But now she tells me they'll be settling here in New Skye after all. Noah wants a home, and she wants to be with him."

"You're still going to have to get some help at that diner of yours, you know. Abby's not going to want to stay there all hours of the day and night, with a husband to take care of."

"You think I don't know that?" His voice was sharp, but Marian didn't take offense. She knew how hard today had been on Charlie. Her own dad had bawled like a baby at her wedding to Jonah.

Maybe he'd known what kind of man her groom would turn out to be.

"I've got an ad scheduled to run in the paper this week," Charlie said, more gently. "I imagine I'll have some applications."

"Be patient with them—they won't be as good as Abby, but they'll get better."

He glanced at her from the side. "You want to apply?"

"Me, a waitress? Hah." She laughed. "That would be your worst nightmare, Charlie Brannon."

He grinned. "You're damn right it would."

The good thing about Baptist wedding receptions was that they didn't have dancing so they didn't last too long. Abby and Noah talked to everybody, cut their cake and toasted each other with ginger ale punch. Then, before Marian realized it, they had disappeared from the room. As the guests started to wander out of the hall to get their coats, Valerie Warren came to the corner where Charlie still sat with her.

"Noah and Abby asked if you could come say goodbye before they leave," the young woman said. "Both of you."

They followed her to the closed door of the pastor's study. Charlie turned the knob, walked right in…and caught Noah and Abby in the middle of a deep kiss.

"Sorry," the big man said, and started backing out, right into Marian, standing behind him.

"Watch where you're going," she told him loudly, with a slap on the back.

"Come on in, Dad." Abby left her husband, with only a sweet blush betraying her embarrassment.

"Hi, Ma." Noah came across the room and put his arm around Marian's shoulders. "Did you enjoy the wedding?"

"Real nice. You looked like a gentleman." She shook her head. "Something I never thought I'd see."

Abby was hugging her dad, with tears in her eyes. "Thanks," she whispered in his ear. "I love you."

"Love you, too, Abby girl." Charlie turned to Noah. "I don't have to tell you to take care of her, do I?"

Noah shook his head, then grinned. "No, sir. That's what the next fifty or sixty years are for. I promise."

Out on the church porch a few minutes later, the snow was still falling, thick and heavy, with flakes the size of biscuits. When Noah and Abby appeared at the top of the steps, a cheer went up from the crowd and birdseed began to fly through the air. Abby held up her bouquet and tossed it high, where it fell apart into a rain of petals and ribbons that showered them all.

Then, with Noah's hand in hers, the bride skipped down the steps to the motorcycle waiting on the drive. They both wore jeans and boots and long coats just right for riding in wet weather, with matching helmets. The crowd laughed loudly as they saw the writing on the back of those helmets—Noah's read "Just" and Abby's read "Married." A tail of ribbons, shoes and tin cans attached to the back of the bike added the final wedding touch.

With a roar of the engine, Noah set the Harley in gear and wheeled down the driveway, leaving a single trail in the thick snow. He drove slowly past the front of the church as Abby waved and the crowd waved back. In a moment, the bike and the newlyweds were gone. The silence of snowfall claimed the day.

"A pretty town." Charlie stood with Marian on the church steps, looking out over downtown, after the rest of the crowd had drifted away. "Especially in the snow."

"A good place to live," Marian conceded. "To raise children."

"To be a kid," Charlie added.

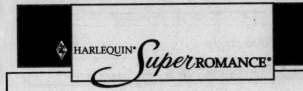

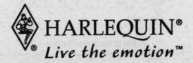

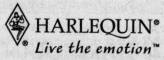

If you enjoyed what you just read,
then we've got an offer you can't resist!

Take 2 bestselling love stories FREE!

Plus get a FREE surprise gift!

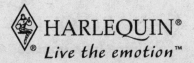

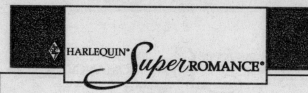

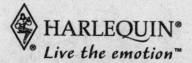